T0266958

Fever

Fever

A novel

JANET GILSDORF

BEAUFORT
BOOKS

Fever

Copyright 2022 by Janet Gilsdorf

FIRST EDITION

Hardcover 9780825309809   ebook 9780825308598

For inquiries about volume orders, please contact:
Beaufort Books, 27 West 20th Street, Suite 1103, New York, NY 10011
sales@beaufortbooks.com

Published in the United States by Beaufort Books
www.beaufortbooks.com

Distributed by Midpoint Trade Books
a division of Independent Publisher Group
https://www.ipgbook.com/

Printed in the United States of America

To Jim, for his endless patience

Prologue

1984 BRAZIL

Dona raised her hand, shading her eyes from the piercing sun, and stared at the rows of corn straight ahead. Marcelo had told her he wouldn't go to the far field today, so he must be in the closer one, beyond the fence line, beyond the lonely cow that swished her tail as she slowly chewed the tangled weeds. The wind, those dry summer gusts that kicked up the dirt and provoked the leaves overhead, blew her hair away from her face. Squinting, she tried to focus as her eyes traveled toward Mr. Queiroz's house. Her husband called him "Boss." Dona called him "Mr. Queiroz." She patted her bulging belly, felt the squirm of the new life that was growing as fast as a pumpkin sprout inside her, and smiled.

Mariana, the usually sunny girl, the child whose smile could melt any heart, called from inside the house. She sounded hoarse. Or mad. "Mama's out here," Dona called back. Her daughter began to cry. She was cranky today. "I'm on the porch," Dona said over her shoulder.

The screen door squealed open and then slammed shut. Mariana, her hair the darkest mahogany, dragged a ragged green blanket across the concrete and grabbed her mother's leg. Her diaper drooped to her knees, her tummy was bare. When she released the blanket, it puddled over her feet. She stretched her fingers toward the sky and cried, "Mama."

The sun had worked its way down to the tops of the mimosa trees along the road. The shafts of early evening light glittered through their branches, then shot like darts between the roof slats over the porch. Dona let out a faint groan as she lifted her daughter to her hip. She combed her fingers through Mariana's snarled hair and kissed her cheek. It was flushed and warm. Her eyes were still a little gooey, and the white parts still poppy pink. They were better, though, than yesterday. Or the day before that.

Dona spotted movement out beyond the fence. He was coming closer. "Marcelo," she called. "Dinner." She opened the screen door and, carrying Mariana, headed to the kitchen.

Dona was eager to eat, to bathe Mariana and put her to bed. The baby inside her would come in about three months and, by the end of every day, Dona was exhausted. The evening heat cramped her muscles, the dusty air clogged her nose. She stirred a pinch of salt into the stew of potatoes, beans, and pieces of chicken, carried the pot to the table, and set it on a potholder over the hole in the tablecloth. The painted roses on the plastic cloth, once ruby red, now looked like overripe mangoes, and the edge nearest the refrigerator had been chewed by a mouse. Someday she would have a proper lace tablecloth, and an oak dining table with six matching chairs, and real china rather than her tomato-stained plastic plates. She glanced around the dreary kitchen. She'd have a broad window beside the stove; a closet for her broom, mop, and bucket; and a toaster, so she wouldn't have to singe the bread over the gas flame.

She heard the clunk of Marcelo's boots on the porch. Inside, he yanked his cap off his head and tossed it at the hook beside the kitchen door. As always, it caught. His belt buckle clinked against the front of the sink while he washed his hands. He soaped them three times. Then he pulled the brush from the cupboard and scrubbed his knuckles and under his nails. One of the many things she loved about him was his cleanliness.

Mariana wouldn't sit on her seat in the empty chair. She kept crawling down to the floor, and Marcelo kept setting her back up on the cooking oil box that they called her throne. "Eat your dinner, little princess," he said. "The stew will make you grow up to be a beautiful lady, just like your mama." The girl whined and then threw her spoon across the table. It bounced off the chipped pitcher half full of milk from their cows and landed on the floor with a dull clank.

"That's enough, Mariana," Dona yelled. What was wrong with her daughter? She thought it must be the red eye. Mariana scrambled down to the floor once more, crawled up on her mother's lap, and sobbed into Dona's neck.

Dona looked into her husband's weary eyes as she slowly rubbed Mariana's back. "I don't know what's gotten into her."

"She's acting like a royal monster." Marcelo shook his head and shoved another spoonful of stew into his mouth.

Dona's hand ran up and down Mariana's spine. "She's hot. Feels like she has a fever."

"A bath and a bit of aspirin will fix her right up."

"I hope so."

Mariana didn't want to sit in the bath basin, either. She climbed out once, twice, three times, splattering water and suds all over the kitchen counter. Dona tried to comb the kinks from her daughter's hair, but the child screamed and swatted at the comb. "What on earth does she want?" Dona asked her husband. Finally, she wrapped the slippery child in a towel and handed her to Marcelo. "Here, you deal with her while I get the aspirin."

Dona tipped one tablet from the pill bottle, smashed it between two teaspoons, and mixed a quarter of the powder with a bit of strawberry jelly. Then, while Mariana squirmed on her father's lap, Dona pinched her daughter's nose shut, murmuring, "Here, sweetheart. A sweet for a sweetheart." When the child opened her mouth to breath, Dona dropped the jelly and aspirin onto Mariana's tongue. She clamped her daughter's jaws shut with one hand and stroked her throat with the other. "There you go, little one. That medicine will help you feel better." Marcelo loosened his grip on Mariana, and she thrashed against his arms. He held her tight again.

Marcelo carried Mariana to her room. Earlier that week they had moved her crib to the storeroom that was now her bedroom. They wanted her to get used to the different sleeping arrangement before the new baby arrived. Their daughter had accepted the move much better than they expected.

Now he laid Mariana across his knees, pinned a clean diaper on her, and slid her arms and legs into her pajamas. He considered her fresh smell, the velvet of her skin, her baby voice when she called him "papa" to be miracles. He laid her in the crib, sat on a box beside it, and began to sing a song his mother used to sing to him.

"Sleep, baby

"At grandpa's house.

"Grandpa doesn't have a mattress ..."

He patted Mariana's head as he sang until she finally drifted off.

When he returned to the kitchen, Dona was scouring the stew pot. He kissed the soft, moist skin along the neckline of her shirt.

She turned to him and said, "That was quite a tantrum. Soon she'll be a big sister. I wonder how she'll handle that?"

"She'll play mother from morning to night. And you, my dear, will teach her to be a wonderful, loving sister."

At the crow of the rooster, Dona woke up. The sun had barely cleared the horizon. She listened to the wind against the bedroom window and to Marcelo's soft snoring beside her. Then she heard another sound. A muffled murmur. Sounded like an animal. Had one of the dogs outside gotten hurt? She turned her head on the pillow and heard it again. "Marcelo," she said, jabbing his back with her elbow. "I hear something. Maybe one of the dogs."

He rolled over, then sat up. "What the hell ..." He shook his head as he padded out the bedroom door.

Dona, too, climbed out of bed. She glanced to the corner of the room, to the place where Mariana's crib stood before they moved it to the storeroom.

Marcelo wandered around the yard, calling for the dogs. In

the kitchen Dona again heard the sound, now a kind of whimper. As she entered the storeroom, the strange noise grew louder.

"Marcelo," she screamed. "Come here." Mariana lay in her crib with her limbs splayed like a frog, her face white as cream. Her breaths spurted out in little bubbly moans. "Marcelo," Dona screamed again. She lifted Mariana, cradled her daughter's limp, hot body in her arms, and ran back to the kitchen.

Her husband dashed through the back door. Dona sobbed, "Mariana ... something's terribly wrong."

He ran his calloused hand over his daughter's fiery head. "We're going to the clinic."

Dona, carrying Mariana, climbed into the front seat while Marcelo tried to start the car. She fingered the cross that hung on a chain around her neck—an anniversary gift from her husband—and prayed. For the engine to catch. For Mariana to be okay. She unsnapped her daughter's pajama tops to scatter the heat. Purple patches, each about the size of a 100 centavos coin, dotted her chest. "Make it go, Marcelo," she cried. "Now she has a rash. A bad rash." He turned the key one more time and, finally, the motor jumped to life, and the car barreled down the rut-filled road.

The car jerked to a stop, and they raced across the dusty parking lot and through the door marked "Emergency." Marcelo nearly ran into a nurse whose arms were loaded with clean linen. "Help us. Our little girl is very sick," he said.

The nurse handed the linen to Marcelo, took Mariana from Dona, carried her into a white-walled room that smelled of rubbing alcohol, and laid her on a narrow bed. "Please wait in the hallway," she said to Dona and Marcelo.

"I'm not leaving her," Dona sobbed.

"I'm sorry, you'll have to wait outside while we do our work." The nurse pulled off Mariana's pajamas. "We'll get you when we are ready."

"Where's the doctor?" Dona yelled.

"Dr. Alancar will be here shortly." She slapped the head of a stethoscope on Mariana's chest, set the earpieces in her ears, and began counting.

"Where is he?" Dona yelled again.

"Please wait outside." The nurse wrapped the blood pressure cuff around Mariana's arm and pressed the air bladder, over and over, in a clock-like rhythm.

Marcelo pulled at Dona's elbow and led her out the door. "Come," he said, "we need to let the nurse take care of Mariana."

They sat in the wire chairs across the hallway from the treatment room. The bulb in the ceiling light overhead was burned out and the one further down flickered. "It's so dark in here," Dona said. "And cold." Why was she so cold, she wondered? It was summer.

A gray-haired man, the tails of his white coat flapping as he ran, dashed past them with a quick nod and into the treatment room.

"That must be him. The doctor," Marcelo said.

Dona nodded and tugged at her pendant, the cross of St. Anthony. Because of that saint's blessing, theirs was a happy marriage. "Please, Holy Father, take care of Mariana and make her better," she whispered.

They listened for sounds from behind the door. Something rattled. Then quiet. A voice muttered, but they couldn't tell what it said. Then another voice, this one pitched higher.

"That must be the nurse," Marcelo said.

"Yes," Dona said. She sobbed into her handkerchief. "I don't hear Mariana."

It sounded as if something fell on the floor. The hallway grew dimmer.

Finally, the door opened. Marcelo sprang to his feet. Dona, unable to breathe, grabbed his arm.

"I'm Dr. Alancar," said the slightly hunched man with ruminating eyes. He was wringing his hands. He cleared his throat. "I have sad news." He took a deep breath. "Unfortunately, we were unable to save your little girl. She has died."

1

1984 MICHIGAN

The results made no sense. Sid straightened her glasses and stared again at the print-out, at the jumble of black digits that littered the white page. She had run these tests on other samples often, and before today the findings had always been logical. This time, though, the pairs of numbers had gone haywire; rather than concordant—both high or both low—as they should be, they were discordant—one high and the other low. She laid the paper in her lap, closed her eyes, and listened to the music from the lab across the hall. The beat of the bass slapped against her head, rhythmic, regular, driving, compelling. She took a deep breath. The air around her, warm and heavy, smelled of fumes from the Bunsen burner.

Why did the tests have to go bad now? She didn't have much time. Her research fellowship would end in less than two years, and the experiments she was doing were complicated. She spent days to weeks preparing the materials for one experiment and then, with each new experiment, needed to prepare more materials. Ultimately, if her experiments succeeded, she could end up with her dream job, doing what she dearly loved: pondering the world of microscopic creatures, following her curiosity about how they caused illness. If her experiments failed, her curriculum vitae wouldn't be competitive for a position as an independent researcher, and her dream would be shattered. Since college, she had longed to be a physician-scientist—a doctor to her patients, and a scientist who could unravel the complex and exquisite ways bacteria cause infections. The fellowship was designed to prepare her to do research and to do it well. But she—and she alone—had to make her work succeed. The results from today made no sense.

Those failed experiments were, of course, not her first encounter with failure; life wasn't real without a few stumbles. She knew that, but it always stung. She had been rejected by her top-choice medical school but then accepted by her second through fifth choices. She had received a D in community medicine because the subject was boring beyond words. There was the fender-bender last spring, the meeting she forgot with her research mentor several months ago. Several previous experiments had also gone awry, and once she fleetingly considered quitting the fellowship. And, of course, there was her relationship with Paul. She and Paul had seemed to be two compatible souls, wandering down many paths side by side. But now, like madcap spinning tops, they had twirled off in opposite directions. The worst part was she couldn't figure out what to do about that.

The thick air stirred. Sid opened her eyes.

Raven peered into her face. "You all right?"

"Yes. Of course." Sid sat up straight and ran her fingers through her hair.

"You look like hell. Sure you're okay?"

"I'm fine. The results of my experiment are cockamamie. That's all."

"Hey, that's an everyday event for the rest of us. You've been mighty fortunate if this is your first messed-up experiment." A tinge of concern etched Raven's usually playful face. Then, like a passing cloud, it disappeared. "You could try making a graph." She smiled. "Eliot says that plotting the numbers on a grid sometimes makes them behave." With that, Raven was gone, back to her lab bench.

Sid gazed out the window into the morning sky, past the tombstones in the cemetery on the other side of the road, past the leafy treetops that scattered the sunshine, past the river beyond that burbled toward the faraway lake. Her eyes wandered back to one of the graves, the tiny one set apart from the others. From that distance, the little head stone, tilted slightly to the right, appeared mossy and long forgotten. That old feeling, the haunted, empty one that had plagued her for years, swept over her once again like an inky, velvet cape.

She turned her eyes back to the lab and glared, again, at the results. Maybe Raven's idea would work. Compared to other third-year graduate students, Raven was very wise. She was correct that images sometime revealed what words or numbers couldn't.

Sid plotted the numbers from her experiment on a sheet of graph paper. When she finished, the grid looked as if someone had blasted it with a shotgun—tiny black #2 pencil dots, helter-skelter, all over the place. She searched for a pattern among the spots, a hint of a relationship among them that would lend meaning to her results. There was none.

She carried the graph to Raven's bench. "See anything significant?"

"Um ... no."

"Me neither." Wonky results sucked the investigative juices right out of her. She preferred the rousing joy of discovery when each new understanding buoyed her spirits and set her mind afire against the next biologic puzzle. Somewhere in those seemingly random black spots there must be meaning. "Let's ask the oracle," she said. "He'll have the answer."

"Or at least an opinion," Raven said. "He always does." They wandered to the far corner of the laboratory.

"Eliot?" Sid called as she approached his lair. It was a clumsy affair he had built by stacking empty Petri dish cartons around the end of his lab bench. The boxes reached skyward, nearly to the banks of fluorescent lights that ran across the ceiling.

"Yeah?" A deep voice growled from behind the cardboard wall.

"Must be crotchety today," Raven whispered.

"When isn't he?" Sid stopped at the opening of what they called "Eliot's Nest" and, with a smirk, read once again the notice duct-taped beside the entrance.

Fever

ATTENTION:

1) Don't use the equipment in here without permission.

2) Don't store your supplies here.

3) Don't borrow anything from here without permission.

4) Do not come in when Eliot Mitchell isn't around.

She knocked on the side of the upright freezer that formed part of one wall of his nest and poked her head around the corner. "Permission to enter?"

"Yeah." His feet were propped on his desk, and he was scribbling on a legal pad balanced on his thighs. The yellow paper looked like an abstract drawing with overlapping circles, crossed-out words, arrows pointed in random directions, and a large empty square in the center. He must be dreaming up a new experiment.

Outside his dusty window, in the cozy amber of the fall morning, the trees cast short, angular shadows across the grass. From beyond, Sid heard the drum cadence and then the trumpet blasts of the university marching band as it practiced for the next football game.

"I have strange results with the antibody experiments and don't know why," she said to the back of his faded green and black plaid flannel shirt.

He waved his arm for them to enter. His hair, acorn brown and wispy, looked as if it'd been caught in an eggbeater. When he finally turned away from the window, his broody eyes darted past hers.

Sid stepped inside. Piles of papers and journals cluttered his desk and spilled from the tops of the file cabinets. The trash bin overflowed with crumpled yellow notes and three empty pizza boxes. That was illegal. They weren't allowed to have food in the lab, but Eliot had declared The Nest to be an office so he could eat undisturbed in there. Eliot didn't like disturbance.

"Sit down," Eliot said.

"Where?" Sid glanced around the crowded space. There were no seats.

He pointed to two stacks of microbiology journals piled knee-high on the floor. "There and there."

Raven giggled. Eliot smiled at her, the tiniest of impish, elfin smiles.

Sid balanced herself on a pile of journals and wondered why he hadn't moved a chair or two in there. Probably because he, like every other hermit in the world, didn't want anyone to hang around for long.

"Maybe you can figure out what I did wrong." She handed him the read-out and the graph she had just drawn and explained, first, her goal in doing the experiment and, second, the techniques she had used, step by step.

He paged through the data, studied the graph. His face was free of emotion. "Um ... this's the negative control, right?" He jabbed his finger at a black dot on the lower left side of the plot.

"Correct."

He scratched his head. "Why do you think these results are wrong?"

"Well ... either both or neither of the antibodies I used should bind. But see ..." She pointed to several other dots on the graph, "... they're discordant."

He looked annoyed. She wished she didn't need his help.

"Sidonie, don't think about what your results *should* be. Pay attention to what they *are*." He paused a moment, then added, "You should know that. It's Basic Laboratory Studies 101."

Sid glanced at Raven. Her friend's dark eyes studied the floor tiles.

"Look, there's no problem with your results." Eliot whapped the graph with the back of his hand. "The only problem here is your expectation of the right results. If you're going to ignore the outcome, you shouldn't bother doing the experiment. You could spend the rest of your whole goddamn life trying to force your results to meet your wrong expectations." His eyes dug into hers. "That's lousy science."

"The antibodies are binding to something," Sid said. She stared again at the graph. "The question is: Why aren't they binding correctly?"

The quiet in the room thrummed as he scrutinized her results. She studied his face. His deep-set eyes were intense, his mouth solemn. What was he thinking? His mind was surely grinding with thought, and she couldn't guess the notions embedded in those thoughts. Suddenly the corners of his mouth turned upward like a leprechaun's. "Gene transfer," he said, and then started to laugh. "You have, for the eight thousandth time in the history of bacteriology, demonstrated that genes leap from one bacterium to another." He pointed first to one and then another of the dots. "See ... altered genes have made new proteins to which the old antibody won't stick. That's elementary bacterial genetics, isn't it Sidonie?"

The world stood still. Her mind choked. Of course. Why hadn't she seen it? Gene transfer was the perfect explanation.

How did Eliot sort it out so quickly when she couldn't? She knew he was a genius and wished she had more of that kind of genius. Heat crept up from her neck to her cheeks. He was absolutely right, but he could have found a kinder way to say it. "Thanks," she murmured. The word sounded like a shovel hitting stone. She pulled the graph from his hands, turned, and left The Nest. Raven's footsteps followed her.

When they reached their end of the laboratory, Raven said, "He's an ass."

Sid sat on her lab stool and nodded.

Raven raised her voice. "He's a really big, thoughtless ass." She started to leave and then turned back to Sid. "He doesn't mean to be mean, you know. It's just that his social skills need some polish." She looked at the ceiling and, in a priest-like, droning voice, said, "We must strive to ignore his rough patches. I think Dr. Joyce Brothers said that." Then she stared at Sid again. "Because Eliot has a lot to teach us."

Sid had just finished asking Raven if she could borrow some HEPES buffer when the telephone rang. Raven picked up the phone with one hand and stretched her other arm toward a bottle on the shelf overhead. Suddenly, she backed away from the bench, and a smile bloomed like a spring rose on her face. She yelled into the phone, "Hey, I'm terrific. It's wonderful to hear from you. What's up?" A moment later, she said, "Hang on a minute."

She covered the phone with her palm and said to Sid, "It's my brother. He's calling from Brazil, from his office in backwater Promissão. Sounds as if he's on the moon with something sizzling in the background."

Then, as she thrust the handset toward Sid, she called, "River, say hello to my friend."

Sid put the phone to her ear. "Ah ... hi, River. Pleased to meet you. Be assured we're taking good care of your sister here in Michigan." She, a stranger, couldn't think of anything else to say to River, another stranger.

"I hope she's behaving herself," he said. "She's capable of pretty crazy high jinks."

River's voice sounded mellow and light-hearted, like a radio announcer telling an entertaining tale. What did he mean by *high jinks*? She glanced at Raven's glowing face and dancing eyes and laughed. "So far Raven has stayed within the boundaries. At least the boundaries of this place." She nodded at Raven. "Here she is."

Raven took the handset. She listened a moment and then said, "Well, happy birthday to you, too. How do you feel at twenty-eight? I feel ancient." Raven laughed. River must have said something funny.

Finally, she said, "Beware of the octopuses, River," and hung up.

"Huh?" Sid winced. "Octopuses?"

"That's code for *be safe*." Raven grinned. "A left-over from when we were kids. For a while we wouldn't get out of bed until we made sure no octopuses were hiding underneath. He called because he won some kind of raffle down there and doesn't know if he has to pay income tax on it."

Raven continued, her voice soft and dreamy. "River didn't say how much money he won. Just like him. Modest. Heck, he might be a millionaire." She carried a test tube to the centrifuge, set it into one of the rotor's pockets, and pushed the start button.

"River sounded quieter than usual. Maybe he's tired." She took a deep breath. "I hope he's okay. He's a wonderful brother. I miss him a lot."

It was the word *miss*, a stubby, piercing word, that hit Sid. Raven missed River. She, Sid, missed her medical school friends from Seattle and her residency pals from Portland. She missed the sibling she should have had; her college roommate, Laurie, and their walks in new-fallen snow; her girlhood cat, Lilac, and the way they snuggled on stormy nights in her bed; and the sweet gin of success when things worked out well. And she missed Paul, or at least some parts of him. She missed the way he laughed—it emerged slowly with a smile and a quiet chuckle and grew into a riotous guffaw. She missed the dinners he used to cook and the nights they watched movies. But missing didn't dictate destiny.

Raven glanced at her watch and asked. "Hungry? It's lunch time."

The lounge smelled less gassy but more fusty than the lab. Raven sank into the easy chair, and Sid settled on Long Green, the weary faux-leather couch that stretched beneath the window. She scratched at the coffee rings on its pea-colored arm and watched while Raven unwrapped her sandwich—pickles, sprouts, liverwurst, and peanut butter on rye—and then took a bite. There was a satisfying harmony to it: quirky Raven, quirky lunch.

Suddenly, the lounge door flew open and a wall of flames burst in. Sid stared into the blaze and, when she understood, she shook her head in disbelief. So crazy, so like him. It was a cake covered with burning candles on a foil-covered tray carried by Eliot. "Happy birthday," he said in a deep, sing-songy but off-tune voice.

"Holy cow," Raven gasped. "How'd you know it was my birthday?"

"A little lark told me." He tilted his head toward Sid and winked.

Then Sid remembered. Last week, she and Eliot were talking about the ages of everyone in the lab. Among the trainees, he was the oldest at thirty years, followed by Sid at twenty-eight. Raven was, then, twenty-seven. "But not for long," Sid had said. "She turns twenty-eight on Tuesday."

Eliot held the burning cake in front of Raven's face. She leaned back in her chair. "Criminy, Eliot, you're going to set me on fire."

"Well, blow out the candles, then. Make a wish first."

Raven thought a moment, took a deep breath, and blew. The flames flickered, and those from the front candles died, sending a puff of smoke upward from each blackened wick. She took another breath, blew at the cake again, and the rest of the flames died.

"Your wish is not granted," Eliot said, pulling the cake away from her face. "Two tries don't count for a win."

"That's okay," Raven said with a shrug. "The wish was to become a beautiful movie star like Elizabeth Taylor. I'll find another way to be famous."

Interesting wish, Sid thought. Her friend had never spoken of a beauty goal before. Raven, with her, wavy coal-black hair and pale buttermilk skin, vaguely resembled Elizabeth Taylor. "Set the cake on the table, Eliot," Sid said as she retrieved Styrofoam plates, paper napkins, and plastic forks from the lounge cupboard.

"Who made that?" Raven asked when Eliot handed her a slice. "The baker at Kroger?"

"No. I did," Eliot said. "Carrot cake is the only thing I know how to cook, besides popcorn and grilled cheese sandwiches."

Sid thought it was kind, albeit odd, of him to bring the cake. When they celebrated events in the lab—notices of grant awards and publication of important papers—someone usually ordered doughnuts. But that was Eliot: different.

He had almost finished eating his frosting when he said, "Speaking of celebration cakes, when are you and that guy friend of yours getting married, Sidonie?"

Sid stared at him, wordless.

Raven laughed. "Are you volunteering to make Sid's wedding cake?"

"She hasn't confirmed the engagement yet. Wasn't he supposed to move to Michigan by now?"

Sid slid her fork into her cake, broke off a piece, and set it in her mouth. It had looked so good earlier, moist, honey-colored crumb with chunks of raisins and walnuts. Now it looked dreary and dry. Why did Eliot have to bring that up? A year ago, when she first arrived at the lab, she had expected Paul might join her within several months. "No wedding soon. I'll let you know when that happens. How much would you charge for a three-layered cake?"

"For you, nothing. It'll be my wedding present."

When they returned to the lab, Raven asked Sid for pipette tips. "I'll pay you back when the next shipment arrives."

Sid lifted a rack of tips from the shelf beside her and handed it to Raven.

Raven started toward her own lab bench, then stopped, and turned back to Sid. "You seemed torqued at Eliot for asking about Paul."

"Well, it's none of his business."

"True ..." Raven paused and then asked, "How *is* your Indiana Jones this week?"

Sid laughed. Raven referred to the first time Sid met Paul. She had run out of soap at the laundromat and spotted a package of Tide on top of one of the driers. She figured the owner wouldn't mind if she borrowed a handful. As she reached into the box, Paul walked around the corner with an armful of wet clothes and asked what she was doing with his detergent. They started talking and ended up going to a movie—*Raiders of the Lost Ark*. That was the night she fell in love with Indiana Jones.

"Oh, Paul is fine this week. Loving his job, still. Went fishing in the Columbia last weekend. He's more like the adventurer Indiana Jones than the professor Indiana Jones."

Alone at her desk, Sid stared again out the window. The fading summer had left dry brown grass on the cemetery lawn, and the approaching winter felt like the promise of a cold shower. Outside, a chickadee, who would bravely stay in Michigan for the duration of the winter, landed on a branch of the redbud tree, hopped about seven inches toward the trunk, and then flew away. Why hadn't she been able to figure out the meaning of the goofy results of her experiment? The answer to the problem was obvious when Eliot blurted it out.

At moments like this, Sid wondered why she had pursued this research fellowship in the first place. By the time she finished, it would eat up three years of her life. Paul used to kid her that she wanted the fellowship because of her relentless ambition, her single-minded determination to be the world's greatest bacteriologist; but now, to her mind, it wasn't the fun kind of kidding. Her mother wondered why her daughter worked so hard at the fellowship when she was already a physician. Raven said she was rightfully, beautifully, following her passion for science. Her own answer was that the mysteries of microbiology fascinated her.

It all started when she first stared into a microscope in her 4th grade science class, saw a swarm of *E. coli* through the lens, and realized that they were alive. "They eat and breathe, like we do," her teacher had explained. "Like my cat Lilac does," Sid had told the class. Sid loved to let her mind wander down the path of interesting microbial questions: how bacteria cause infections, how the immune system controls them, how to harness that control for the benefit of patients. She wanted every experiment to turn out perfect, though, and befuddling results were as annoying as bossy postdocs like Eliot.

She wandered over to Raven's desk and picked at the cuff of her sleeve at the place where the buttonhole was unraveling. "I'm still bothered by Eliot's comment about my being a lousy scientist."

"Well, that's Eliot being Eliot. Let it go."

"He might be right. Sometimes I wonder if I should quit. Maybe I should forget about this laboratory research stuff and go back to Portland, back to being an ordinary doctor."

"No." The word came sharp and fast. Raven's mouth looked set in cement. "Don't quit."

Sid pulled her long-neglected knitting from the basket at her feet on her living room floor. As she untangled the yarn, the phone rang. It was Paul.

"What are you doing right now?" he asked. "At this very instant?"

She trapped the receiver between her shoulder and her ear and continued on a purl row. "Ahh ..." The navy-blue yarn on her needles would be a sweater for Paul. A surprise for Christmas if she finished it in time. "I'm just knitting." She had started the sweater shortly after she moved to Michigan. The back and fronts were done, but she was having trouble finishing the sleeves. The problem was inertia—a body at rest tends to stay at rest. She just wasn't motivated anymore.

Paul told her about his trip up the Columbia to fish. "I caught nothing, but near the John Day Dam, Steve reeled in a big salmon. A chinook."

"What did you do ... eat it?"

"Of course. It was delicious. I could send you some of the leftovers."

She laughed. "I bet they're good. But they're yours. Enjoy."

She heard Hector barking in the background. He was a friendly hound, that Hector. He was probably gazing out Paul's picture window, yowling at another dog outside.

Paul told her about his solution to an engineering problem at work. "The boss loved it." He talked about the remodeling project in his wing of the building, about the mixed-up bathroom plumbing and the fire extinguishers that spontaneously sprinkled from time to time.

Ultimately, she told him about the discordant antibodies/gene transfer fiasco. "I really wish I'd come up with that solution myself. Next time, I'll be quicker."

"Atta girl. Don't let the turkeys get you down."

"I'll try to keep them at bay, especially the turkey named Eliot."

She could picture Paul in his apartment. He'd be slouched in his easy chair with his bare feet propped on the footrest, a bag of sour cream potato chips in his lap, and a beer in his hand. He liked polo shirts and likely was wearing the taupe one she gave him before she left. It was his favorite until he dropped a loaded hot dog down his front. Now the shirt had a ketchup shadow just north of his navel. He wore it anyway around the house.

"I called with my good news," he said. "The boss told me today that I'm being promoted yet again. To manager of our group. And it includes a nice salary increase."

Good news? Sid thought. Yes, for him it was terrific news. But for them as a couple? The promotion would further guarantee that he'd stay in Portland, at least for a while longer. She had no way to know if she'd be able to find a physician/scientist job there when she completed her research fellowship.

"And the group manager's boss, the section manager, is getting up in age, so I could move to that position in just a couple years. Actually, that's a pretty good bet."

He'd be chained to Portland forever. "That's great, Paul. Congratulations. I'm proud of you." She was honest about that. She was happy for him, pleased when he did well. She wanted him to be successful. She wanted everything to work out beautifully. Was that ever possible?

"Come back to Portland, Sid. I need you here."

"I can't do my research training there. You know that."

The faint whir of the refrigerator fan broke the silence. Finally, Paul spoke. "With my raise, we could afford a decent house."

Sid laid the knitting in her lap, leaned her head against the back of the couch, and stared at the crack in the corner of the ceiling. The thought behind his words was familiar. During their senior year, her college roommate had decided she wanted to get married. "I'm ready," Laurie had said. "Wed now, work for a couple years, and then start a family." Laurie had caught the marriage bug, and Ted, her boyfriend at that moment, was the target. His timeline seemed to mesh well with hers and, as far as Sid knew, their marriage was solid. But she, Sid, was not ready. Sweet-enough guy Paul was very ready, but she wasn't.

"A house would be nice," she said. She rolled up the knitting and returned it to her basket.

After she hung up, she poured herself a glass of orange juice and tried to think about a Portland house. Three bedrooms, a wood-burning fireplace, rhododendrons in the garden, friendly neighbors. Those were key elements, but in her mind, she couldn't make the picture warm and complete. She just didn't care about a house. She looked around her living room at the stack of microbiology journals on the coffee table she had bought at a used furniture store, the rubber tree plant beside the sofa, the knitting basket on the scatter rug from the Goodwill, and, on the bookshelf, the vase Laurie had made in a pottery class. For now, her apartment was fine, a good home base during her fellowship.

The next morning, Sid returned the bottle of HEPES buffer to Raven. "Here's the ... hey, what's wrong?"

Raven sat at her lab bench, sobbing. "I just talked to Mom. She's worried about River. Says he sounded different when she called him. Distracted. Almost sad." Raven looked up. "He was quieter than usual when he called me yesterday. Something must be wrong."

"What?"

"I don't know. Girl trouble, maybe. I hope he's not sick. Maybe he caught one of those weird jungle diseases."

"He didn't tell your mom, or you, what's bothering him?"

"No. He wouldn't. He's always been kind of secretive."

Poor Raven. Her brother was so far away. She had talked about him so much. Sid wrapped her arm around Raven's shoulders. "Let's go visit him."

"Visit him? In Brazil?" Raven turned her face toward Sid. Her eyes were wide with disbelief.

"Yeah. My mother sent me a check—for Labor Day, I guess—and it's enough for two airplane tickets. I think my passport has three more years until it expires."

"You'd do that? I mean, go with me? Pay for the trip?"

"I'd love to. Friends are friends, after all. Besides, I need a break."

2

1984 BRAZIL

The air over the tarmac was hazy and hot when Sid and Raven descended the aluminum steps from the plane. A searing gust tossed Sid's hair into tangles, and the humidity smoothed the wrinkles in her slacks. She took a deep breath. The smell of the weeds beyond the fence, the tint of the sky, and the free-wheeling clouds overhead reminded her of eastern Washington. For a moment, she expected to turn and find her mother standing beside her. Her mom would ask why she had gone all the way down to Brazil for a vacation when she could have gone home to Pendleton.

"We made it," Raven said. She stomped her feet on the con-crete. "I've been scrunched in that seat for too long. My poor body might permanently be a pretzel."

Inside the smoke-filled terminal, the room quavered with chatter. All Portuguese. Not a word of English. Sid scanned the crowd for someone who looked like Raven, for a man with black-as-tar hair, alabaster skin, graphite eyes, and a toothy smile, although he might be glum if something was wrong. Most of the guys—at least a hundred of them were packed into the small waiting area—fit that general description, except they had ruddy, tea-colored skin instead of Raven's ghost-white complexion. They flapped pieces of cardboard covered with hand-scribbled names over their heads, shoved toward the deplaning passengers, and shouted, "Renato." "Bruno." "Victor." "Ruth."

Suddenly Raven rose to her toes, thrust her hands high into the air, and screamed, "River." Her voice could have split a tree. Across the room, a tall young man—as Sid had predicted, a masculine replica of Raven, including the winning grin—waved and elbowed his way toward them. He threw his arms around his sister, lifted her off the ground, and spun her around. When he set her back down, he looked toward Sid.

She held out her hand. "Hi. I'm Sid. I'm so glad to finally meet you in person." His palm was surprisingly cool considering the heat in the terminal. His face, though, was warm and alive, and his handshake firm with confidence. He didn't look sick at all.

"Let's be off to Promissão," River called, pointing toward the door. "It's about an hour and a half from here."

Out in the parking lot, they crammed their suitcases, and themselves, into his rusty Volvo. As they rumbled through the countryside, Sid watched the scenery from the seat beside River. They passed wooden hay carts that stood empty along the highway and fields carpeted with the green nap of young plants; they passed a railroad crossing where pink flowers grew between the rails and a tall wire contraption with a red cloth dangling from its top straddled the ties. The place was different from rural Michigan, or rural Oregon for that matter—about a hundred years different. And while it was fall in America, it was spring in Brazil, and the land shimmered with new life.

Sid stole glances at River in profile and saw in him Raven's nose and the slope of her forehead. "What's the story with your names, anyway?" she asked. In the year she had known Raven, she had never asked. "River and Raven. Rhythmic, alliterative. Sounds like a nature song."

"Sort of is," Raven said from the back seat. "They're the fruits of our parents' overly active imaginations. According to family lore, when I was only two hours old, my wailing reminded them of the squawking black bird that roosted in a manzanita tree beside our cabin. And 'River' suits my brother perfectly. He's like a ribbon of water flowing insistently but quietly to the sea."

Sid looked at River again and didn't see flowing water. "What on earth does that mean?"

"Oh, you know, he's steady and resolute, in a wordless way."

River chuckled, said nothing, and gripped the steering wheel as he stared straight ahead at the road.

"Our early life was a fairy tale. I may have told you before about the commune where we grew up," Raven continued. "It was a splendid place, among the redwoods of Anderson Valley, California."

Ahh, Sid thought. She hadn't heard about the commune. That explained both Raven's breeziness and her earthiness.

"River and I were constant companions. We did everything

together: climbed trees and trapped field mice and gathered huckleberries. In our little cabin, our beds were so close that when a nightmare jolted me awake, I would reach over to him. Then he would rub my arm and whistle a tune—my favorite was 'Yankee Doodle'—until I went back to sleep."

Their young lives, fun and simple yet charmingly complex, were so very different from Sid's. They were country kids, she a town mouse; their parents were free-spirited, hers were rule-bound; they had each other, she had no one.

River steered the Volvo around the corner and up a dusty road. He leaned toward Sid and glanced out the window and then looked again at the road. A few minutes later, he did it again. Then he slammed on the brakes saying, "Ah-ha. Here it is," and made a sharp turn into a grassy yard.

"What's this?" Raven asked.

"Where we get dinner. Best sausages in all of Brazil."

The place smelled of uncooked muscle and bone. Hams wrapped in string mesh hung from hooks on the ceiling, as did ropes of stubby sausages. Slabs of dried beef shanks lay stacked like cordwood on the counter. River bent over a pile of pearly pink coils, each separated from the other by a sheet of waxed paper. "Here we go," he said.

Sid stared at the raw meat and wondered how long it had been there. The coils were still pink and glistening, not the dull brown of aged knockwursts, so it must be fresh. "Are they spicy?" Her stomach, unsettled from the long flight, may not tolerate zesty food well.

"Garlic and peppers is all," River said. "But not hot peppers. At least, not very hot." He nodded to the butcher and held up his index finger. "Uma linguiça." To Raven and Sid he said,

"They're gigantic. I think one will do."

Back on the road, Raven said, "River really loves Brazilian food. He's learned Portuguese and is pretty good at it. Mom and I wonder if he's found a Brazilian beauty yet. Huh? River? Any girlfriends?" She socked him on the shoulder.

He shrugged and continued to stare ahead. He waved to a hitchhiker, who led a dog tied to a piece of rope, and then turned the Volvo onto a lane lined with swaying palm trees.

"This's pretty fancy," Raven said.

"We're not there yet," he answered.

He stopped the car beside a small, red clay dwelling. A broad-leafed tree towered over the house, casting stippled shade on its corrugated metal roof and its sandy dirt yard. Several cats, tails erect, strutted across the porch. "Scram," he called and waved his arms at them. "Damn felines. The last people who lived here must have fed them, and they haven't forgotten. At least they keep the mice out."

Inside, he led them to the narrow area behind the kitchen. "This is the guest bedroom," he said. Two army cots filled the space between the back door and the shelves of canned food and cleaning supplies. A neat stack of folded sheets, a towel, and a wash cloth sat on each cot. Even the bathroom was spotless. Sid wondered if River had always lived alone. His place was more tidy and well-stocked than she expected from a bachelor.

"Hey, River," Raven said when she finished eating the dinner of sausages, oranges, and crackers. "Tell us about that money you won in the raffle. Mom says you'll have to pay US taxes on that."

"Right. I heard. Cibele, my office manager, talked me into buying a ticket from some kind of fundraiser to support an art school in São Paulo. And I won. First time I've ever won anything."

"How much?" Raven asked. "Are you a millionaire."

He chuckled. "Rein in your fantasies, Sister. Only about $2,500. I wisely used it to pay off my car loan." He poured himself a second glass of wine. "Speaking of Cibele, tomorrow is a holiday at the office, so I don't have to work. She invited us to her house for lunch. You'll like her. She's a cool lady."

"What are we celebrating?" Sid asked. She was starting to feel more relaxed. Maybe it was River's unassuming, gentle nature. He wasn't a demanding person. Maybe it was just being away.

"It started as a joke and somehow it stuck. Today is Emancipation Day in Ohio, so the regional boss, who's from Toledo originally, calls it an official holiday."

"Weird."

"Yes, he is." River's elbow knocked his glass, and the red wine splashed across the table and down to the floor. "Shit." He dashed to the kitchen and returned with a handful of towels.

"I meant," Sidonie said as she slid her feet away from the wine spill, "it's strange to celebrate Ohio holidays down here."

"That, too."

After dinner, Sid nestled into the bean bag on the living room floor and listened to River and Raven reminisce. They laughed about their Aunt Margaret and their wayward cousins, worried about their even more wayward father.

The meal had lulled Sid into a smooth, easy languor, and the conversation flowed like gently falling rain. River and Raven seemed to know what the other was about to say before it was said. She thought of the flight from Michigan, of the view out the window at the tops of the clouds below that looked like a field of ashes. She had imagined skipping through the powder and kicking up a plume of ash dust. Then it made her feel light. And free. Now, she felt as if she were embraced by the cloud fluff, even lighter and freer. She hadn't felt that way for a long time. Not since the early days with Paul.

That night, Sid lay in her cot in the pantry and listened to Raven breathing. "Are you awake?" Sid whispered.

"Yeah."

"River looks okay to me. What do you think?"

"Yeah, he looks good. He's a bit ... subdued, I'd say. Nothing major. Maybe Mom was over-worrying."

The road to Cibele's home, like all the roads Sid had seen near Promissão, was riddled with ruts, and curls of dust billowed behind each car they passed. The sky was the color of bluebonnets and clear except for the thin, wispy clouds that stretched back toward town.

River stopped the Volvo beside a fence of tree branches that surrounded a garden of ankle-high seedlings. As Sid followed River up the path to the house, she stepped over a puddle and then another. From the corner of her eye, she watched a creature—a small squirrel? a big chipmunk?—dart from bush to bush. Cibele's place was quaint in a ragged way: the pocked and peeling stucco on the house matched the rust-colored dirt, the porch sagged, and an unpainted shed stood beside an old car suspended by its axles on cinder blocks. An abandoned gray and squash-colored fur coat was wedged under the car's front wheels.

She smelled onions. Must have come from behind the curtain that flapped against an open window. It was a smooth but intense scent, more like sweet, caramelized onions than tangy raw ones.

She wondered about Cibele. Was she old? Did she speak English? She stepped over another puddle and suddenly stopped. The heap of fur under the old car moved. She took two steps forward. The hairy pile raised its head. Then it stood up. A dog. He wandered toward her. She stopped again. He was the size of a small German shepherd, and his dusty coat looked full of mange. Would he bite? Was he rabid? She glanced at River. He raised his eyebrows and shrugged.

"River," Raven commanded. "Is this guy friendly?"

River stooped, stretched his arm toward the animal, and called, "Here, buddy. Do you belong to Cibele?"

The dog, his nose bobbing, his scraggly tail wagging, inched toward River. If a dog could smile, he'd look like that, Sid decided.

The screen door slammed. A young woman had stepped onto the porch. "Aqui, Lauro. Aqui." The dog turned toward her, dropped his now motionless tail between his hind legs, and slinked away from them. When he plopped down at the woman's feet, she patted his head and called out, "Hello. Welcome to Promissão. Lauro is my greeter."

Sid had expected a tired, dowdy, fifty-year-old secretary, but the woman's smooth skin was the color of seasoned copper pots, and her ebony hair was tied into a relaxed knot at the back of her neck. When she turned to open the door, her purple and red printed caftan swirled on her trim frame and brushed the tops of her shiny pink slippers.

River introduced the women. "Pleased to meet you, Raven. And you too, Dr. Royal." Cibele nodded toward Sid.

Sid hadn't checked with River about title protocols. Would she embarrass his friend, or him, or herself if she asked to be more informal? She shot a questioning glance at River. He apparently understood and nodded back. "Please call me Sid," she said. "Here, I'm not a doctor. I'm River's friend."

Once inside the house, Cibele motioned them into the living room and pointed to a woman seated near the window. "This is my sister Ana. She lives down the road and wanted very much to meet you. We don't get to know many Americans, except, of course, for River. Ana's an excellent cook. She helped me with the lunch."

Beaming, Ana rose from her chair and shook their hands. "We hope you are enjoying your visit."

"Yes," Sid said. "It's a beautiful country. And this is a beautiful home."

Contrary to the outside, the inside was stunning. A woven rug—with olive leaves and creamy berries against a claret-colored background—covered the plank floorboards, and a cowhide was draped over the couch. Wooden bookcases lined one wall, and vases and jugs of rough-finished, smoke-stained porcelain stood among the volumes. Sid stared at the pottery, admiring their asymmetric shape and the flinty glazes.

Cibele crossed the room, lifted one of the jugs, and handed it to her. "Our uncle Carlos made them."

Sid cradled it in her hands. It was lighter than it looked, and its handle was set at a strange but striking angle, snug against the open mouth. "It's beautiful. Your uncle Carlos is very talented."

Cibele smiled. "Sit, por favor," she said as she motioned toward the couch. Sid lowered herself onto the cowhide. Raven sat beside her.

River had been right about Cibele. There was a lot to like about her. She moved with the ease of yards of silk gliding slowly from its bolt to the floor. Was she the Brazilian girlfriend Raven and her mother had hoped for River? She was beautiful, her clothes elegant. Sid looked down at her own scruffy shoes and baggy socks, at the legs of her wrinkled khaki pants. Then she glanced at River, who leaned against the bookcase, quiet as he listened to the women chatter.

Cibele's voice was buoyant and self-assured. She asked about the town in America where they lived, where they grew up, what they studied in school, what they did for fun.

Raven explained that she liked to go to movies and to ride the local bike trails when the weather was good. Sid didn't know what to say. "Well, in my spare time I like to knit," she finally said. "And read." Was that really all she did for fun? A quick mental survey of past weekends confirmed it. Knitting the sweater for Paul. Reading. Shopping at Kroger's and Walgreen's. Working. Mostly working. In Portland, she and Paul used to visit galleries and attend concerts from time to time. That was then.

Ana said she enjoyed cooking and caring for her son. Cibele said she liked to weave and nodded to the end of the room, to a large wooden loom hidden in the shadows, with blue-gray and chartreuse-green fabric arising from the warp threads.

"Did you weave this?" Sid asked, brushing her hand over the thick wool nap of the runner on the coffee table.

"Sim ... ah, yes. A while ago." Cibele flashed a demure smile and, seemingly embarrassed, quickly changed the subject. "And I play with Ana's son," she said quietly. "Little Gilberto." She pulled a framed photo from the bookshelf, pointed to the smiling child in short pants, and handed it to Sid. He looked about three years old and, leaning forward with his right knee bent, was poised to kick a soccer ball.

"Gilberto, he's good with the ball," Cibele said. "But now he is sick. He has red eye."

Sid looked at River for clarification.

"We'd call that *pink eye*," he said. "And, yes, Gilberto is a rugged little soccer player. He beats me every time."

Sid pictured River sliding across a grassy field, his muscled legs stretching to follow the ball.

Ana stood and announced that she needed to get back to her son. "My husband will need my help, soon, with Gilberto."

Back at River's house, Raven and Sid relaxed in the living room and tasted the drinks River had mixed in an old Mason jar: slices of lime smashed with sugar and rum poured on top. Sid took a cautious sip. The sweet of the sugar neutralized the sour of the lime, and the alcohol added a lively kick. She liked it.

Now it was Raven who lay in the bean bag chair, her bare feet braced on the couch beside her brother. "These are really good," she said after her second drink.

"Sure are," Sid said, still sipping on her first. "In your next life, River, you could be a bartender."

"Thanks," River laughed. "I think I'll stick to my regular job."

The twins chattered as if they were squirrels chasing each other through the treetops. "Remember the creek?" Raven giggled.

"And that huge fish you caught with only a half an angle-worm on the hook?" River chuckled.

"Remember that snotty Jennifer who waited for the school bus with us?"

"And Witch Hitchens? Was she our second- or third-grade teacher?"

"Second, I think. And mean."

Something stirred in Sid. She wondered if it was jealousy. Or longing. Maybe yearning for the sibling she'd lost. She slipped into her own reminiscences—twirling her fingers in an infant's curly hair, listening to the shrieks of a two-year-old calling her name, smelling the fresh-as-pure-air fragrance of a baby. These memories—were they really memories at all or had she imagined them?—were gray and vague, like a street scene on a foggy evening.

Raven held out her glass for another drink.

River shook his head. "You've reached the end, Sister," he said. "Four is more than enough. These things are wicked strong."

Raven giggled. "And wicked good."

3

1984   BRAZIL

River stood at the stove working a skillet. Even from the rear, he looked a lot like Raven. Same long waist, same round butt, same arm motions as he shoved a spatula under the eggs that sputtered in his frying pan. Whorls of turbulent, lampblack hair curled against the back of his collar. His voice, albeit lower, was Raven's voice, feisty and windswept. And engaging. Very engaging.

"Get away." He grabbed a towel and swatted the tiny flies that swarmed over the sink. "Shit, I forgot to close the window screen." He slammed it shut. "They're awfully pesky. Between the flies and the cats, you're going to think I live in a slum."

Sid sat at the table with her elbows resting on the top and one leg curled beneath her. She nursed the warmth of her coffee cup with her hands. It had been years since she had eaten a leisurely breakfast in her pajamas. In college she had usually grabbed two stale doughnuts while Laurie slept and then dashed from their dorm room to her early morning classes. As a medical student, she bought pastries, which tasted like jelly-coated cardboard, from hospital vending machines before the early morning rounds. During her residency, if she ate breakfast at all, it was an uncooked Pop Tart. This morning, soothed by the eggy odors of River's little house, she felt wonderfully lazy.

"Tomorrow's our lab meeting," Sid said. "Wonder how everyone's doing?" She blew on her coffee to cool it.

Raven, also in her pajamas, sat across from Sid and cradled her head in her palms. "The topic of the lab is off limits," she muttered. She stumbled into the back room and returned with two Tylenols. She popped the pills into her mouth, moaned "headache," and washed them down with a swallow of orange juice.

"Yeah, still, I wonder," Sid said. "Dr. Evans will be worrying about the lab finances. Eliot will be holed up in his nest, paging through microbiology journals and questioning the validity of what other scientists have published. I wonder who he's annoying now that I'm away?"

"Miss him?"

That word again, like a steel-pointed arrow. Miss. Miss him. Why did Raven ask that? She looked at her friend, at her half-mast eyes, her swollen lips.

Sid sometimes thought that if she and Eliot had lived on a different planet, somewhere deep in outer space where only nice people existed, his keen intellect, his creativity, his single-mindedness—everything about him—might have appealed to her. But they lived on Earth, and the real Eliot, distant and critical, had been wearing her down. He was one of the reasons she was in Brazil. "No," she said, "I don't miss him." She sipped her coffee. "Eliot needs to hear the old bromide about catching more flies with honey than with vinegar. That's what my Belgian grandmother used to say."

"Flies?" River, still stirring the eggs, called from the stove. "Did you find more flies in here?"

Sid shook her head and laughed. "No, we were talking about a guy in our lab who gets on my nerves. Need any help?"

Raven wrapped her arms around her head again. "When it comes to Eliot, you need a skin transplant, Sid. Ask for one that's thicker than the one you've got."

Sid glared at Raven. Her friend was unusually testy. Maybe driven by a hangover?

"Uh ..." River laid a hand on the shoulder of Sid's pajamas. His fingers were strong and electric. "You could set the table." He handed her three plates, three knives and three forks. He unrolled three sheets of paper towels and set them on top of the plates. "These will do for napkins."

After they sat down at the table, River passed Raven a plate of buttered, somewhat charred, bread.

Raven frowned. "Burned the toast, I see. Did you cook these eggs at all? They look slimy."

The toast tasted fine to Sid. And so did the eggs.

"Burned toast?" River asked. He looked puzzled. "It's done just right. Who likes raw toast? You?"

"No, I don't like raw, but not carbonized either," Raven said.

"And, the eggs are scrambled," River said. "Yes, they're moist. Dry scrambled eggs are like eating sawdust."

"They're too runny. See?" Raven tipped her plate and a stream of egg juice ran downhill.

"Sister, your usually sunny disposition seems to have darkened." He flashed a playful grin. "You're free to dine elsewhere."

Sid ate her toast and eggs without a comment. The twins' squabbling felt like the pull of a slingshot right before it releases its stone. She didn't want them to quarrel; she liked them better as loving siblings. River and Raven also remained silent.

"On a different note, want to go on a field trip after breakfast?" River finally asked. "I have to visit several farmers out near the reservoir."

"I've been wondering about your job," Sid asked. "What exactly do you do?"

"I work for an agricultural program through the US Agency for International Development," he answered. "We teach local farmers modern agricultural practices: how to plow their fields efficiently, which seeds to plant, what fertilizer to use. That kind of stuff. It's great."

"Did they grow crops in your commune? Is that where you learned about farming?"

"Well, our community had big gardens, but all I learned there was to distinguish the weeds from the vegetables. Yanking up dandelions and Bermuda grass was my job. We'll be gone a couple of hours. I have new seeds to show the guys."

"Sure, I'll come," Sid said.

"Ah, count me out," Raven said. "I'll stay home and tend my throbbing head."

"You sick?" Sid pretended to be naive. Of course, Raven was sick. Hung-over kind of sick.

"Well, too much fun, I guess." Raven said.

"Too much *rum* is my bet," River said. "The diagnosis is bottle flu. Do you agree, Doctor Sid?"

Sid shrugged.

Raven ignored them both. "I'll just laze around here a bit longer. You two go ahead."

The clouds, which dropped to the horizon ahead of them, threatened rain. As he drove along the dusty roads, River explained the crops that grew in the passing fields: sugar cane, cassava, corn. He recited the names of the tiny villages they passed through: Ursina Diana, Juritis, Brejo Alegre.

"They sound musical, like operas or something," Sid said.

"Yeah," he laughed. "They kinda do." He explained the struggling economy of the region and the limitations of agriculture and hydroelectricity and cattle ranching to provide decent wages. "It's beastly hot in the summer down here, and those folks are out in their fields in the worst of it. The weather is unpredictable for the crops, and the politics of the hydroelectricity plant range from muddy to ugly, and yet the farmers here manage to scratch out a living." His fingers tapped the steering wheel as he talked. Sid watched the expressive gestures of his hands, remembered their gentle touch on her shoulder.

This was how it used to be with Paul, she thought, back when they shared ideas with each other, enjoyed being together. Paul, too, was confident, kind, smart.

"If you haven't noticed yet, the folks here are the happiest humans you'll ever meet." A smile inched across his face. "They enjoy their lives. Like Cibele and Ana. Like the farmers we're about to meet." He pointed out the window. "Like those fellows out there." Two young men, laughing, stood up to their knees in grass, one with a scythe in his hands, the other, a rake. Even from the car, Sid could feel the comradery that filled their hilarity.

He turned onto a dirt road and, after about ten minutes, parked behind several pick-up trucks. Beyond, ten or twelve men stood in the shade of a pole barn or leaned against the fence, smoking.

Sid climbed out of the car and followed River toward the men. Dry grass, stippled with occasional tufts of green, carpeted the ground. As they walked through the farmyard, she heard a car door slam. She turned. A woman walked quickly toward them. It was Cibele.

River waved to her. "She's my translator. I'd be lost without her help with the technical language. Her father and grandfather are farmers, and she grew up with the lingo."

Cibele didn't look anything like a farmer. Her silk tunic billowed in the breeze; its green and blue print, like watercolor brush strokes on a camel-colored background, echoed tints of the sky and the distant treetops.

Sid continued to follow River toward the gathered men. Three steps later, the ground gave way under her left foot, and a barb of pain shot through her ankle. Her arms flailed as she tried to grab onto something, anything, to keep from falling. River leaned toward her and clutched her elbow. "You okay?"

"Yeah. I must have stepped in a hole. Thanks for catching me."

He held her elbow as they continued to walk. His grip was strong. "You're limping," he said.

"I think I turned my ankle a bit. It'll be fine in a minute." He was a convenient crutch. As she hobbled forward, she tilted against his side, felt the warmth of his body.

"Want to go back to the car?"

"Oh, no. Let's keep going." She wanted to stay with him, wanted to watch him do his work.

When they reached the farmers, he guided her to a stump and let go of her arm. "Here's a good place to sit." Then he began talking to the men as he passed out samples of corn seeds from his backpack. Cibele stood beside him. Through her, the farmers asked questions, and through her, River answered. What kind of yield could they expect? How many bags of seed per hectare? When should they plant? When would they be able to harvest?

When the farmers had finished asking questions, Cibele walked over to Sid. "It's good to see you, again. Sore leg?"

"Twisted ankle. My foot fell in a hole." Sid asked about Ana and the little boy, Gilberto.

Cibele's face glowed as she described her nephew's antics. "He's what we call a rocket child." Then she said, "Come. I'll introduce you to our friends."

The nearest men, five of them, nodded as Cibele called to them. Cibele laid her hand on the arm of the tall, somber man with the straw hat. "This is Marcelo," she said. "He's the lead assistant to Mr. Ayrton Queiroz, who owns a large farm near here."

Marcelo shook Sid's hand. His eyes were deep and dark and seemed to cling to something far away and sad.

"And this is ... Felix ... Hermann ... Philippe ... Thiago."

Sid shook their hands. Each man's skin was rough with calluses, and each grasp was as vigorous and assured as River's had been at the airport. While Cibele chatted with them in Portuguese, Sid studied their tanned faces, the intensity of their expressions, the earnestness of their voices. From the way they responded to Cibele, they clearly respected her.

When the men returned to their trucks, Cibele said, "That first one, Marcelo? His little daughter Mariana died about two weeks ago. It's been terribly hard on him and his wife. They are expecting another baby in a couple months."

Sid looked at Marcelo again. His sad face, his stooped posture, his blank eyes all spoke volumes. She knew that look, had seen it before in the grief-stricken parents of her dying patients. Before she could say anything, she heard River call. "Ready to go?"

River appeared at her side and asked about her ankle.

"Still a bit sore. It'll be fine by tomorrow."

He offered his arm again. As she leaned against him and limped back to the car, she once more felt the warmth of his body. The familiar, haunting echo crawled over her like a specter at midnight. Her sobbing mother, the disbelief, the emptiness, the fury of the silence when no words would come. "Tell me about those seeds," she said.

"They're a new hybrid, developed at the University in São Paulo. Should give higher yields than the seeds these guys have used for generations."

"Sounds important." The leaden shadow from long ago began to dissipate. Slowly.

"It is. I'm excited about helping the people here maximize the yields from their crops. They're not highly educated. Not at all. But they're fast learners and willing to try new varieties in their fields. They have no reason to trust me, though. That's where Cibele is invaluable."

At the car, he helped her into the passenger seat. She held onto his arm a bit longer than necessary and searched his face for a response. But he offered no smile; she saw no sparkle in his all-business eyes.

"There you go." He pulled away from her and slammed the door.

They followed Cibele's Chevy away from the farmyard and down the dirt road. About three miles later, Cibele stopped behind a string of parked vehicles. She climbed out of her car and walked back to River's Volvo.

He leaned out his open window. "What's up?"

"Everyone's here for a funeral. I heard about it from the guys back at the farm."

Sid leaned her head against the back of her seat. She didn't want to hear about another person dying.

"Anyone we know?" River asked.

"Yes," Cibele said. "Eduardo Setti's young daughter, Luiza."

Sid closed her eyes. Another child. Another devastated parent. First Marcelo, and now someone named Eduardo.

"Oh, god. That's awful." River's face darkened. "What happened?"

"Come on. I'll explain on the way."

He turned to Sid. "Eduardo is one of the farmers in my district. Want to go to a funeral?"

Not really, she thought. But she didn't want to wait alone in the car, either. "Okay."

He helped her out of the passenger seat and offered his arm once again. Hanging on to him, she tottered toward the crowd in the graveyard.

Cibele explained as they walked that Luiza had woken up with a fever and purple blotches on her legs and was dead by that night.

Fever and purple blotches. Sid tightened her hold on River. The ashen shadow began to gather over her head again.

"You're a doctor, Sid," he said. "What might have happened to her?"

"Hard to say. Sounds like sepsis of some kind." She gripped River's arm even harder. Sepsis was bad. Often really bad. "How old was Luiza?"

"About two years," Cibele said, shaking her head. "Just a baby."

Sid stopped walking and leaned against River.

"Ankle too sore?" he said. "We're almost there."

"It's fine. Let's go."

At the graveside, she continued to lean against him and the rigidity of his muscles. The priest mumbled a blessing and sprinkled holy water over the child's plain wooden casket. The onlookers crossed themselves and mumbled a response. A girl in a white dress placed a bouquet of flowers on the casket's lid. She appeared to be about five years old. Could she be the dead child's sister? Sid stared at the girl's tear-stained cheeks, at her shiny black hair and delicate hands, at the pretty young girl who would carry the ghost of her lost sister forever.

A group of women—Sid guessed they were Luiza's mother, grandmothers, and aunts—wailed even louder as the little box, buoyed by ropes in the hands of six young men, disappeared into the hole. The women were all dressed in black mourning clothes.

Then River let go of Sid's elbow. Abruptly. Matter-of-factly. "Will you be okay standing here for a moment? I want to speak with Luiza's family." He edged into the crowd, wrapped his arms around one of the weeping women, and spoke into her ear.

She nodded her head as she sobbed. He whispered something more to her, and she nodded again.

Now it wasn't her ankle that bothered her most. It was the empty expanse of an absence. The inexplicability of it all.

As they returned to their cars, Cibele wandered over to Sid. Dark glasses masked her eyes. "How's your leg?"

"It'll be okay."

"You know, she's the third little child to die like this in the past two weeks."

What? In this tiny little place? "Three deaths in young, healthy children?" Sid said. "In Promissão? Over two weeks?"

"Yes. Marcelo's daughter Mariana was the first." "What's going on?"

"No one knows. They got sick, high fever and listlessness, and then they died. Within a day."

"How about the local doctors? What do they say?"

"All we have is Dr. Alancar. I don't know what he thinks of it."

"We could ask him."

4

1984 BRAZIL

They had cleared the breakfast dishes from the table when River proposed a walk along the shore of the reservoir. "It's like a giant lake, but much less interesting. The river was dammed back in the '70s during an electrification project, and its waters spread like lava over the surrounding farmland. Biology alert: there aren't a lot of trees. But we could do some fishing if you'd like."

Raven set the skillet she had been drying on the counter. "What kind of fish?"

"Nothing you've heard of. But they're good to eat."

"Fine with me," Raven said. "So, we'll have fresh fish for dinner?"

"Well, maybe. Fishing is no promise of catching."

"Sounds fun, but I'll have to pass," Sid said. "The ankle is a little better, but I think I wouldn't be a good hiking companion." She pulled up the left hem of her slacks. The ankle was puffy.

Alone in River's house, now eerily quiet, Sid limped from room to room, trying to figure out what to do while River and Raven hiked and fished. She hoped River would tell Raven what was bothering him. A walk by the water was a good venue for that. She set the clean breakfast dishes in the cupboard and scrubbed the stove top. She wiped out the bathtub even though it didn't need cleaning. Then what?

She kneeled on the floor in the living room in front of River's bookcase. *The Stand, The Eye of the Needle, Tales of the City, The Stories of John Cheever.* None appealed to her. When she spotted *The Valley of the Horses*, she thought it might be a good choice. It was half hidden beneath a stack of agency reports, the only book on the bottom shelf. Even though River had told her to help herself to anything in his library, she felt a twinge of discomfort as she dug it out from under the papers. The book was shabby, with a tear in its paper cover and a coffee cup ring centered over the title.

When she flipped open the front cover, a photo fluttered like an injured bird to the floor. She reached to retrieve it. The picture was dark as if it had been taken inside a cave. She began to shove it back between the pages but then stopped and studied it more closely. The cave was actually a smoky bar filled with people. She gazed at the faces. Every person was a man. And, several were kissing. In the corner of the picture, a guy with pale skin and dark, thick hair that fell into his eyes—the guy looked a lot like River—sat at a round table in front of two bottles of beer. He was kissing a man.

She turned the photo over. On the back, sloping script, in blue fountain-pen ink, read, "Hey Riv. Great night. Hope to do it again, soon. Fernando."

She slapped the cover shut, trapping the photo between the pages. The book felt like fire in her hands and fell to the carpet. She scrambled to her feet. Everything was suddenly, stunningly, glaringly clear: River's gentle but emotionally distant greetings, the way he moved away from her rather than toward her, his disinterest in responding to her, albeit subtle, advances. And his personality change, the new quiet and apparent sadness that worried Raven and their mom.

Her mind leapt from tangled thoughts to jumbled logic— not River. Can't be true. Must be someone else. Who was Fernando? She felt hollow as a kettle drum, and a distant echo of a warning song from a cymbal rang through her head.

Secrets should stay secret. Private things should remain private. She didn't want to know his secret, didn't want it to be real. But she was a scientist, and the evidence was clear. She wedged the book back under the papers on the shelf. She wanted to wash her hands—to scrub them until they bled—but she couldn't wash away the truth. She felt like a fool. A silly, blind fool. Did River realize she had tried to flirt with him? She hoped not.

Did Raven know? She and their mother had speculated about a girlfriend. Of course Raven didn't know. But that was the explanation for the sadness she and her mother had detected in his voice.

What would Raven think? Would she dump her brother from her life? Abandon the boy who whistled Yankee Doodle when she was scared?

She certainly couldn't mention this to Raven. She couldn't

Fever

bring it up with River. Nor Cibele. River's secret was now also hers, and she was alone with it.

She limped out the door and down the path to the road, trying to escape the throb in her head. Everything was gray—the other buildings, the trees, the fences that ensnared the yards, the cats that slinked through the grass—even though the sun glistened high in the sky. Where had the color gone?

Sid was nestled in the bean bag chair trying to read *The Eye of the Needle* when she heard a car slow as it approached the house. It pulled into the side yard. They were home. Her new, unwanted knowledge was about to meet its key players. The knowing—River's secret, her secret—had to remain unspoken. It belonged to both of them, and yet they couldn't share it.

"Hey, what'd you do while we were gone?" he called as he stepped in the front door. "I hope you didn't get bored."

"I've been reading." She waved *The Eye of the Needle* at him.

"See what Raven caught?" He held up a stringer. A foot-long, silver-scaled fish dangled before her.

"Raven caught that?"

"I sure did." Raven walked through the door. "According to River, it's a curvina fish. It'll be our dinner."

River held his fish knife in his hand when he leaned through the kitchen door and stared at Sid. "You okay?"

"Yeah, I'm okay." She was mostly okay, as okay as anyone could be while carrying River's secret as well as the responsibility, and the awkwardness, of keeping it.

"You've lost your usual verve."

"I'll be fine. Maybe tired." To her, he was now a completely different person. Apparently, so was she. "Can I help with anything?"

He ducked back into the kitchen and returned with a juice glass and a bottle. "You can help by drinking this. Maybe it'll bring your verve back." He poured three fingers of red wine and handed the glass to her.

She took a sip. He was such a kind person, and she was such a fool. Being gay was a hard way to live and, besides her loss of innocence and the need for it to remain clandestine, that bothered her most. He had to be furtive. Always hiding. She knew people who were fired for being gay, who went to jail for showing public affection with a lover. A person should be able to love whoever he loved, freely and fully. *She* should be able to love freely and fully, but that wasn't working out, either.

And then there was the specter of AIDS. She'd read about the bath houses in San Francisco and had seen medical papers about the devastated immune systems. Kaposi's sarcoma. *Pneumocystis carinii* pneumonia.

Had he spent time in the Bay Area? He and Raven grew up in California. He would have graduated from high school in Santa Rosa with his sister. He had gone to college at Sonoma State. Not all that far from San Francisco. How about Fernando? Did he live in Brazil? In Promissão? Was he still River's friend? The prospect of River with AIDS was terrifying. It was a death sentence, and its possibility yet another awful secret for her to carry.

She watched his body move between the kitchen and the dinner table. He seemed healthy. His clothes—and they weren't brand new, but rather seemed fairly worn—fit him well, unlike the pants and shirts that fell off the skeletal figures with "slim disease" pictured in the newspapers. His arms and face, the only skin she could see, were free of the puffy, violet, quarter-sized eruptions of Kaposi sarcoma. She wished that could free her from worry about AIDS.

"Soup's on," River called. "Or, rather, fish's on."

"Boy, is this good," Raven said after everyone was seated and had begun to eat.

"Sure is." Sid tried to sound enthusiastic, to sound as naive to the truth as she had been only hours ago when River and Raven had walked out the door with their fishing poles. Now she watched, and listened, as the twins chatted about the angling expedition, about the one River caught that got away, about the waves on the reservoir and the difference between the taste of the curvina and bass or brook trout.

"This is sweeter than bass, not as musty," Raven said as she spiked a piece of fish on her fork and waved at her brother.

"Maybe," he said, tilting his head and thinking and remembering. "I'd say brook trout are cleaner tasting, and this is a tad gamier."

Sid remained silent. The conversation was so ordinary. As if nothing were different. This is going to be very hard, she said to herself. Very hard.

Sid couldn't sleep that night. Thoughts of sickness spun through her mind. She tried to remember what she had read in the Centers for Disease Control report about how AIDS was spread. By blood. By sexual contact. Not through the air, not by touching the hands of people with AIDS. Not by contaminated food nor water. Not by sitting at the same dinner table eating fish prepared by River. Not by drinking wine from a clean juice glass that may have been his glass the night before. Not by his hand on her shoulder. Not by the soap on the bathroom sink. Silly, she said to herself. You don't even know if he's infected.

Then images of dead children marched through her mind. Mariana, Luiza, the third child. What was the cause of their sudden illness? A poison? An infection? Could it be treated? Prevented?

She heard Raven breathing from the cot beside hers. Air moved smoothly in and out of her friend's sleeping body, the gentle, regular breathing of slumber. Innocent Raven. Unaware Raven.

5

1984 BRAZIL

The afternoon Sid and Raven decided to hike toward town, the clear blue sky reached toward eternity, out to where the quiet of space stretched without end. Did worry exist in outer space, Sid wondered. Probably not, she decided. Planets and asteroids and moons and the rocks that rotated around Saturn in its rings don't have brains to hold any worry nor neurons to spread it. Those inorganic bodies, unlike people, don't have secrets that can't be shared.

"Is your ankle up to walking?" Raven asked.

"Yes, it's fine now." She pulled up her pant leg to show Raven that the swelling was gone.

They stopped for a moment outside a small bar and listened to the bossa nova that poured out the front door.

"What do you think?" Sid asked, nodding toward the bar.

"Sure," Raven said. They walked inside, selected two seats on the open-air patio out the back door, and ordered rum with lime juice.

Raven took a sip and scrunched her nose. "Well, River's were better."

"Absolutely," Sid agreed. This one was too sour while River's were as sweet as the best limeade.

The wind kicked up dust in the field next door and rustled the bushes beside their table. The bouncy music, the shocking yellow tablecloths, the rattle of Portuguese, the cracked, almond-tinted plaster on the church across the street were, to Sid, Brazil from central casting. And she loved it: the colors, the food, the energy all of it. As a bonus, the sense of liberty that banished the ghosts of the lab was exhilarating. Or should have been. A tiny, naggy voice in the back of her head, however, whispered that time was fleeting. Experiments were waiting to be done back home. She shook away the voice and took another sip of her drink.

On the walk back to River's place, they wandered through an open market, past tables loaded with mangoes and papayas, bananas and pineapples. Overhead, purple, blue, and orange printed fabrics, pinned to the wires that crisscrossed the top of the arcade, flapped in the breeze. Children chased each other among the stalls, turning here, ducking there. One boy skidded to a stop in front of Sid. Tiny flies fluttered around his moist eyes as he stared into her face. Before she could swat them away for him, the child was gone. She'd seen pictures of tropical eye flies in her medical textbooks, but never in person. The thought of them made her blink. And blink again.

They stopped at a booth of hand-painted scarfs. Sid fingered the smooth silk. "Do you like this one?" she asked Raven as she held a creamy one covered with deep plum and apricot blooms.

"It's yummy. Will match your coat."

Sid bought it.

Beside the scarves was a table of knitted sweaters and shawls. Sid ran her fingers over a cardigan. The yarn was coarsely spun and the color of beige sheep. She touched another, the bright orange and red one. Then another, almost the same blue as the sweater she was knitting for Paul.

Next to the knitting table was a game booth. "Bet you can't hit the plate," Raven said.

Sid watched a man fling coins at about twenty emerald green, pressed-glass plates that stood on a sand-covered platform inside the booth. She eyed the dishes, calculated the slopes of their rims. "I bet I can." She fished her wallet from her snakeskin handbag, the one she liked so much, the one Paul had given her for her birthday. For a brief moment, the memory of that evening when he'd surprised her with the bag flashed across her mind: the delicious dinner at an expensive restaurant and, later, the opening of a play at their favorite theater. She was in love with Paul then. Deeply in love.

She handed a Brazilian one *real* bill to the vender, and he handed her three coins. She turned them over in her palm. They were lighter than she'd guessed, were made of foil-covered cardboard rather than metal. She pitched the first into the center of the cluster of plates. It slid across the top and fell to the sandy platform. She hadn't realized how shallow the plates actually were. She needed to throw the coin at a different angle, to make it skip like a flat stone across the surface of a lake. The second one slid more slowly across the dish but, again, landed on the gravel.

"Last chance," Raven said. Her smile was full of mirth. It delivered a teasing challenge.

Sid studied the plates, tilted her head from side to side for a better bead on their depth, and lobbed the last coin. It glided to the plate, swept across it, and stopped just short of the edge.

"Hey, you did it," Raven yelled. "I can't believe it."

"Me neither," Sid laughed. Back when she played games—hearts as a child with her neighbor friend, bridge with Laurie and the dorm girls, and Scrabble with Paul—she never won. The attendant handed her a fuzzy, stuffed duck, about the size of a football. "Parabens," he said, nodding and smiling.

She didn't know what that word meant. "What did he say?" Raven shook her head.

A man standing beside her smirked. "He said 'congratulations.' Next, he'll want to sell you more coins."

"No more for me." As they walked away from the booth, Sid dangled the toy duck in front of Raven's face. "What on earth will I do with this?"

Raven shrugged. "I don't know. But he's kind of cute."

When they turned a corner in the center of the market, Sid thought she heard her name. She looked around at the rows of vendors hawking sandals, blankets, plantains, and plucked chickens that dangled by their feet from rusty wires.

"Raven, Sid."

Who was calling? She looked down the rows, again. Then she saw her. Cibele. She was waving from amid a group of women at a table piled with cheeses.

"Greetings," Cibele called. "Are you enjoying the market?"

"Oh, yes," Sid answered as she and Raven neared the cheese stand. She held the duck in front of Cibele. "See what I won by tossing coins at plates?"

Cibele laughed. "Let me show you around. I'd like you to see my favorite places here."

Together they wandered through the rows of stalls, stopping to examine leather purses, embroidered handkerchiefs, more knitwear, carved wooden bowls. As they passed a jewelry stand, the vendor motioned to Sid and extended a necklace toward her. In the sunshine, the veins of orchid pink and pistachio green stood out like interwoven rivulets from the gray of the stones.

"Wow, that's beautiful." Raven fingered one of the pebbles. "What are those little stick things hanging in the middle? They look like miniature French fries. Think they're real gold?"

A price tag dangled from the necklace. Sid and Raven calculated the cost in dollars. Sixty bucks. "Probably brass," Sid said as she fingered the stick things. But she liked the necklace. Was sixty dollars reasonable? She wondered if she was supposed to haggle over the price. She had no stomach for that.

"Here, try it on." Cibele signaled to the lady in the stall who muttered something in Portuguese, unhooked the ends of the necklace, slid the clasp together behind Sid's neck, and stepped away. A wide, warm grin spread across her face.

"You absolutely have to buy that," Raven said. "It's perfect for you."

"Where will I wear it?" Sid didn't dress up much, especially since she'd moved to Michigan. "To Thursday morning lab meeting?" she laughed.

"Wherever you want. It's gorgeous."

The lady in the stall pulled a hand mirror from beneath the counter. Sid gazed into the chipped glass and viewed the necklace from face on, from the left, then the right. She liked the muted colors of the stones and the way they fell like flattened marbles across her collar bones. It was a comfortable weight. The sales lady made clucking noises as she bobbed her head and grinned.

Cibele asked the lady something in Portuguese. The lady answered. Cibele shook her head. "Too much." Cibele then apparently quoted another offer to the lady.

Back and forth they quibbled, their voices rising and falling, their heads turning from side to side. Cibele started to walk away from the stall. The lady trotted after her, jabbering and fluttering her arms.

In the end, Sid bought the necklace. Cibele had bargained the price down by a third. Sid thanked her, and Cibele waved her hand as if shooing away a mosquito. "That's the way we do business here. It's a game."

As they walked away from the jewelry stand, Sid handed the toy duck to Cibele. "Maybe your nephew will enjoy this."

"Why don't you give it to him yourself? Come to my place. Gilberto and Ana are there."

"You go, Sid," Raven said. "I'm heading back to River's to take a nap and then help him make dinner."

"Show Ana your new necklace," said Cibele.

Sid removed its newspaper wrapping and handed the beads to Ana. Gilberto, seated on his mother's lap, reached for it.

"No, no, little one," Ana said. She set him on the floor and held the necklace toward the window. She slowly slid the beads through her fingers as the sunshine caught their colors. "This is beautiful." She glanced at Sid. "And it will be lovely on you, Dr. Royal. The stones pick up the gray-green of your gorgeous eyes."

"Please call me Sid. We're friends, after all."

Ana handed the necklace back to Sid. She seemed to be thinking about something. Finally, she said, "Could I ask about Gilberto's eyes. See ..." She turned her son's face toward Sid.

Sid sat down on the floor beside Gilberto. He leaned his head against his mother's leg. "How old are you, Gilberto?" Sid asked. He stared at her with serious, albeit pink-rimmed, eyes.

"Tell her you're almost two and a half," Cibele said.

He buried his head in Ana's pant legs.

"He's timid of me, a stranger. That's to be expected. Here." Sid passed the duck to Cibele, "You give it to him."

Cibele swung the stuffed duck in front of Gilberto. "Here's the toy Sid brought for you." He lifted his head, then spread his hand toward it.

"Quack, quack," Cibele squawked and made the duck's head bob.

Gilberto giggled. He was a beautiful child, fresh, curious, full of magic. He scooted to Cibele, grabbed the duck by one orange leg, and slammed the animal against the rug.

"No, Gilberto. You have to be nice to the duck." Cibele's voice was stern and her face twisted with horror. "He's your toy. Sid gave him to you to play with, not to hurt."

Ana grabbed the duck from her son and cradled it in her arms. "He's a gentle duck, Gilberto."

Gilberto grabbed it back and cradled it against his chest. "Duck," he said.

"So sorry," Ana said. "He's been sick with the red eye and isn't himself."

"He's only two and has a long way to go to learn all the rules of the world." Sid'd been examining Gilberto's eyes while speaking with him. Indeed, the whites were inflamed, and dried matter was crusted on his lower lids. Otherwise, he seemed fine. "Has he had any fever? Is he eating okay?"

"No fever. And he's eating fine."

"Children often get pink eye when they have colds. If you're worried about this, you should check with his doctor." Did he even have a doctor? Sid didn't know what kind of medical care was available there in rural Brazil, although Cibele had mentioned the name of the local physician.

"If he gets sicker, we'll take him to the clinic," Ana said.

Soon Gilberto was wandering around Cibele's living room, making his new duck dance on the couch, on the bookcases, on the chairs. He thrust it into Sid's lap and then laid his head on the duck's back. She patted the boy's cheek. His skin was smooth and buttery, with the smell of fresh apples.

"He's a charming young fellow," Sid said. "With a sparkling personality. He'll grow up to be a genius."

"You're a pediatrician. I'll bet you say that about every little boy."

Sid chuckled. "Well, it's true that I enjoy all children. They are beautifully natural, and the young ones haven't had their native spunk disciplined out of them yet. They are, after all, innate little scientists, curious about everything around them. They explore their world at every turn."

Treasures are what kids are. That's what she had said to Paul when they had talked about children. Unbridled, imaginative, beloved by their parents. He couldn't understand why her love for children didn't translate into her yearning to have some of her own. And she didn't understand why the two, the love and the yearning, had to be linked. For her, the other good thing about children was that she, as a pediatrician, could pass them back to their parents when they were cranky, needed a diaper change, or whenever she was finished examining them.

"Time for us to go," Ana said. "Gilberto needs a nap. Thanks for the toy ... Sid."

As Ana and Gilberto walked out the door, Cibele excused herself and returned with a tray of glasses. "Iced tea?" she asked. "You must be getting thirsty." After she passed a glass to Sid, she said, "I hope I'm not prying, but are you married?"

"No." The question was a strange one and seemed to have leaped out of nowhere.

"Well, I ask because I think you'd be a wonderful mother. You obviously understand and enjoy children, and you are so even-tempered with them. Someday."

Sid swirled the ice cubes that floated in her tea. Even though she thought of Cibele as a friend, she was a very new friend, and thus, would ordinarily not yet be privy to Sid's personal life. The world expected her to become a mother, but she wasn't sure. Occasionally visions of motherhood flashed through her head: being pregnant, breastfeeding an infant, lugging a baby through the grocery store in a backpack, singing a lullaby to her child as she stroked his head. She never spoke of such visions with anyone.

Something about that afternoon, though, made Sid chatty. Maybe it was being in laid-back Brazil or in the company of a warm, broad-minded person like Cibele. Maybe it was because her hidden secrets seemed suddenly tiny compared to River's massive secret. "Actually I've been dating a man for several years, and children is the big issue between us. He wanted to get married a year ago and start a family right away. I wasn't ready. And still am not."

"Not ready?" Cibele asked.

"No. For a long time, in addition to being a pediatrician, I've wanted to be a scientist. And I needed several years of additional training to do that. Paul was unhappy about my decision to move to Michigan for that training. He has tried to be supportive, but clearly he is unhappy."

"Are you still a couple?"

"Well ... I'd say a tenuous one. He still lives in Portland, Oregon—he has an excellent job that depends on his living there, so he can't move—and he pouts about my living in Michigan. He wants to be a father, and he'd be a good one. I'm just not ready yet to be a mother, and he can't accept that." After a short pause, she added, "I'm really not sure how that will all turn out."

Cibele sighed, looked at her hands, and then said, "Most women here long to be mothers. I do, and when the right man comes along, it'll happen. I hope."

Sid twirled her ice cubes again. "Speaking of children, I'm very curious about what happened to the girl whose funeral we attended. Is it common for a child here in Promissão to die suddenly like that?"

"No, it's very uncommon." Cibele looked at the top of the window. "Children die sometimes from pneumonia or diarrhea. But this seemed different. So sudden. Luiza was well until a day before she was dead. And those purple spots ... we've never seen anything like that before."

The purple spots. Purpura? Sid wondered. It could explain the death of a child. And an otherwise healthy child. And suddenly. "I'm eager to meet the doctor and ask him about it."

"Tomorrow," Cibele said. "We'll go tomorrow."

6

1 9 8 4   B R A Z I L

After another breakfast of River's eggs, Raven said, "We need an adventure. Sid missed seeing the lake. Let's go for a ride, Sid." She turned to River. "Can we borrow your car?"

"Should I trust you with it?"

"Of course you can trust us." Raven pretended to be mildly offended. "Sid will be the copilot. Does that meet your approval?"

Sid hoped she didn't have to witness another spat between them. She wanted to tell Raven to lay off her brother, wanted to say that the teeny slight he had fired at her was completely unimportant considering his situation. But his secret was a secret, so she had to remain silent.

"While you are on your adventure, you should stop at the Mosteiro de São Alonzo. It's an ancient, working monastery. And have my favorite bauro sandwich at my favorite restaurant, Mocotó. You can drop me off at the office before you head out," he said. "Okay?"

"Better remind me how to get there," Raven said.

Sid watched River trace the route on the map with his pointer finger—the road to the lake, and then the little road to the monastery, and then the bigger road to the restaurant. His hands were strong, those of a self-confident, secure person, and their digits were steadfast as they moved over the paper.

"Raven, beware of the octopuses," he said as they headed out the door.

From the highway, Sid saw the water, a distant slice of silver sparkling in the sun. Then it disappeared but reappeared again after Raven turned the car onto a dusty, curvy road. They drove past plowed fields and patches of trees. When they arrived at a rim of beach dotted with weeds and trash, they stopped and watched a fishing trawler chug slowly forward several hundred yards off the shore.

"What do you think?" Raven asked. She started to walk along the water's edge, gingerly stepping over a rusty bucket and then a broken hobby horse half buried in the caramel-colored muck.

"About what?" Sid followed.

"About Brazil. Promissão. The lake. Anything and everything."

"Well, Brazil is beautiful. Promissão is small and comfortable and earthy. I've seen nicer lakes." And the "anything?" Did she mean River?

Sid's shoe sank into a pile of sludge hidden by the rushes beside the water. When she pulled it out, the mud made a sucking sound. Maybe Raven was playing matchmaker.

Even if River weren't gay, Sid could see that the two of them wouldn't be a compatible pair. He was easygoing and laidback, the feral son of hippies; she, on the other hand, considered herself focused and single-minded, the only child—only surviving child—of proper Belgians who had assimilated into upper middle class America very quickly. River was funny in a mature, comedic way; she knew she wasn't funny at all. He lived in Brazil; she was committed to completing her research training in Michigan. That was still her goal despite her experiments going sour. "If you're wondering what I think of River, I find your brother to be a generous, dear fellow," she added.

On the way back to Promissão, they drove past a sign to the Mosteiro de São Alonzo. "Isn't that the monastery River suggested we visit?" Sid asked.

"I think so." Raven turned the steering wheel hard to the right.

From a distance, its golden, plaster-sided chapel glowed like a fireball in the bright sunlight, and its bell tower rose heavenward above a crowded cemetery. "I think River has befriended several of the monks here," Raven said. "He mentioned them a couple times, said they went fishing together." She pulled the car alongside the monastery and stopped in the shade of the only tree in the parking lot.

River and monks? Could the Fernando in that fateful photo of River at the gay bar be a monk? No matter how Sid twirled the thought, the monks didn't fit well with what she knew of River.

"Does your brother have a religious streak to him?" she asked.

"Oh, gosh, no. Believe me, he doesn't. He just likes to take the kids from the mission school fishing in the reservoir with the monks." Raven stepped out of the car. "Let's go in."

Sid sensed an inexplicable force in the solemnity that surrounded the building. The air was crystal clear, and it smelled of strangely scented dust. Maybe nutmeg. Maybe cumin. The subtle odors reminded Sid of her pious grandmothers. Her parents had been raised Roman Catholic in Belgium, but they hadn't attended mass in America ever as far as Sid knew. But both grandmothers had rosaries dangling over their dressers and spoke fondly of the priests of their parishes. Sid glanced up at the colorful windows of muted stained glass, at the images of the baby Jesus and Mary and shepherds. They were dark except for a candle flickering in the center pane and looked like those in her maternal grandmother's church. She thought of that grandmother's bowed head during mass, the way she chewed on the wafer when she returned to their pew after communion, the delicate way her wrinkled hand made the sign of the cross.

The churchyard in Brazil was serenely quiet, except for the chipping of a squirrel high up on the bell tower's roof. From behind the chapel, a second squirrel echoed. When they reached the ornate wooden door, Raven rapped the metal knocker against its plate. Nothing happened. She rapped again. No one came. "Let's try the back," she said.

They walked around the building to a short, wood-sided hut attached to the abbey. The windows were open. The air now carried a yeasty smell. Sid peered through the screen door. Inside, three monks, their brown robes dusted white with flour, were baking bread.

"Bem-vindo." The monk nearest the door waved a wooden spoon.

"Hello. We speak only English." Sid said the words slowly, deliberately.

"Welcome to our bakery." He waved the spoon again and laughed. His English was excellent.

One of the other monks hauled four thick loaves from the brick oven, which had been built into the wall. He balanced them on a well-used baking peel and then set them on a counter. The third monk, up to his elbows in dough, bent over a wooden trough the size of a baby's bath basin and kneaded.

"My brother is River Saunders." Raven leaned her forehead against the door screen, dislodging the flies gathered there, and stared inside.

"River's a good fisherman," the monk with the wooden spoon said. He sliced two slabs from one of the fresh loaves and handed them through the door. "Have some bread."

Sid bit into the warm, hard-crusted wedge. "Yes, very tasty. Thank you. Could we buy a loaf?"

"Sim." He slid a loaf into a paper bag and passed it out the door.

"Let's try to find the restaurant River talked about," Raven said when they returned to the car.

Back on the road, Sid leaned out the open car window and took a deep breath. The odors of the fresh bread in her lap mingled with the smells of the wildflowers along the ditch. The wind was dry against her cheeks. Michigan, home of bewildering experimental results and squabbles with Eliot, seemed a world away. She loved the simplicity of the Brazilian countryside. "This place is so wonderful."

"Indeed. I'm so grateful you made it possible." Raven flashed a sincere smile.

According to the map, the café was about fifteen kilometers ahead. River claimed they served the best sandwich in the entire country. It seemed a long way to go for a sandwich, Sid thought, but, as Raven reminded her, the drive was part of the adventure.

The Volvo's wheels bounced over potholes that dotted the dirt lane as they rode past farmyards, fences, and telephone poles that either leaned into the road or away from it. Raven gripped the steering wheel, and Sid braced her arms against the dashboard. They turned the corner beside a cluster of trees and spotted, ahead, seven or eight concrete buildings.

"What are we looking for, again?" Sid asked.

"Mocotó." Raven kept her eyes on the rutty road.

"There it is." Sid pointed to a low celery-colored structure with a bright blue roof. It looked a bit iffy. She hoped it would be clean and the food safe. She had to trust River's recommendation.

Inside, the air smelled of barbeque, butcher shop, and Pine-Sol. The floor was clean and the room well-lit. They found seats at a table near the kitchen and studied the hand-written menus.

"What did River call those sandwiches?" Sid asked.

"Ah ... started with a B, I think."

She looked, again, at her menu. Under the word "sanduíches" was the word "Bauru." That must be it. They ordered one each.

The waiter slid two overloaded paper plates onto their table. Each of the hollowed-out buns was filled with three slices of tomato, a hunk of lettuce, a sliver of pickle, and melted cheese, and the meat stuffing hung like a ruffled skirt around the edges. "I wonder what kind of animal this came from?" Sid poked the meat with her fork. "Maybe it's best not to ask."

"Cow?" Raven also prodded her sandwich. "Or horse? I don't know if they eat horses down here. We'll have to ask River."

Sid took a bite. A stream of meat juice trickled down her chin and puddled on the front of her T-shirt. "Ugh." She dabbed at the stain with her napkin and smeared it into an even wider smudge, a red-brown bull's eye on a lemon-yellow background. "At least this is one of my crummy tops."

"We can try to wash it out in the sink at River's," Raven suggested.

"Yeah. I really don't care, though. It's an old thing I got when I was in college. I should, however, change into a clean one before Cibele and I visit Dr. Alancar this afternoon."

The meat tasted like rare roast beef. It was good—very good—but Sid wouldn't give it the award for the best sandwich ever.

Cibele parked her car in front of a stucco building that glowed like an apricot, turned to Sid, and said, "This is the clinic." They walked inside. "Dr. Alancar's office door is around to the left."

Inside, four wire chairs lined the wall beneath the window. Three slats on the venetian blinds were bent, and dust bunnies nested along the floorboards. Cibele knocked on the inside door. When it finally opened, a gray-haired, slightly stooped man stepped into the waiting area. His clinical coat hung from his shoulders like a large jacket on a small hanger, and his stethoscope looped from one pocket. "Welcome," he said. His voice was warm and kind.

Cibele placed her hand on Sid's arm. "Dr. Alancar has been the doctor in Promissáo for a long time. He probably delivered every person in this town under age thirty ... including me."

His smile, slow to dawn, was polite.

"Dr. Alancar, this is my new friend, Dr. Sid Royal."

Sid shook Dr. Alancar's hand. His grip was firm and self-assured.

"She's a pediatrician from the United States. Sid and her friend are visiting River Saunders. My boss. Do you know him?"

"No." Dr. Alancar shook his head. "I don't know him."

"Dr. Royal is interested in learning how pediatrics is practiced here in rural Brazil," Cibele said.

"Well." Alancar looked baffled. "It certainly wouldn't be the same as you do in the United States. I've never been to America, so I really don't know, but I'd bet a fair amount of money I'm correct in that."

Cibele chuckled. Sid nodded.

"Would you like a tour of the clinic?" he asked.

The first stop was the emergency room, which was the size of River's kitchen. "We see patients of all ages here, newborns to the very elderly," Dr. Alancar explained. A gurney stood in the center of the room. Shelves and cabinets lined each wall. When he touched the switch, bright light from the lamp over the gurney flooded every corner. "Our job here is to stabilize the patients as best we can. If they need further care, we transfer them to a larger hospital, usually the one in Ribeirão Preto. As you know, I'm a general physician. The hospital at Ribeirão Preto has several pediatricians."

He opened one of the cabinets. Inside were rows of endo-tracheal tubes of all sizes, each inside a sterile package. "We are able to intubate patients young and old," he waved his hand at the tubes, "but we have no ventilators, so we have to use Ambu bags if the patients aren't breathing."

"How far is that other hospital?" Sid asked.

"Um." He thought a moment. "It's about 270 kilometers. Takes a bit over three hours."

Long way, long time to hand-ventilate a child, Sid thought. Worse yet for a larger adult. "How about radiology? Can you take chest or bone X-rays?"

"Yes, and we process them by hand, in tanks of developing fluid and fixer. We don't have much of a laboratory, either. We can do a urine dip stick looking for an infection or renal wasting of glucose, and we can spin a capillary tube of blood to check for anemia, but that's about it."

"Vaccines?" Sid asked.

He explained that they were usually given by the public health nurses. "We give only the basic childhood immunizations, DPT and polio," he said. "And now MMR. The coverage in the region around Promissão isn't good enough, but it's slowly getting better."

"Here's what might be called the pediatric ward." He ushered Sid and Cibele into a sunny area off the emergency room. One of the five cribs held a sleeping baby attached to an intravenous drip, and a woman—Sid presumed she was the child's mother—sat in one of the five rocking chairs. Dr. Alancar introduced the woman to Sid, who shook her hand. "Many of the children hospitalized here, including this little one, have diarrhea. After a day or two of IV fluids, they are usually fine to go home. We expect to discharge this child," he nodded toward the baby in the crib, "tomorrow."

Standing there among the hospital cribs drew Sid back to her days of training in pediatrics. The long days and longer nights on the wards. The desperately ill children and their desperately worried parents. She'd loved the challenge of making diagnoses, of searching for the missing pieces of a diagnostic puzzle, an X-ray, a laboratory test result, a physical exam finding, an obscure item in the medical history, that would bring everything together. She'd loved watching troublesome symptoms steadily dissipate in response to her treatments while evidence of a healthy child steadily returned until the little patient was hanging onto the crib rails, jumping on the mattress, and yelling for ice cream. She'd almost forgotten, and didn't want to forget again, the joy of being a doctor.

They returned to Alancar's office.

"Cibele told me about the deaths among young children here recently," Sid said. "What do you think is going on?"

Dr. Alancar's face grew solemn and his head bobbed. Then he shook his head slowly. "I don't know."

His words were halting. Sid couldn't tell if that was due to his imperfect English or reluctance to discuss the deaths.

"Children sometimes die here. From diarrhea. From pneumonia. Or measles," he said.

"Is that what the dead children here had?"

He shrugged. "They had high fever and a purple rash. Within a day of getting sick, they died. That's what I was told." He took a deep breath and then continued. "Two died at home and the third shortly after she arrived at the clinic. I was called to care for that child, but by the time I got here, it was too late." He paused. Then he said, "They were little children. Only two and three years old or so."

"And the purple rash?" Sid asked.

Dr. Alancar nodded. "It's what you say ... purpura."

"Excuse me?" Cibele asked. "What's that?"

"Purple blotches on the skin," Sid answered. "It's not good." She looked out the window to the field across the parking lot, to the fluffy clouds that dotted the sky, to that dreadful night so long ago. Then she turned back to Dr. Alancar. "Sounds like some kind of infection. What kind of germs might have caused it?" she asked. "Bacteria? Or viruses? Do you think the deaths were all caused by the same thing?"

Dr. Alancar, again shaking his head, said he didn't know. "They died too fast. Too fast to transfer them to Ribeirão Preto where they can do the right tests." Then he added, "All three had red eye about a week before the fever."

Red eye. Pink eye. Cibele's nephew had "red eye." That was four days ago. Sid turned toward Cibele. "Gilberto?"

"Yes." Cibele paused a moment, then her face curled. "Oh, God. Do you think ...?"

Sid turned to Dr. Alancar. "You must see pink eye, here. Often."

"Oh, yes, a lot. We have all these tiny flies that crawl into the children's eyes and irritate the membranes."

"How about treatment? Antibiotic drops? Is that what you usually use?" That's what Sid prescribed for her patients if the eye drainage looked like pus.

"No. The drops are expensive. And the pink eye usually clears up on its own."

Cibele spoke quickly, her voice tense as a spring. "Would those drops keep Gilberto from getting the fever and the rash?"

Sid shook her head. "Probably not."

"How can I get those drops?"

Cibele and Sid turned to Dr. Alancar. He cleared his throat and said he thought he had some in the clinic's pharmacy. "Does the boy still have the 'red eye'?" he asked.

"Yes, he had it yesterday when I saw him, but it was getting better," Cibele said. "No fever then. Other than the red eyes, he seemed fine."

Dr. Alancar walked them out to the clinic pharmacy and, after unlocking the door and rummaging through the shelves of drugs, showed Cibele a small bottle. He explained how to drip the fluid into the eyes of a squirmy toddler. As he rattled off words in Portuguese, he gestured with his hands. He squinted his eyelids shut and spread the left one open with the fingers of his left hand. He held the bottle upside down in his right hand and pretended to squirt the medicine into his own eye.

Cibele had asked it the drops would prevent the fever and purpura and death, even if that illness was related to the pink eye. Sid doubted it. If it were an infection, fever and rash would mean it had spread beyond the eye. Eye drops might kill germs on the eye, but they wouldn't get into the blood, wouldn't kill the germs that percolated through a child's body.

Cibele thanked Alancar for the drops. She was effusive in her gratitude. "We need to do whatever we can to keep Gilberto healthy," she said. "People around here are scared about this mysterious illness. Three dead children in just a couple weeks. That's too many."

Indeed, thought Sid. Although the eye drops probably wouldn't do it, there must be a way to prevent the children from dying. Sid's mind whirled. If it was an infection. If it was caused by bacteria.

After the several decades, her mother's wails still echoed through her thoughts. "If only we had known. If only she had the antibiotics earlier. If only ... if only ..." The sick children in Promissão needed to be treated sooner. "The local parents need to bring their children to the clinic early, as soon as they notice the fever," Sid said.

"Yes," Dr. Alancar said. "If we could give antibiotics by vein early enough, hopefully that would stop the illness's relentless march to death."

"We need a pamphlet," Cibele said. "People here will read a message on a pamphlet."

It was a small office with two tiny, grimy windows and the smell of old dust. River's desk was a government cast-off of nicked steel. The phone sat on the top, amid piles of paper and an unwashed coffee cup. Cibele's desk was a small table, laden with ledgers and an old typewriter, wedged against a wall about a foot from River's desk. That was it. Two employees.

A barrel full of seeds stood beside the door. Corn seeds. Sid scooped up a handful and let them flow like rain between her fingers back into the barrel. A file cabinet leaned against one wall and a map of the state of São Paulo was tacked to the opposite wall. Cibele explained that the little red pins stuck in the map marked the farms River had visited. There were at least two hundred of them, scattered in all directions around Promissão.

Huddled together over the table, Sid and Cibele designed a flier to pass out in the clinic. Cibele typed the message on the old Underwood and, at the bottom, Sid sketched a thermometer and a pudgy child with dark blotches on her arms and legs. She printed large, shaded letters across the top of the page: "FEVER."

"Ah, Sid. The word in Portuguese is febre. F-E-B-R-E."

"Right." Sid started over, with new drawings and the correct word at the top.

"You're a good artist," Cibele said.

"Not really," Sid said. "But it'll do. How do we get copies?"

"The town office has one of those duplicating machines. They'll let us use it, but we need to provide the paper." Cibele opened the middle drawer of the file cabinet and pulled out a ream. "The United States Foreign Agricultural Service is happy to donate this."

Cibele drove them to the center of town. She stopped in front of a squat building with a sign that read, "Delegacia de Polícia Promissão." A patrol car was parked out front. "Here we are."

"This is the police station?" It looked like an abandoned warehouse.

"Yes. Police station. Mayor's office. City Hall. Everything. All Promissão's government agencies are here."

A row of trees, with leaves the size of luncheon plates, lined the street. Something moved above Sid's head. She looked up. A bird, big, brown, and white, swayed on a branch near the top. Maybe a hawk? Probably a hawk of the Brazilian variety.

"It's downstairs," Cibele said as they entered the building. "Watch your step. The light has been burned out for at least a year."

Sid grasped the handrail as she followed Cibele down the steep, dark-as-a-coal-mine, musty-smelling stairwell. At the bottom, Cibele opened a door and walked in. "Olá" she called to the lady behind the desk. "Sid, this is Fabiana." Then, in a soft voice, she explained that Fabiana's granddaughter, Mariana, had been the first child to die of the mysterious disease. "Mariana's father, Marcelo, is Fabiana's oldest son. Remember him? You met him on the farm with River. The family is devastated, as you can imagine."

Yes, Sid could imagine that; she knew it well. The woman, Fabiana, had managed to get herself out of bed that morning, change from her nightgown to her street clothes, and go to work. For a person whose grandchild had died so recently and so cruelly, that was a major accomplishment.

As Cibele and Fabiana spoke in Portuguese, Sid heard her own name and turned toward them. Fabiana smiled at her, a brave but desperate, half-hearted smile beneath dark, puffy eyes. Then she pointed to a photocopier in the corner.

A half-hour later, they handed a stack of leaflets to the police receptionist. "Give one to anyone who might be involved with young children," Cibele said. "Parents. Grandparents. Aunts. Uncles."

Across town, in the clinic, Cibele dabbed her eyes as she set a stack of the fliers on the table in the patient waiting room. The nurse stroked her hand and murmured, "These deaths are so terrible. So very, very terrible." Cibele nodded, silently.

Back in the car, Sid said, "We need wider distribution." Traffic in the clinic seemed slow. Maybe fifteen patients a day.

"How about the farmers River and I visit?" Cibele said. "They are fathers, and they care a lot about their children."

Sid liked that idea. "And give them to the teachers," she said. "And the monks."

7

1984 BRAZIL

The morning of their last full day in Promissão—Saturday—River again made breakfast. The three of them sat around his kitchen table drinking coffee and, as Raven and Sid had every morning since they arrived, eating toast and eggs. "I get them from the lady down the road," he said of the eggs. "Pretty cheap. From real chickens."

What did he mean by 'real chickens?' Sid wondered. What other kind of chickens were there? It might have been a nod to her city-ness. She had to admit she'd never eaten farm eggs before; she only knew the kind that came in a cardboard carton from the supermarket. Now that he mentioned it, she thought she could taste the farm in the eggs. Was it straw? Or barnyard dirt? Or chicken poop? She swallowed the egg and took a bite of her toast. Stop it, she told herself. Your imagination is in overdrive. She finally decided they tasted like every other egg she'd ever eaten but with deeper flavor.

Halfway through the second pot of coffee, they heard something banging at the door. It sounded insistent.

"Who's that?" Raven asked.

"Got me." River rose from his chair and headed toward the living room.

The front door creaked as it opened. "River?" a woman's voice called. "River? Are you home?"

They heard muffled sounds from the doorway, and then River rounded the corner from the living room followed by Cibele. She was crying. "My sister ... Ana ... her baby ... is very, very sick." Her hair was no longer tucked into a neat bun against the back of her neck but fell across her shoulders like a cascade of India ink. Her long turquoise skirt swept over her ankles as she walked, and the image of a fan-tailed peacock sprawled across the front of her shirt.

The story spilled from her in weepy sputters. The eye drops had made his 'red eye' go away. But then Gilberto started vomiting. "This morning, when my sister woke up, he had fever and purple patches all over. His arms and tummy and little legs." Cibele pinched at the skin of her arm. "They were everywhere. Just like that picture you drew on the flier, Sid."

"Oh, no." Sid leaped from her chair. She reached her hand toward Cibele.

Cibele continued in Portuguese, a rapid tumble of foreign sounds. The only word Sid understood was "clinica." River explained that Ana had taken the baby to the clinic.

"What?" Raven's voice wavered, and her eyes darted from Sid to Cibele to River and back to Sid. "Sounds like the sickness those other children had."

As River handed Cibele a cup of coffee, his entire arm shook. Sid had been in Brazil for almost a week, and she'd never seen him edgy. He had been, in fact, the opposite of edgy.

Cibele set the coffee on the table and grabbed Sid's hand. "Please come. I'm so worried about Gilberto. Maybe Dr. Alancar needs you. You know about the purple spots."

The room was silent except for the sound of a tree branch scratching against the roof.

Sid glanced at Raven and then at River. How could she help Dr. Alancar? He was an experienced physician and, as Sid had seen during her visit to the clinic, an excellent clinician. He was a general practitioner, though, rather than a pediatrician. Is that what Cibele meant? Cibele wanted her to come. That was enough. "Let's go," she said.

The children's ward seemed smaller and more cramped than when she'd visited earlier. The five cribs, now empty with clean folded linens on their bare mattresses, still lined the walls, and the five wooden rocking chairs still crowded the middle of the floor. The smell of ampicillin and rubbing alcohol rode the breeze from the open window into every corner.

"Onde está Gilberto?" Cibele asked the nurse. "Where's Gilberto?"

The nurse said something Sid couldn't understand. Her words were slow and quiet, almost a murmur. Cibele's eyes widened and then clamped shut. Suddenly, she sank like a deflated balloon to her knees, grabbed handfuls of her hair, and began to scream. It was a piercing shriek, the kind of animalistic noise that made Sid want to cover her ears with her palms. With each scream, Cibele pounded her fists against her thighs and then wrapped her arms around her waist and rocked back and forth. Over and over.

Time stopped. The screams echoed. Sid could barely stand to watch Cibele. She turned toward River.

"The boy's dead," he said, his voice barely above a whisper.

Dead. The word landed on Sid with a sickening thud. She leaned against the doorway, afraid she might faint. Gilberto was the vibrant little boy with the twinkling eyes who walked the toy duck along the sofa at Cibele's house just a few days ago. Cibele had said the pink eye was getting better. What happened? Sid felt the clutch of that old, familiar, wrenching ache. Now he was dead. With purple spots on his skin.

The nurse steered the sobbing Cibele toward one of the rocking chairs. She patted Cibele's head, spoke to her softly in Portuguese. Such a beautiful language. Such a terrible message.

"Onde está Ana?" Cibele sobbed. The nurse answered. Sid couldn't understand that, either.

River leaned toward Raven and Sid and quietly said, "Ana's in the treatment room with Gilberto's body. She won't leave him."

The nurse disappeared and, moments later, led Ana into the room. She stood her in front of an empty rocking chair and nudged her to sit. Ana's eyes, dull and empty, stared at Cibele. Sid couldn't tell if she saw her sister. Did she see anything?

Raven began to cry, and River wrapped his arm around her shoulders. Sid took a deep breath and closed her eyes, working to quell her own tears. She had spoken to many parents, aunts, uncles, and grandparents about their dying loved ones, the children who were her patients. But this time was different. She wasn't the doctor here. Now she was just River's sister's friend. And Cibele's new friend.

The nurse held a bundle wrapped in a clover green blanket under one arm. She handed it to Ana. Sobbing, Ana clutched it to her face and then held it out in front of her. The bottom of the bundle opened and something—it was white with several patches of yellow-orange—fell to her lap. It looked soft and fuzzy. The toy duck Sid had won at the fair.

River nodded toward the door, and Sid and Raven followed him outside. After the deaths of her patients, Sid had handled the medical measures: examining the child to be sure the child was no longer living, signing the death certificate, writing a death note in the patient's chart, requesting permission for a postmortem exam from the parents, notifying the medical examiner if a forensic autopsy might be legally mandated, making sure the body got to the morgue. Here, helpless in a hopeless situation, she had to leave Ana and Cibele to themselves.

On the porch, a man, puffing on a cigarette, ambled away from them. He turned and started to pace back toward them. Dr. Alancar's eyelids were swollen, and his back stooped even more than when Sid first met him. He walked with a faint limp. Perhaps he'd been up all night trying to save little Gilberto.

He greeted them, told them that Gilberto had suffered a cardiorespiratory arrest soon after arriving at the clinic and hadn't responded to the resuscitation efforts. "He had fever and purpura. Like the other children."

"And," Sid added, "pink eye."

"Sim. The eye drops didn't keep him from getting sick, as you expected."

Sid nodded. It would be the germs in Gilberto's blood that had killed him, not the ones in his eyes. What kind of germs were they, anyway?

"Were you able to draw blood cultures from Gilberto?"

"Não." He shook his head gravely. "He died too fast. And, as you know, the clinic doesn't have a good laboratory."

As they said goodbye to Dr. Alancar, the wind picked up and strands of wispy clouds raced across the sky. It was an awkward farewell, the end of a terrible morning. Another devastated family. An unspeakable, dark emptiness would permeate Cibele's world. It would haunt the gorgeous rugs and vases and books in her beautiful living room and take years to fade away. Maybe it never would. Gilberto would forever be the little boy in Cibele's picture, a determined smile on his face, foot raised to kick the ball. Forever two.

What would they do with the toy duck? Bury it with him? Maybe give it to another child. Or throw it in the trash. Why did that silly question stick in her mind? It was absurd. Completely beside the point.

8

1984 BRAZIL

Sid, Raven, and River walked slowly down the steps from the clinic porch. They didn't speak, their thoughts too dark and muddled to render coherent words. Gilberto was dead. Sid turned back for one last glance at the clinic and saw movement in the shadows behind the trees. It disappeared over the horizon, and she understood. Two women had staggered forward, clinging to each other. Ana and Cibele.

Sid looked at Raven, then at River. Another set of siblings. Such a gift.

As they headed to River's car, a pick-up truck roared up the driveway and jerked to a dusty stop on the gravel parking lot. The driver's door flew open, and a young woman almost fell from the front seat. She dashed over the pebbles, yelling, "Meu bebê é doente." In her arms, she cradled what looked like a small child wrapped in a shawl. A toddler-sized leg dangled from the heap she carried as she raced up the steps to the clinic.

"She said her baby is sick," River explained.

Dr. Alancar, still on the porch, held open the clinic door for the frantic mother and then turned back to Sid, Raven, and River. He motioned for them to return. They walked back into the clinic and watched the nurse lift the child from the mother's grip and dash into the treatment room.

Dr. Alancar said, "Dr. Royal, perhaps you could help me here."

Sid didn't hesitate. She hadn't taken care of a seriously ill child for over a year, but she hadn't forgotten what to do. It wasn't until the next day that she realized that she had no authority to practice medicine in Brazil. Dr. Alancar could take care of that if an issue emerged. She followed him into the treatment room. River and Raven waited with the mother in the hallway.

The little girl that rested on her back on the gurney looked about two years old—about the same age as Gilberto. Dr. Alancar slapped the head of his stethoscope on her chest and listened. She didn't move. Even when he shoved a tongue blade into her mouth, she didn't resist and didn't gag. Purple patches, coppery plum in color and the size of petunia blossoms, dotted her thighs and arms. Sid raised the hem of the child's dress and laid her fingers on her abdomen. She guessed the fever to be about 105 degrees. Three tiny flies darted around the girl's filmy eyes. Sid waved them away.

"She's Izabel," Dr. Alancar whispered as he prepared to insert a needle into her left hand. "She's dying, just like all the rest."

"We should get blood for a culture," Sid said.

"No laboratory ..." His voice faded away.

"How about ..." Sid paused a moment and then said, "I'll take the blood back home and test it in our lab." It would be unthinkable to simply walk away without trying to learn what was killing this little girl—these children.

Dr. Alancar turned toward her, and his head tilted with doubt.

She knew it was a crazy idea, and his gray face told her he wasn't sure he should, or could, go along with it.

Finally, he spoke to the nurse, who shook her head, but opened and closed several drawers and then disappeared into a closet. She returned with what looked to Sid like a very old blood culture vial.

"She needs an antibiotic, right?" Sid asked.

"Sim. Ampicillin. It's the only antibiotic here."

Sid held Izabel's arm steady—unlike her feverish abdomen, the child's hand felt waxy and cold, like a doll's vinyl hand—while Dr. Alancar worked at the IV. He had to wiggle the needle to coax its tip into the vein, and as soon he hit it, burgundy fluid flowed into the syringe attached to the needle. He pulled on the plunger until the blood reached the ten milliliters mark, unhooked it from the needle, and handed it to Sid.

The syringe felt warm as bathwater, living person warm. Inside was precious fluid, the liquid of life. It might hold the key to what was killing the children. She squirted the blood into the culture vial and gave it a quick shake. She nodded to Dr. Alancar, a signal that he could open up the intravenous line. Soon, the crystal clear IV fluid ran through the tubing and into Izabel's arm.

The girl's skin, white as the bleached draw sheet that covered the gurney, had sprouted even more purple spots. The nurse took her blood pressure. Too low. Dr. Alancar pulled a vial of epinephrine from the crash cart and shot its contents into the IV tubing. The nurse took her blood pressure again. Still too low. The nurse mixed a vial of ampicillin with a vial of diluent and handed it to Alancar. He injected it into the child's vein. The purpuric blotches were growing, inching across her pale skin like spilled grape juice, and her breaths had become weak, little gasps.

Sid slapped a small mask over the child's mouth and nose and pushed air into her lungs with an AmbuBag. "ABC," she recited to herself. Airway—check. Breathing—check, with assistance. Circulation—check, but poor. The girl's heart was still beating. But her blood pressure just wouldn't budge upward.

She grabbed the top of the child's thin cotton shift and then paused a moment. It was a pretty little dress, custard yellow with a row of ruffles around the neckline, but it was in the way. She yanked at the front, and the lightweight fabric ripped from neck to hem. "How about another IV line?" she asked. "An intraosseous?"

"Yes," Alancar said.

She had never inserted an intraosseous line, but when she was a medical student, she'd seen one placed in a badly dehydrated baby. She attached a syringe to a large bore needle, pulled off the plastic cap, and thrust the needle into Izabel's shin bone. She then pulled back on the plunger. The pressure felt right—tight but with a little give—and when she saw the tell-tale dark red blood bubble into the bottom of the syringe, she connected the needle to another bag of IV fluid. She opened the valve full tilt and let the liquid flow, as fast as it would go, into the little girl's bone marrow.

Still the blood pressure was too low. "Can you think of anything else?" Dr. Alancar's eyes pleaded for a new idea. She had none. Even if they had been in Michigan, in the high-tech emergency department, with modern equipment and well-trained emergency physicians, the blood pressure might not have responded. She looked at Izabel's pasty face, now puffy from all the fluids, at her swollen eyelids, her diminutive nose and blue lips. The blotchy skin of her tummy above the elastic of her flower-printed panties was now clammy cold, and her fingertips were gray. But she was still beautiful. So fragile, so precious, so very, very sick, but still beautiful. Like all children.

Her blood pressure continued to slide downward. "No pulse," Sid muttered to Dr. Alancar.

He flopped his stethoscope on the child's chest and listened. "Nothing." He shook his head.

Dr. Alancar started the chest compressions while Sid continued to squeeze the Ambu bag to push air into the little girl's lungs. For eighteen seemingly endless minutes, they alternated: one rhythmically thrust a fist against the child's breastbone, square between her little brown nipples, over and over, while the other held the cup of the Ambu mask against the child's face. When one paused the compressions, the other squeezed the air from the bag into the child. Sid counted. "Thirty-three, thirty-four, thirty ..." They traded places every sixty pushes. Finally, they stood back and waited. No pulse. No heartbeat. Absolutely no response.

The nurse slumped into a chair and sobbed into her hands. Dr. Alancar pulled the sheet over the baby's face and said something under his breath that Sid didn't understand. A curse? A prayer? Then he walked into the hallway to tell another mother her child had died.

Sid, holding the blood culture vial in her hand, stood beside Izabel's tiny, motionless body. Those memories from long ago once again swept over her like murky flood water. Another little girl, another place, another terrible disease. Her head throbbed, and her knees felt like pudding. She turned toward the wall and wiped the tears from her cheeks.

Yesterday, Izabel, like that other girl from long ago, was a vibrant child, likely playing with a doll on the floor of her parents' house. During the night, she'd developed a fever; today, the purple blotches spotted her skin; and now she was dead. The fifth child in Promissão to die in less than four weeks.

Izabel's mother would bury her baby, just as Ana would bury Gilberto and Marcelo had buried Mariana. Then what? Sid knew what, at least for the mothers. Her own mother had sat at the kitchen table in the middle of the night, a half-empty bottle of Silver Satin at her elbow, a wine glass in her hand. Mother had stayed in bed for days. The crying. The terrible, aching sobs. Sid shook her head to bury the memory. If only Sid's mother had been more watchful. Was Izabel's mother watchful enough?

Through the door, she heard Izabel's mother's screams. Something pounded against the wall. A male voice spoke. Was it River?

Sid rounded the corner in the hallway and saw Izabel's mother folded over in her chair, her face almost in her lap. River and Raven sat on either side of her, their arms around her back.

Sid squatted in front of her and touched her knee. "I wish we could have helped her," she said. River translated her words into Portuguese.

The mother nodded and grasped Sid's hands. She brought Sid's fingers to her lips and then, still sobbing, stared off into the distance. Her hands, warm with her tears, were somehow assuring. Sid leaned closer to her and said nothing. No words would make a difference.

After the nurse led the mother into the treatment room to say goodbye to her daughter, Sid remained with River and Raven in the hallway. Raven gave her a hug, and River slipped his arm around her shoulders and pulled her toward him. How could they know so well what she needed most right then?

Sid still held the vial of blood, and she gave it another shake. She could not grow viruses in her laboratory. But if the blood contained bacteria, she could grow them. Then she might be able to help the children here. It was worth a try.

9

1984 MICHIGAN

From the window of the airplane, Sid watched the graceful funnel of Point Pelee stretch southward until its tip disappeared into Lake Erie. She wondered what would be at the absolute end of that point. A single grain of sand? A glob of seaweed? Maybe a beached beer can. A person could stand, she figured, with a foot on either side of the tip and watch the earth dissolve to nothingness between her legs.

The miniature world far below throbbed in steadfast normality. Two tiny freighters, one up-bound toward the mouth of the Detroit River, the other down-bound toward Lake Erie, churned through the water, plowing forward, ever forward, their silver wakes trailing aft like comet tails. On the land, highways threaded between the fields, carrying tiny trucks that bore goods from town to town. It was tedium as usual in Michigan, while down in Brazil, children were dying.

Her thoughts circled around the dead children, and her head began to throb as her mind rewound the horror of Izabel's death. Every step. Nothing they did could keep her alive. What more could, or should, they have done?

And Gilberto. At first, at Cibele's house, she hadn't realized that his pink eye might be the prelude to the fatal illness. But even if she'd thought about the possibility, what could she have done? She considered a number of options—give him antibiotics, draw his blood for a culture, draw his blood for other tests, examine him three times a day, etc. She rejected every one of them as impractical or impossible.

She wondered how Cibele was doing. Would she be back at work yet? River would be a comfort to her, just as he had been to Raven.

After the complex—delightful and then dreadful, terrific and then terrible—trip to Brazil, she was now almost home, back to the routine of her life and the work in the lab. And Eliot. A least three weeks of experiments with the antibodies lay ahead, and he would be bossing her through every hour of it. She wasn't looking forward to that.

And then there was Izabel's blood. She didn't know if any bacteria would grow from it. Very likely not. Without knowing what caused Izabel's death, no one could know how to prevent the mystery illness or how to treat it. It all seemed so hopeless, and yet the children were dying.

She gazed out the airplane's window at the fields and towns below and wished she could remember more clearly Brazil as it had been early in the visit: an enchanting adventure through shops seemingly painted with Day-Glo crayons, contrasted with the disintegrating alabaster churches that still harbored ancient ghosts from the past. The food and the markets, the birds and the bossa nova, the sing-song of Portuguese conversation day and night. And then those evenings in the company of River and Raven, their easygoing humor, the ebb and flow of their conversation, their indelible bond.

After the dark times of the past day, thoughts of the dying children had perched on her shoulders like vultures breathing sour air down her neck. They were ever present, whispering petulant reminders in her ear. She could force those thoughts away for a few moments, but they *always* skulked back.

She hadn't slept well the night before and had listened to Raven toss and turn until four in the morning. Raven wasn't easily rattled, but she'd been with the mother when poor little Izabel died, listened to her screams, watched her pound against the wall. It was a good thing River had been there. He would know what to say to Izabel's mother. And, of course, he'd had a lifetime of comforting his sister and could do it better than anyone.

Now, on the plane, Raven, her lips still, her eyes closed, dozed in peace in the seat beside Sid. A book, *The Name of the Rose*, was splayed open on her lap; shadowy monks and misty cathedrals and moldy Bibles dressed its cover. Raven may never have been as closely involved with death as she had been in Promissão. At least not the death of a child. It was, after all, against the natural order.

Sid clutched her large handbag against her chest as she had during the entire plane ride, felt the scratch of its snakeskin on her arms. The silk scarf she had bought at the market and tied to one handle seemed a symbol of something, but she wasn't sure what. Ordinariness, maybe, in the simplicity of a scarf? Or virtue in its quality? Hope in the brilliance of its colors? Innocence because it was trouble free? Beauty in its sheer splendor? All of that.

The flight attendant leaned toward her. "Ma'am, you'll have to stow the bag for landing."

Before she shoved the bag under the seat in front of her, she ran her fingers yet one more time deep inside, down to the bottom. Still there. She felt the fabric of the T-shirt, the crummy one stained with meat juice from the Brazilian sandwich, and wrapped inside was the firm, rounded form of the tube of blood. Less than a day ago that blood had been racing through the dying child's arteries and veins, dripping through her tissues as it ferried oxygen to her skin and heart, brain, and muscles, and then carried waste away. Now, it was merely a biologic fluid, a suspension of cells and plasma in a glass vial. But still precious.

It was a long shot. A very long shot. She knew that. Even if bacteria had caused the little girl's illness and were floating in that blood sample, the probability that the germs survived the trip to Michigan was low. The blood had been in that tube for over a day, packed in the bottom of her bag. As each hour passed, the oxygen in the sample had decreased and toxic metabolic products had increased. All in all, the likelihood that she would be able to grow bacteria from that blood, assuming germs had been there in the first place, was very low. But she had to try. For Gilberto's sake, and Ana's and Cibele's, she had to try.

The flight attendant made an announcement. Raven's eyelids flew open.

"We're about to land," Sid said. "See," she pointed out the window, "the Fermi towers." Smoke, or steam, or whatever that cloudy mist was, drifted in lazy trails upward from the reactor's cones and disappeared into nothingness over the river. "Remember, no mention of the blood," she whispered. "Not a word. And if the customs guys ask about it, don't say anything. I'll do all the talking. You can pretend you don't know me."

Raven nodded. The slow movement of her head told of her uncertainty, of her edgy anxiety. "Are you sure this is a good idea?" It was Raven who was usually the carefree risk-taker. But not this time.

"Of course. It's important. We have to know what killed her."

"Are you sure this is legal?" Raven's voice was a mere whisper.

"I don't know, and I'm not going to figure it out right now."

"I don't want you to go to jail."

"Oh, for Pete's sake. No one's going to jail."

"Well, I did once, and it wasn't any fun."

Raven in jail? That was news. Surprising news. "When? What was that all about?" Sid looked at sweet, wholesome Raven, at her wavy jet-black hair that hung in her dark, now troubled eyes and couldn't imagine her friend shackled, dressed in an orange jumpsuit, sitting in a cell.

"It was during my lost years. Had to do with a rally in Haight-Ashbury. Started out peacefully but then grew ugly, and my friends and I landed in the San Francisco slammer."

Lost years? Lost from what?

"Mostly I remember how filthy it was. Grime everywhere, and my cell smelled like a cross between an outhouse and a moldy basement. There was no privacy—the open toilet stood in the corner of the cell—and while I peed, anyone who wandered by could watch. You'd really hate that, Sid. Anyone would, but particularly you."

Raven was right about that. Sid would hold her urine for a month before letting a stranger watch her pee.

"Fortunately, I had to sleep on that lumpy foam mattress for only one night. Actually, I didn't sleep at all but stared at the cracks in the ceiling, more scared than I've ever been in my life. I worried I'd never get out, that they'd send me to San Quentin forever. My mom used to say that California is the place for second chances," Raven said. "Back then, I thought she meant the Gold Rush or all the immigrants from Asia. But it's more than that. The place is full of people realizing success after they've stumbled. And boy, had I stumbled."

She had trouble believing such a story, but Raven never altered the truth. Still, it didn't fit the Raven she knew. "How'd you get out?"

"In the morning, River, our mother, and Mother's cousin— he's some sort of lawyer—talked to the cops, and I was released. No charges."

River to the rescue. He was a rescuing kind of guy. She, though, had no intention of being arrested. She just needed to stay calm through customs and immigration and keep the blood out of sight.

After landing, they wound their way through the jet bridge and down the steps to the immigration/customs area. Sid led the way to the line snaking away from the sign that read "United States Citizens." While they waited, Raven fidgeted.

"Are you still nervous?" Sid asked.

"Yes."

"Well, quit it."

"I can't."

When she reached the head of the line, Sid handed her

passport to the immigration agent and watched him flip the pages.

"Citizenship?"

"United States."

"Where have you been?"

"Brazil."

"The purpose of your visit?"

"Vacation."

"Welcome home." He pressed a stamper against the page and yelled, "Next in line."

Sid headed into the customs area while Raven spoke to the immigration officer. Soon Raven joined her. As they neared the luggage area, Raven whispered, "So far, so good."

Ignoring her, Sid pulled her suitcase off the turning carousel and headed for the line at the US customs station.

While they waited, a stubby dog darted from suitcase to briefcase to shopping bag to purse. Sid's palms grew sweaty, and her heart pounded. She knew what he was about. She directed her eyes away from him and willed him to ignore her.

A burly customs agent grasped the leash while the beagle stopped at each passenger and sniffed. When he reached Raven, the dog nosed her suitcase. In the front, in the back. Then he sniffed her carry-on bag. Her face turned icy white, and she looked as if she might pass out.

Would the scent from Izabel's blood be on Raven? Couldn't be. She'd had no contact with the vial. So why was the dog so interested in Raven's luggage? The agent put something green into the dog's mouth. Must be a treat—a small dog biscuit? Or a piece of candy? Maybe a pill. He must have given the dog a secret signal too, because it moved on.

When the beagle reached Sid, his nose tracked straight to

her purse. After one sniff he plunked his butt on the tile floor. The agent gave the leash a tug, but the dog refused to budge. The agent pulled the leash again, but the dog remained seated.

"Ma'am," the agent said to her. "We'll have to search your purse. Follow me, please. Do you have any fruits, vegetables, meat, drugs, or other illegal imports?"

"No, sir." The calm she had so carefully fabricated suddenly evaporated.

The agent placed her bag on a stainless-steel table, pried it open, glanced into its interior, and slipped his hand inside. She held her breath and watched as he pulled, item by item, her belongings from inside. Her car keys, her wallet, and her make-up case. A pen, a tiny flashlight, and a month-old chocolate bar. Then her boarding pass and her paperback book with a folded sheet of Kleenex marking where she'd stopped reading. She felt woozy and leaned against a pillar.

He dug to what must have been the bottom of the purse and started to pull out something that was light yellow. Fabric. The meat-stained T-shirt. He jostled the purse and pulled again. The shirt must have gotten stuck on the inside zipper. Sid took a deep breath and held it. She wanted to sit down before she fainted.

Suddenly a little boy broke away from his mother's side and raced toward the beagle. "Mommy, a doggy," he yelled. "Look at the doggy." The beagle pulled back from the table, strained at its leash, and stretched toward the boy. The agent, his right hand still inside Sid's handbag, yanked on the leash in his left hand, yelled a command, and the beagle instantly lay down on the floor. The boy kept running, and when he reached the dog, he began patting its head. Gilberto had been a little younger than this boy.

The agent removed his hand from inside Sid's purse. He

squatted beside the boy and explained that the dog's name was Scout. "He's working right now," the agent said. "We'd better let him do his job."

The child's mother dashed to his side, stooped, set a large Mickey Mouse pillow on the floor, and pulled the boy to her chest. "Honey, that dog isn't like Riley. We can't play with that doggy."

The agent returned to Sid's purse and slowly pulled the yellow T-shirt by one of its sleeves. As it emerged, the dog began to whine, and his neck hairs pointed toward the ceiling. Sid felt her heart banging inside her chest. He'd found it.

Finally—after what seemed like a year to Sid—the agent had tugged the shirt free from the purse. He held it up. Only the shirt. No tube of blood. Where was it? Not on the table. Nor the floor. Had it fallen out of her bag somewhere between the plane and customs?

The agent pointed to the stain on the shirt. "Do you know what this is, ma'am?"

She stepped toward him. "Meat juice." She could barely hear her own voice. "From a drippy sandwich I ate a couple days ago in Brazil."

The agent waved the stain near the dog's nose. A low rumbling snarl burbled from deep inside his chest. "That must be what he's reacting to." He laid the T-shirt back on the table. "Good sandwich?" he asked.

"Yes, sir. A terrific sandwich."

The agent gave another signal to the dog and led him away. Over his shoulder he said, "Sorry to bother you, ma'am. Please proceed through customs."

She stuffed her belongings back into her purse. Raven appeared at her side. "Where is it?" her eyes asked.

Sid couldn't answer. They weren't safe yet. She carried her suitcase toward the customs desks. Her hands trembled when she passed her papers to the officer. She felt sweat dotting her forehead. Where on earth was the blood?

The agent looked up from the papers. "Are you okay, ma'am?"

"Yes, I'm fine." She tossed her head, tried to look nonchalant. "I have a big problem waiting for me at home, so I'm a bit flustered."

The officer glanced at her declaration papers, slammed his rubber stamp on the top sheet, and motioned for her to pass. Then, with her head held high, she strolled out into the corridor. Now she was free.

When they exited the terminal, Sid settled on a cement bench and waited for the parking lot shuttle. She gripped the handbag to her chest. Raven sat beside her.

The suspense was eating her hollow. She looked around, at the teenager smoking by the curb, at the old lady waving to a passing car. No one suspicious. Was it safe to check?

"Where'd the blood go?" Raven whispered.

"I don't know." She opened her purse and dug down to the bottom. Her hand zigzagged from the left to the right, beneath the T-shirt. Her fingers felt the flashlight, the pen, the wallet, the make-up case. Then something firm and smooth as glass. The size of a thin cigar. "It's here," she said and cradled the tube in her palm, still inside the bag.

"Unbelievable," Raven said into a sigh. "How'd ..."

"It must have rolled away from the T-shirt while the agent was pulling it out."

"You are so damned lucky."

10

1984 MICHIGAN

Sid unlocked the door and stepped into the darkened laboratory. The full moon, bloated and blotchy, hung high in the sky outside the window and cast its eerie, chalky light on the centrifuge, the shelves of reagent bottles, the boxes of agar plates stacked against the cold room wall, and the curled pages of the calendar that dangled from a nail above her desk. The lab odors, acrid but familiar, were uplifting. At last, she was home.

She snapped on her gooseneck light and settled at the benchtop that held her lab notes, the Bunsen burner, and the wooden cup with her pens and pencils. She took a deep breath and pulled the tube of Izabel's blood from the bottom of her bag.

She cradled it in her palms and shook her head. Izabel's

family would now have to plan a funeral for their little girl, the precious child who, only two days earlier, had probably played with her cousins. The oxblood-colored liquid, now in the tube, had been inside her. Sid shook her head again to dispel such thoughts. She needed to concentrate now on the sample, which had come a long way from the clinic in Promissão. It had weathered the storm of the sniffer dog and the day-and-a-half lapse since she collected it. She didn't know if the blood harbored bacteria. If so, she didn't know if they were still alive. If they were, she didn't know if they would grow on her laboratory agar.

As she began to streak a wire loopful of the blood onto an agar plate, she heard the door creak open.

Who was it? The cleaning guy left at midnight, so it wouldn't be him. Maybe one of the graduate students. Or a prowler. She held her breath, and her hands, grasping the agar plate and the inoculation wire, trembled like twigs in a tempest. She watched a shadow on the far wall grow larger as the figure neared her bench. A tall person rounded the corner.

It was Eliot. She stood up, and he jolted to a stop.

"Hey, what're you doing here?" he asked. "I thought you were in Brazil."

"We arrived a couple hours ago."

"Well, the question remains: What the hell are you doing here in the middle of the night?"

She sat down and continued streaking.

He edged closer to her bench.

"Have a good time in Brazil? And what are you streaking, there?" He leaned toward her. "Looks like blood."

"Brazil was an interesting adventure." She flamed the wire

loop to re-sterilize it, dipped it into Izabel's blood, and began to streak it across another agar plate.

"Sidonie, what's up? You're pretty evasive. What on earth are you culturing at three in the morning?"

She kept streaking. How could she tell him? What should she tell him? Anything? Finally, she reluctantly turned on her stool, stared into his questioning face, and explained the mysterious illness. She told him about Luiza and Gilberto, about the little girl, Izabel, who died in the clinic in spite of her attempts with Dr. Alancar to save her, and about the blood sample she'd brought back.

"You did what?" He spit the words at her. He waved his arm at the vial of blood in her hand. "That was incredibly idiotic. You realize, I hope, that blood like that could be insanely dangerous. How'd you get it past the customs guys, anyway?"

"They didn't know about it." Sid glared at him and his overblown reaction. She, the infectious diseases physician, knew better than he, the Ph.D. microbiologist, the dangers of working with someone else's blood. Very early in medical school, she'd learned to respect bodily fluids for their infectious risks and had practiced the appropriate precautions every time she encountered blood, diarrhea, coughed-up phlegm, and weeping wounds. The probability that this blood was a danger to her, or anyone else, was vanishingly low, and she was using appropriate sterile technique. She had no reason to fear it. Nothing, especially Eliot, was powerful enough to keep her from culturing that blood.

"'Didn't know'? How could the customs officers not know? It's their goddamn job to catch people smuggling contraband into our country."

"They didn't ask me. I didn't tell them." She gripped the

vial with both hands, held it secure so he couldn't grab it away from her. "I kept it stashed in my purse. And it isn't contraband."

"Don't you have to declare stuff like that? God knows we have to untangle a mile of red tape when we send bacteria to England. You can't, for example, just saunter into the United States with a vial of smallpox or anthrax in your pocket, I would hope. Bringing that blood here was really, really stupid."

"Look, Eliot, I have no idea what's in this blood. Chances are good—are very, very good—it's sterile. Blood usually is." He hadn't been there. The images clawed at the back of her mind: Izabel's cold skin and raging purpura, her mother's screams, Cibele's sobs, Ana's dead eyes. "Will you help me with this, or not?"

"Help you? What, for God's sake, do you have in mind?"

She gave the vial a shake.

"Sidonie, what are you going to ..."

"We'll try to culture bacteria from it."

"We? What do you mean '*we*?' What's my part in this crazy scheme?"

"Ah ..." What *did* she want from him? Approval? Respect? Insight? Not lab expertise—her clinical training ensured she knew better than he how to identify bacteria from clinical specimens. "Your part is to provide good cheer." She returned to streaking out the blood.

"I don't think much of this hare-brained plan of yours." A scowl creased his face.

"Look ..." Her patience with him, Eliot the Road Block, Eliot the Always-Knows-Better, was running thin. "Something killed that little girl. Probably an infection. We need to know the cause, so we know what to do with the next sick child. Besides, it's very unlikely any bacteria would grow at this late date."

"Right." He shook his head. "The 'something' that killed that child, and the rest of them, of course, might not have been an infection at all. Could have been a poison. Or contaminated food. Maybe bad water."

"Her symptoms were very consistent with an overwhelming infection. So the question should be *what caused the infection?* and not *did she have an infection?* I think she had an infection, and I intend to find out what caused it."

"You *think* she had an infection. I'm afraid you've wandered into belief territory, Sidonie, and have left behind the land of scientific evidence."

"The 'think she had an infection' is a hypothesis, Eliot, and I'm in the process of gathering the scientific evidence to prove it. I don't understand why we're having this conversation." She set the agar dishes in the incubator and walked away before he could answer.

For the next week, several times a day, she squatted before the open incubator and pulled the agar dishes from inside. She stared through their clear plastic lids, searching for a miracle, for bacteria to sprout like petite, mystic dew drops on the smooth agar surfaces. She removed the tops of the dishes for a closer look. She tilted them to change the angle of the light that bounced off the agar's gel and reflexively waved the dishes beneath her nose to catch any telltale odor.

"Anything yet?" Eliot asked whenever he passed her at the incubator.

"Nothing," was her forever answer. Each morning, after finding no bacteria on the agar, she pulled the tube of Izabel's blood from the fridge and dripped a couple drops onto fresh dishes, hoping something would grow. Over and over. Day after day. Maybe tomorrow, she kept thinking. She wouldn't give up, couldn't let the possibility of finding whatever was killing those children slip through her fingers like sluice water.

"You seem to be *willing* something to grow on that agar," Eliot said one afternoon when she was kneeling at the open incubator. "That won't help. Bacteria don't grow on faith. Nothing does."

She set the dishes back inside and slammed the incubator door shut. "I just have to wait a little longer."

At the end of the week, Sid and the rest of the lab group gathered for their regular meeting. Dr. Evans, the chief of the laboratory, passed around a box of bakery muffins and asked if the autoclave had been repaired yet and if the key to the cold room had been found.

Then Dr. Evans announced the news from the National Institutes of Health—their most recent grant application had not been funded. A communal groan filled the room. "Shit," Eliot muttered, "skunked again."

Sid tapped her pencil against her knee. The lab needed the money. They had to maintain the equipment, pay the salaries, and buy the supplies to conduct their research. Molecular materials were expensive. Everything was expensive. Now they'd be on an austerity plan until they could get another grant funded. As Dr. Evans explained the new priorities in the lab, she twirled her pencil between her fingers. Her Brazil project was eating up resources.

Eliot slapped his palm against the conference table. "I have the solution to the money problem," he said. "How about we set up a donation campaign, and everyone who gives a thousand bucks gets a mutant bacterial strain named after them? We could even send them some kind of certificate and a clone of the strain growing on a slant tube."

Raven rolled her eyes at Sid, and Sid rolled hers back.

"Well, I applaud your creative thinking and entrepreneurial spirit," Dr. Evans said. "But I don't know a single person, including bacteriologists, who would want a mutant anything named after them. It has a bad vibe."

Eliot shrugged and returned to filling in the "D" and the "o," of the *Detroit News* masthead, and the "9" and the "8" in 1984.

Everyone had brought a "show and tell" to the meeting. Sid set one of her agar dishes on top of her note pad. Her leg jiggled with anticipation.

When Dr. Evans called Raven's name, she pulled the chart of her newest results from between the pages of her notebook and held it up for everyone to see. When it was Eliot's turn, he passed around a printout from an immunoassay run.

When it was finally her turn to speak, Sid handed her agar dish to Eliot. "Take a look."

He lifted the lid. Then he moved the dish closer to his face. He turned it ninety degrees. Then forty-five degrees more. He squinted and tilted the dish to get a clearer view at a different angle. "I'll be damned," he said.

He handed the dish back to her. "Congratulations. You finally coaxed something to grow." He paused, then added. "Wonder what they are. Considering the specimen, which was probably dirty, I'd bet the annual federal budget that they're contaminants." He gestured with his outstretched arms. "Maybe something dropped from the air onto the agar, or maybe that culture tube from Brazil was grubby, or your wire loop wasn't sterile enough, or you breathed on the dish. Maybe they were in the agar to begin with ..."

At times like this, she detested Eliot. She wished he could be pleased with her results. Why did he have to jump to the dark conclusion that the bacteria were unimportant contaminants rather than the cause of Izabel's illness? They'd have a better idea about that eventually, when she identified what kind of bacteria they were. But for now, he should be excited for her. If these were *his* results, from a sample *he* had nurtured for so long, he'd be prancing around the room in victory laps.

"Let me see that." Raven pulled the agar dish from Sid's grasp. "Holy cow. I can't believe it. *Something's* actually growing in there. That's amazing. What are they?" She passed the dish back to Sid.

"Don't know yet. All I know is that they stain Gram-negative and are rod-shaped." Sid handed the dish to Dr. Evans.

He glanced at the agar. "What am I looking at?"

"They're bacteria from a Brazilian child with a strange infection," Sid said. "I mentioned last week that I would try to grow something from her blood." His eyes were quiet, and his face silently suggested disinterest. Or skepticism. He was a busy man with many responsibilities; he probably wasn't paying close attention to what she said. He handed the dish back to her, announced the end of the lab meeting, and strolled out the door.

"Hey, we need to throw a party," Raven said.

Sid cupped the agar dish in her hands as it if were a broken bird. These bacteria, more than all the others she had worked with, seemed terribly fragile. One false move—if she dropped the plate on the floor, or mistakenly ditched it in the incinerator bag, or ran it through the autoclave—and they might disappear, lost forever. A tiny part of that sick, and now dead, little girl from Promissão still lived. Right there on the agar dish. Alive and growing. She felt a tear crawl down her cheek. She wiped it away and closed her eyes. She couldn't let Eliot see her cry.

Eliot turned to Sid. "I've seen other scientists—really good scientists—go down dead-end rabbit holes while chasing a wrong idea, an erroneous result, even a contaminant. I did it myself when I was a doctoral student—wasted six months on a wayward mold that grew with the bacteria and threw off all the growth character-istics. Sidonie, I don't want you to waste your time. You have to acknowledge that the thing growing from the Brazil blood might not be what you think it is and then be ready to quit."

"Look, I have to do this. It's about dying children, Eliot. I fail to see how I can ignore that."

Sid started out the door of the conference room when Raven stopped her. "Until we figure out what they really are, those bacteria need a nickname," she said. "We need a shortcut for talking about them in the lab. *The bacteria from the sick little girl in Brazil* is too big a mouthful."

Sid turned back into the room. "Any ideas?"

"How about Royal, after you?" Raven said. "The 'Royal' strain."

"Interesting thought," Eliot said. "Has a kingly ring. Even contaminants can use noble nicknames until you sort it all out."

"No." Sid had no intention of attaching her name to those bacteria.

"Well, then, give them the name of the patient they came from," Eliot said. "Like other strains we have around here—Eagan, Rabinowitz, Durst."

"Absolutely not." Microbiologists had been naming bacterial strains after patients for decades, but this was different. She'd held Izabel's little arm, felt her clammy skin; she'd drawn the blood as the child was dying. "We can't do that. We just can't."

"What was the kid's name?" Eliot asked.

"Iz ..."

"Stop. Raven, no." Sid shot her friend a frown. She turned to Eliot. "I'm not going to tell you." He was trying to trick her. "It'd be a despicable betrayal of her if we name the bacteria after that little girl. She was a person, not a germ."

"I've got it," Raven finally said. "Brazilian purpuric fever strain. In honor of the disease it might have caused. Purpura on the skin. High fever. And from Brazil."

"What's purpura?" Eliot asked. "Sounds like a kind of plaid or something."

"It means purple blotches on the skin," Sid answered.

"BPF for short," Raven said. "Very zippy." Then she added, "You know, the deadline for late-breaker abstracts for the International Microbiology Society meeting is in a couple days. You should put together an abstract about the outbreak."

"Good idea." In fact, Sid thought it was a terrific idea. "Someone at the meeting may have a useful suggestion about what the germ—the BPF strain, Raven—is. Or at least thoughts about how to further proceed in figuring it out."

Eliot remained silent. The shadows in his eyes said it all. He thought they had gone way too far without knowing the significance of those bacteria. Sid thought differently.

She set the dish back in the incubator and returned to her desk. She stared out the window, her mind awash once again with memories from Promissão. River and his breakfast eggs.

Cibele and Ana. Dr. Alancar. Izabel, the little girl whose germs were growing on the dish in the incubator, her pale skin and pretty, thin cotton dress. Her anguished mother who had kissed Sid's fingertips. With a few more tests on the bacteria, hopefully they'd know what killed her.

Dr. Evans' announcement regarding the failed grant application worried the entire lab. He hadn't said anything to Sid about money to pay for her Brazil project. Earlier it didn't matter. But now that bacteria were growing from Izabel's blood, she'd need lab supplies for the tests to figure out their full identity and why they caused such overwhelming infections. Finally, she mustered the courage to speak to him.

Evans was in his office on the telephone. She waited until he finished the call and then knocked on the open door.

"Come in," he said. Gray-haired, with his glasses slightly atilt on his face, he looked like the modern-day executive, searching for additional grant money and managing complicated projects, seated behind his desk. She explained her thoughts about the germs in the blood from Brazil, how she needed to identify them to know if they truly represented an infection in the little girl. She skipped over the part about sneaking the blood into the country. "This is really important, Dr. Evans. The answer to those children's deaths may be growing on that agar dish."

His mellow eyes spoke of encouragement in a kind, grandfatherly way. "So you assume these bacteria caused her infection?"

"Well, I can't assume anything. Her symptoms were very consistent with a terrible infection, and these bacteria grew from her blood."

"Sidonie, as the mentor for your research fellowship, I need to know where your focus rests. Are you committed to learning to do the state-of-the-art type of research that will reveal the basic mechanisms behind how microbes cause infection, or are you committed to clinical medicine?" The question hung in the air like a bad smell. "This blood from Brazil sounds like a clinical question to me."

Sid took a deep breath. That's why Dr. Evans's face had seemed dull during the meeting. He had doubts. "Well, I see the project as both. Yes, it's a clinical question. Whatever is growing on that dish may have caused the little girl's death or may have nothing to do with her illness. But for now, it's all we have, and we should follow that lead."

He seemed disinterested. She felt the tears rise over her eyes. She couldn't cry, not in front of Dr. Evans. She had to keep it scientific. She blinked away the tears and took another deep breath. "In addition, the Brazil bacteria could possibly be something new and of fundamental importance to the whole field of bacteriology. It could represent a new organism, a new mechanism in pathogenesis, a paradigm shift in how we think about infections. Hard to know about that, but I'd really like to try."

Evans' nodded, slowly and deliberately. "What are your next steps?"

She explained the biochemical tests she planned to run on the bacteria, and the experiments to see if the BPF bacteria killed infant rats. She even detailed the test to determine if serum from healthy people killed the bacteria. "I'll need to use some of the laboratory's supplies to do the experiments, though," she said. "Would that be okay? If this project develops into something expensive, I'll write a grant application to get the resources to pay for it."

He smiled. The wrinkles beside his kind eyes deepened.

"Okay. You convinced me. Keep doing the work, Sidonie. Your fellowship award has adequate funds to pay for supplies for a little while longer. If those experiments turn up something important, we'll find money somewhere to pay for it. Keep me posted on your progress."

As she left his office, she felt dizzy with relief. He'd affirmed that she was doing the right thing. Heading back to her laboratory, she wove through the halls of the microbiology department, past the walk-in freezer, past the media preparation room, past the autoclave room, past the shelves of old journals, past the wooden cabinet full of clean glassware. The place felt as comfortable as home.

Her love of microbiology had started when, as a college freshman, she attended, on a lark, a lecture by a heralded visiting professor. She took a seat near the rear of the auditorium and listened while the speaker, Dr. Bausch, told of the ways bacteria make trouble for people. She detailed how they move from place to place and evolve to survive wherever they land. How their toxins drill into human cells and disarm vital metabolic pathways. How they "talk" to each other through molecules that latch onto receptors and set a series of vital chemical reactions in motion, similar to the way sound tweaks an ear drum and sends an electric signal to the brain. "It's the language of microbes," Dr. Bausch had said, in her rich New York accent, to the audience of a thousand. "A beautiful, purposeful language."

Dr. Bausch's words, erudite and engaging, had spoken to Sid just as the utterances of the muses had spoken to ancient Greeks, and she wanted to be just like her. She vowed, there in the stiff auditorium seat, to devote her life to knowing everything about the fascinating ways bacteria do what they do.

And she admired Dr. Bausch's appearance and her stately presence. Her suit was the color of an eggplant, its purple so dark it headed toward midnight. A string of pearls had looped across her ash-gray blouse like dots of white smoke, and dainty, wire-rimmed glasses framed her sparkling eyes.

After the talk, she had looked up Dr. Bausch's bibliography in the library. Louiselle Bausch was her full name. Her manuscripts were published in the most prestigious biomedical journals and were as compelling as her speech had been. That's what Sid hoped her papers—the ones she'd write when she obtained usable lab results—would be: evocative, learned, world changing. Maybe she, too, would be as extraordinary as Dr. Bausch.

Sid walked into her lab and turned the corner to her bench. Now, those tiny specks of life that sat on the agar plates in the incubator needed to multiply a lot before she would have enough to figure out what kind they were. The waiting would be difficult. It always was.

11

1984 MICHIGAN

Sid stood outside Eliot's Nest and knocked on the nearest box. The cardboard container sounded hollow under her knuckles.

"Yeah?" he called.

She edged around the corner. "I need serum for the killing tests. Will you be a donor?"

"Who'll draw the blood?"

"I will."

He jerked his head, a surprised look on his face, toward her. Had he forgotten she was a physician?

"You'd better not miss. And it better not hurt." He didn't look happy.

"I've drawn blood from many tiny babies, so getting some

from big, old you will be simple. Roll up your sleeve."

"Which arm?"

"Your choice."

She laid her supplies on his desk and tied a piece of plastic tubing around his upper arm. "Make a fist," she said.

She ran her fingers over the veins at the bend of his elbow. They were huge, would be an easy stick. She tapped on the main vein, felt its spongy recoil. His arm was warm and velvety, not scaly like the snakeskin she had expected. She dabbed an iodine-soaked pad over her target. "Little poke," she muttered and then plunged in the needle.

He didn't move. Not even a tiny flinch. The blood flowed easily into the tube. She glanced into his face as she pulled back on the syringe's plunger. Expressionless, he stared out the window at the flakes of snow that meandered past the glass.

"I'm going to take fifty milliliters. Okay?"

He nodded.

"You're a good sport," she said. "You've got plenty of blood, you know. Won't notice at all that this little bit is missing."

This venipuncture was different from all the others she had performed. The others had been from patients. This was from Eliot, and it seemed a violation of some cosmic moral principle to touch him, to jam the needle onto him, to feel the heat of his blood in the syringe in her hand. They were at the forty-five milliliter mark.

"Remind me what you're going to do with it." He was still gazing out the window. Then he turned toward her.

"Bacterial killing test. I'll mix the serum from your blood with the BPF bacteria to see if they survive. If they do—that is, if your serum doesn't kill the BPF strain but kills a control strain—then something about the BPF protects it from death by your serum."

He sat perfectly still as he stared out the window, his arm resting on his desk, the needle in his arm. "It'll be a gene on a plasmid that makes them resistant to being killed."

The blood had reached the fifty milliliter mark on the syringe. She pulled the needle from his arm and pressed a gauze square over the needle hole. "Here, hold this. I don't believe for a minute it's a plasmid. I think it's the endotoxin."

"Prove it isn't the plasmid. Those little freelancing strings of DNA, and the genes they carry, leap between bacteria, you know. A rogue plasmid could certainly explain a new deadly quality to an old bacterium."

"No, you prove it is. First I'll prove that your blood kills the control strain but not the BPF strain. Later, I'll prove why, and my bet is that it's related to an altered endotoxin in the cell wall."

He chuckled. It was a sinister, deep-throated snigger. He lifted the gauze, watched a bubble of blood ooze from the needle hole, and slapped the gauze back against his skin. "When are you doing those rat experiments?"

"I infected them yesterday and bleed the animals tomorrow."

"Can I see how you do that?"

This was the first time Eliot had been interested in learning anything from her. Did she want him in the rat room with her? Maybe he'd be in the way and slow her down. For sure he'd offer unsolicited advice. "Why? Are you planning to do rat experiments?"

"Oh, I don't know. I might."

"Well ... okay. I could use help with the tubes."

Sid had just finished washing her dinner dishes when the phone rang. "Oh, hi, Mom," she said. She pulled a chair toward the wall phone in preparation for a long, and taxing, conversation.

"I was cleaning up after supper," she said. To her mother's next question, she replied, "Scrambled eggs and a salad." And to the one that followed: "The salad had an apple and walnuts in it so, yes, it was plenty. And healthy." She wished her mother would focus on something other than her meals. But misdirected focus had been a problem for her mother for years. She'd lost appropriate focus on everything since that disastrous day long ago.

"I ran into Laurie at the drug store. Do you stay in touch with her?" Her mother's voice was a monotone.

"Not much. We have little in common anymore." She and Laurie had been very close while undergrads in Eugene, living in that messy, crowded room in Carson Hall. But passing time and lengthening distance had driven them apart. "I hope to see her next time I'm in Oregon."

They talked about the weather in Michigan and in Oregon. "Remember that red raincoat you used to wear as a kid?" her mother asked. "I found it the other day, buried in the back of the closet in the front entry. That coat was cute on you."

Through the phone line, Sid heard the clink of ice cubes against glass. For certain it was a highball. Possibly the second or third of the afternoon, and it wasn't very late, Oregon time. The drinking was worse since Sid's dad had died.

"So, what do you hear from Paul?" her mother asked. "When is he moving to Michigan? Surely there are jobs for engineers in Michigan."

Sid took a deep breath. "It's complicated, Mom. Paul's work

is very specific to the plant operations in Portland. And the pro-motion he recently received makes it financially impossible for him to move to Michigan." She desperately wished her mother also wouldn't focus on Paul. Something—anything—other than Paul or her meals. "We're trying to work it all out but ..."

"It's sure taking a long time. I still don't understand why you left Portland."

"My fellowship is in Michigan. You know that."

"Yes, but I don't understand it, and your father wouldn't either, if he were still alive. Are there no research fellowships in Portland? You could have gotten a good job as a doctor there. And leaving Paul ..." Her mother's voice trailed off. Then she caught it again. "He's such a good man, Sidonie."

"No, there are no fellowships in my field in Portland." Sid sighed. They'd been over this before. "The situation is difficult for both of us, Mother. Maybe too difficult to resolve. It's not like we're engaged or anything." She sighed again and said, "Oh ... thanks for the check. Cute card."

Sid should have dropped the conversation right there, but something in her made her push it further. "That was very kind of you, but not necessary. My fellowship stipend is enough to pay the bills, so you really don't have to send me money. I never thought of Labor Day as a gift-giving holiday."

"Well, I don't need it. Your father would want you to have it. Besides, that fellowship stipend of yours can't be terrific, espe-cially since Paul isn't there to share the expenses. Buy yourself something special."

As Sid opened the heavy door to the rat room, she heard the skittering of little feet on the bottoms of the cages. A rodent head hit a water bottle with a clunk. Then another. They were spooked, or maybe curious, wondering what she had in mind for that day. The light from the fluorescent lamps overhead, programmed to make the animals think it was now midday in the windowless basement room, cast shadows that stretched and dipped and turned on the cinderblock walls as she shoved the equipment cart over the rubber threshold and between the cages to the procedure table. Eliot followed.

The smell sent a clutch into her throat. No matter how many times she had entered that room, she gagged at the stink of the rat poop, feed pellets, disinfectant, and cage bedding. The rodent dander made her eyes itch, and the mother rats would bite if she came too close to their razor-like teeth. Her isolation gown and rubber gloves were hot and clumsy, and the mask would grow soggy from her moist breath within a half hour. Why did she do this? To unearth the mysteries of the BPF strain. Success at that was worth the discomfort of getting there.

While she arranged the tubes and needles and syringes, along with the Sharpie pens and notebooks on the stainless steel table, she said, "Want to bet on whether or not the BPF strain has survived in the baby rats' blood?"

Eliot stared into the cages, at the nervous rat mothers and their wiggly, six-days-old offspring. "I'm too impoverished to do any betting." He held up his thumb—same size and shape and color as the infant rats. "How the hell will you get blood out of them? They're teeny."

"Intracardiac," she said. "We'll stick a needle into their hearts and withdraw a milliliter of blood."

He stepped backward and leaned against the handle of the cart. His face was the color of an eggshell. His eyes were huge.

"You okay?" she asked. He'd better not pass out while they were taking the samples. She didn't want to have to revive him as they worked. She needed his help.

"I guess so." His voice was thready.

"Look ... I'll draw the blood from their hearts. You'll handle the tubes." He hadn't fainted yet. "It's a tiny needle. They tolerate it pretty well."

She set a cage on the table and lifted the lid. The mother rat glared back, her beady eyes glistening and suspicious. Her whiskers twitched, and her tail slapped the cage's mesh wall. "It's all right," she said to the rat, "we'll be gentle with your babies."

She grabbed the mother rat's tail and, in a smooth, swift arc, swung her into a clean cage. Then she lifted one of the babies out of the dirty bedding material. Shortly after they were born, she had cut two little notches in that baby's left ear and none in the right. "This is infant number L2R0 from mother M1," she said to Eliot. "See, it says 'M1' on her cage." He seemed stable now, unlikely to collapse. "Label a tube with the mother's and the little rat's numbers and hand me one of those syringes—one with the needle attached."

The mother rat raced in circles across the walls of her clean cage. A frantic look twisted her face. She knocked against the spigot of the water bottle. "Settle down," Sid said to the scared rodent. "Your babies will be back soon."

She cradled the tiny animal in her left hand. Its skin was warm and soft, and its belly as pink as a rose petal. Its eyes were closed, and it wiggled in places one wouldn't think an animal could wiggle. She gripped the skin of its back, immobilizing it against her palm. Only its tiny fingers and toes could flex. Then she ran her pointer finger along the bottom of its ribs, searching for her target.

Eliot handed a syringe to Sid. She stuck the needle's tip into baby rat L2R0 beneath its breastbone and slid the needle into its heart. The animal, locked in her fist, didn't move. She pulled the plunger of the syringe and watched the blood, red as rubies, inch up the inside of the syringe's barrel.

If, as she expected, the baby rat's blood didn't kill the BPF bacteria she had injected two days earlier, those bacteria would be circulating inside the animal, just as they had circulated inside Izabel, from her little heart to every cell in her body and then back to her heart. Round and round, like a ring within a circle, like a wheel within a wheel. That's what had killed Izabel, earlier generations of the bacteria that were now in this rat's blood. Generation after generation, like another wheel within a wheel. The rhythm of her favorite song rang through Sid's head.

When the blood reached the one milliliter mark, she pulled the needle from the rat's chest, massaged its rosy skin—"to speed up repair of the needle hole," she told Eliot—and then loosened her grip. The animal squirmed, realigning its shoulders and pelvis. When she set the baby in the clean cage, the mother poked her nose against its back and then flipped it over.

Sid twisted the needle off the syringe and squirted the blood into the tube in Eliot's hand. "Give it a shake to keep the blood from clotting," she said.

One by one, she bled each baby rat. Ten rats per mother, three mothers. Repeatedly Eliot handed her a labeled tube. Repeatedly she squirted in the blood. On about the thirteenth baby rat, her mind began to wander. Maybe it was the heat and dank of the stuffy rat room. Maybe the fact that she was tired following her mother's phone call and a sleepless night thinking about Paul. He was a man every mother would want her daughter to marry. Kind. Thoughtful. Responsible. Stable. More than adequately gainfully employed.

Was that enough? Sid also wanted him to be proud of her tenacity and scientific expertise and to admire the commitment with which she approached her research. She wanted him to value the results of her work and, if necessary, to be willing to sacrifice parts of his life for it. She knew it was a big order.

Eliot started to talk. At first, she ignored his muttering. She couldn't hear it very well. His sodden mask and the whir of the ventilation system blurred his words.

Two baby rats later, his chatter began to irritate her. "What are you saying?" she asked.

He raised his voice. "I was a child and she was a child/In this kingdom by the sea."

His jabbering continued while she felt along the rib edge of the rat in her hand and stuck a needle into its heart. "And this was the reason that, long ago/In this kingdom by the sea."

When she handed Eliot the syringe full of blood, she said, again, "What on earth are you saying? And, to whom?"

His voice was louder. "A wind blew out of a cloud, chilling/My beautiful Annabel Lee."

Annabel Lee? By the sea? Then she remembered. The dreary tone, the ominous rhythm, Poe at his finest.

"That's kind of creepy," she said, laughing.

"Creepier than standing in this cave and sticking needles into baby rats' hearts?" His eyes peered from above his mask and glittered.

He must be the first person ever to recite poetry in a rat room.

When Sid had her results, she knocked on the cardboard box outside Eliot's nest.

"Yeah?" he called. He was back to being grumpy. Maybe her new data would sweeten him up. Or maybe he'd dismiss it as rubbish. No matter what, he'd have lots of suggestions for how she should have done it differently.

"I've got the results from the rat experiment. And from the killing tests with your blood. Want to see them?" She handed him two pieces of paper.

"That's impressive." Eliot was smiling. Truly smiling. "You don't have to be a statistical wizard to see that the rat blood killed the control strain but didn't touch the BPF strain. And," he shuffled the papers and read the final one, "my serum didn't kill those steely BPF bacteria. You'll run a chi-square test to know for sure that the differences are significant, right?"

There it was. The predictable suggestion. Did he think she *wouldn't* do the appropriate statistical analysis? Did he think she was an idiot? She pulled the paper from his hand. "Of course." She heard the bitterness in her voice, wished she didn't have to be bitter, wished he weren't so controlling.

She looked, again, at the results. She thought of the hours and hours of work devoted to those experiments. It all boiled down to only two data tables, each containing four squares, with one number per square. Suddenly she felt very tired.

He might have sensed her disappointment, because he said, "Actually, this is great, Sidonie. These results are astounding. They securely clinch your case that the BPF bacteria survive in blood."

"And can kill people." As she spoke, she tried to hide the sadness in her voice from him.

He smiled again. "Could be." It wasn't a patronizing smile this time. Was he, indeed, capable of a genuine smile? Apparently, the answer was yes, rarely, for she'd just seen one.

12

1984 MICHIGAN

For Sid, evenings usually brought welcome peace to otherwise hectic days. On most nights, she ate a simple supper, did a little knitting, read the newspaper and articles from medical journals, and then went to bed. She assumed the upcoming night would be the same. She turned on the radio and, while she ate a take-out hamburger from the cafe down the street, listened to *All Things Considered*. The chimes of its theme song, familiar and comfortable, rang over the airways, and then the voice of Noah Adams, smooth and resonant, cut in. "In San Francisco, city officials have ordered all bathhouses closed due to the high-risk sexual activity in those venues."

Sid set the half-eaten burger on its wrapper. High-risk sexual activity meant high risk for AIDS. It was spreading among gay men like a prairie fire, unremitting and without remorse. How about River? Was he okay? It was none of her business, but every time she heard or read about AIDS, she thought about him.

As she picked up her burger, the phone rang. From her seat at her kitchen table, she reached toward the phone on the wall.

It was Paul. He sounded weary. "Yeah, tough day at work. I had to sack a guy," he said. "That's never pleasant."

"Is he a jerk?"

"No, not at all. He just isn't capable of doing the work. We went over it again and again with him, and he just didn't get it. I don't understand how someone as well educated as he is could be so obtuse. Absolutely no ability to plan or follow through or initiate the obvious next step." Paul sighed. "So my day was crummy. How was yours?"

She told him about the hoarfrost that coated the trees when she first got up. "It was beautiful, as if the trees wore white, sequined dresses."

"Well, I went golfing yesterday morning. No hoarfrost in Portland."

"Speaking of balmy weather, I'm going to send you copies of some of the photos Raven and I took while we were in Brazil."

"Good. I'd like to see the place."

"It's lovely. Promissão is a little village, thousands of miles from the nearest five-star hotel. But it's bucolic."

"Bucolic is good. I guess. And so are five-star hotels."

"I'd take the cot in River's storeroom any day. More interesting."

"Each to his own."

"Of course, the bucolic, at least the peaceful, pleasant part, dissolved when Gilberto and Izabel died. Then it turned tragic."

"Sid, I think we should get married."

Sid sighed. Headlights from a passing car shined through the kitchen window and swept across the wall. "I know that's been on your mind." They had talked about the possibility before—several times—and always left it as an open question.

"Not on yours?"

"I have lots on my mind right now."

Then she explained the results of the serum killing and rat experiments with the BPF strain. She went into great detail: why Eliot's serum should kill the bacteria, why Eliot's poetry was so charming. She summed it up by saying, "I was right, Paul; the immune factors in blood can't kill that mean germ."

"O k a y." He drew that little word out to four syllables.

She decided to abandon the science talk and described the armloads of old clothes she'd piled on her front porch for the Goodwill to pick up. "It's about time I ditched that stuff." Then she explained the smoke-flavored hamburger she was eating for dinner. She did not tell him about the closing of the San Francisco bathhouses nor about her concern for River.

The line was silent. Then Paul said, "Sid, any plans yet for another trip to Portland? Last time we talked about it, you were vague."

She took a deep breath and let it out slowly. "My work here is consuming me."

"I know, but ... just thought I'd check."

She leaned her head against the edge of the window. "Paul, I really wish you could understand how important this project is to me. Children are dying, and I need to get to the bottom of what's killing them so we can stop it."

"How about at the end of your fellowship? Will you come back then?"

He sounded playful, again. She wasn't. "I don't know. I have no way of knowing what kinds of jobs may be available for me then."

"Portland will always need good infectious diseases doctors. I heard about a new clinic in Southeast for indigent kids. That sounds right up your alley."

He sounded like her mother. Her clinical work was all that mattered to both of them. The lure of research was beyond their understanding.

"Paul, I love my work in the lab."

"I know you do. And you work very hard at it. And it's paying off."

"Is that bad? What's wrong with ambition? What's wrong with persistence?" Some people valued her ambition, people like Raven and Dr. Evans. Probably even Eliot. "If I abandon my research, I'd regret it forever."

"Forever is a very long time and full of possibilities."

After she said goodbye to Paul, she picked up the now cold, half-eaten hamburger. But she wasn't hungry anymore.

She liked the way Paul viewed the world as a pragmatist and his easy, breezy sense of humor. And he clearly was fond of her, at least fond of the idea of her being his wife. Was that love? He had told her he loved her, and she believed him. Did she love him? Yes. At least one kind of love.

She thought of her various loves. There was Dr. Bausch, for her example as an excellent woman scientist. And Dr. Evans, for his patience with her as a junior scientist. There was Raven, for her friendship; River, for his kindness; Paul, for his love. Was her love for Paul the kind that led to marriage? She wasn't sure of that. She guessed she might not know what type of love led to marriage.

She couldn't use her parents as yardsticks. Had they loved each other? Certainly, although they didn't express it much. Her father was a good caretaker, and her mother needed care. Was that love?

By the time she got into bed, she'd realized the evening, indeed, hadn't been peaceful at all. She drifted off to sleep, still wondering about Paul.

13

1984 MICHIGAN

Time. It inched forward, slow as a sloth. Sid's bacteria took longer than she wanted to reproduce in the incubator. The shipment of Petri dishes was late. She dropped a flask full of bacterial growth medium, and it shattered on the floor, so she had to start over with a new batch. She'd jammed the end of the inoculation loop into an agar plate with so much oomph that it had snapped, and she had to borrow one from Raven until a new one arrived. All because she was distracted.

Her mind sizzled with images from Brazil: the gathering at Luiza's grave site, Gilberto cavorting around Cibele's living room, Dr. Alancar thumping on little Izabel's chest, the blank stares in the eyes of Mariana's father and grandmother, Cibele as she sank to her knees on the clinic floor and screamed.

As the hours and days trudged along, she thought of the Earth turning 360° in one day, and of its immensity. The world was too big for her to change, and the hopelessness of that depressed her. A car bomb at the US Embassy in Beirut slaughtered twenty-four people. The Beauty Queen Killer raped and murdered his way across America. A PEMEX oil storage tank exploded in Mexico and killed hundreds. Motorcycle gangs massacred each other in Australia. A female cop in London was shot by a Libyan diplomat. Typhoon Ike drowned thousands in the Philippines. Children were dying from a mysterious illness in backcountry Brazil.

Promissão was much smaller than the rest of the world, more manageable. Surely she could do something to keep those kids from dying.

It was dark when she reached her apartment. At that time of year, it was always dark when she left work. And cold. The fall chill in Michigan always bit into her like a mad dog, but now even more so. She remembered Brazil with its September spring, the silky air, the swaying palms. Her thoughts swung back, again, to the dead babies, and stalled. As she walked from the parking area to her front door, she watched the blue-gray clouds drift across the silvery full moon. That same moon hung high in the sky over Promissão. Those children would never grow up to know the awe of the moon.

A gust of hot air greeted her in the entryway. She hung her coat in the closet. The day's mail—this week's issue of *The New England Journal of Medicine*, a Horchow Collection catalogue, the electric bill, and a letter from the National Democratic

Party—lay scattered on the floor below the letter slot. Beneath them, she found another letter, an onion-skin aerogram. Foreign stamp. Lady-like handwriting in navy blue ink in the upper left corner said "Cibele Barbosa." She must have gotten the address from River. Sid tore open the letter.

My dear Sidonie,

I write to bring you greetings from Promissão. It was a treat to meet you during your visit, and I truly appreciate your being with us when Gilberto died. I hope your return travel was safe.

My sister Ana spends several hours every day at Gilberto's grave. This is very hard for her. She can't sleep. Neither can I. Everyone in our town is terrified that another baby will die.

We're still passing out the fliers you and I made. I had to print 100 more copies yesterday. Even though they didn't help Gilberto, maybe they will help another child. We want no more deaths. It's a horribly bad thing when precious children have to die.

I hope you will return to Brazil soon. I look forward to seeing you then.

My warmest blessings,

Cibele

In her reply letter, Sid again thanked Cibele for her kind hospitality and tried to comfort her in her grief.

Two weeks later, Sid received another letter.

My dear Sidonie,

Thank you so much for your recent letter. I read it to Ana, and she sends her greetings. She still goes to the cemetery every day, but, instead of crying the whole time she is there, now she sings to Gilberto. She says she doesn't want him to ever forget her songs.

Another baby died yesterday. Same sickness as the others. He had the red eye and then developed a high fever. By the next day he was dead.

I've been speaking with the mothers of Promissão. They know you are an American doctor who studies infections, and they ask me, over and over, what they can do to protect their children from dying. Should they feed them special food? Keep them indoors all day? They'll do anything you suggest.

Please, Sid, tell us what to do.

My warmest blessings,

Cibele

At lunch, Sid settled into the lounge's easy chair. Raven sank into Long Green and once again picked at the coffee stains on the couch's arm.

"It's impossible to get rid of them," Sid said about the couch's stains as she cut up her apple. "I suggest you quit trying."

"I don't believe in the word 'impossible.'" Raven unwrapped her sandwich and then offered Sid a Fig Newton.

"No, thanks. Your naiveté is charming, Raven, and totally unrealistic." Yes, Raven was naive about many things, including her twin brother's biggest secret. Sweet ignorance. Raven chewed her sandwich without a clue.

"That's what Eliot says. He thinks I was raised in Shangri-La instead of northern California." The lounge door opened. Eliot walked in. "Well, speaking of impossible," Raven laughed. "There he is."

He leaned against the frame of the doorway and stared at Sid. "I've been hunting for you."

"Well, I'm here, eating my lunch."

"So I see. Where's the big rotor for the centrifuge?"

"I have no idea."

"It's on my bench," Raven said. "Go ahead and take it."

He stomped out, slamming the lounge door shut.

"What's bugging him?" Raven asked.

"I have no idea," Sid again said.

They ate in silence until Raven looked up from reading a notice that lay on the lunchroom table. "Say, did you see this? Looks interesting."

Sid glanced at the paper.

Grand Rounds, 8 a.m.

Wednesday, October 10, 1984

"The Magic of Cephalosporin Antibiotics"

Dr. Joseph Miller, University of Pennsylvania

She read it again. October 10—tomorrow.

The auditorium was packed by the time Sid arrived. During the course of the lecture, she heard about older cephalosporin antibiotics, how they killed many bacteria but not some of the most dangerous, how they were generally safe, how they were only available in pills. The most exciting information, though, was about a new cephalosporin drug. Cefotaxime. Dr. Miller flipped to the figure on his next slide and explained how well it killed the bacteria that caused bad infections in children. He flipped the slide again. "The most valuable feature of this drug," he said, "is that it is given by vein, thus providing very high blood levels, much higher than was possible with older, similar drugs given by mouth."

Thoughts raced through the circuits of her mind as if they were sparks jumping from one live wire to the next. A new drug. Designed especially for children. Effective against a broad range of bacteria. Images of Izabel as she lay dying. High levels in the blood of the patients. Would it work in Promissão?

In the afternoon, the phone in the lab rang. Sid answered.

"River here. How are you, Sid?"

She reached for her stool and sat down. His voice sounded metallic and very far away. But it was gentle like a warm summer evening with candles and cheesecake. "I'm fine. Where are you?"

"In Promissão..."

She pictured him at his office, imagined his lanky body pacing the floor and his trim fingers twisting the phone cord as he wandered.

"I'm calling for Raven, but I can tell you. We had another child die here."

"Oh, no." Her pulse was now racing. "Cibele wrote to me about the death of a little boy. Is this yet another?"

"Yes, a little girl from south of town. I thought you'd want to know. Apparently, this child's illness was like the others." He told her what he knew. Three years old. Pink eye several days earlier. Died within a day of getting sick. He paused and then continued. "I know her father. He's one of the farmers who use our new seeds."

"Was Dr. Alancar able to care for her?" she asked.

"He never saw the child alive. Cibele said the little girl died in the truck on the way to the hospital."

She wondered if the parents had seen the flier she and Cibele made, and if they knew to bring the girl to the hospital at the very first sign of illness. River wouldn't know the answer to that.

"This has gotten utterly awful, Sid. So many people dying. And they're all little kids."

They seemed to line up before her, the row of dead children. Now, seven.

"Is my sister there?" He sounded worn out.

"Tell her I called. Oh, and Cibele sends her greetings." He paused, then added, "One more thing."

Sid reached for the handle to shut off the gas to the Bunsen burner. River's call was getting long, and her lab bay was getting warm.

"Have you ever heard of something called the GHA?"

"Well, yeah. If you mean the Global Health Alliance."

"Maybe. One of the farmers—you remember Marcelo, the fellow whose daughter was the first child to die—told me that someone from an international agency by that name—I think he said GHA—had been asking him and his wife questions about their daughter and that mysterious illness."

What were they doing there? "What kind of questions did they ask? Do you know?"

"No, but I could probably find out. What is GHA anyway?"

"A group of epidemiologists who track new and unusual diseases all over the world. It's headquartered in Madrid. Probably Dr. Alancar notified the Brazil National Health Agency of the illnesses and deaths, and they contacted the GHA to help figure out what's going on."

"So that's good."

She didn't know what to say. She'd never worked directly with the GHA but had heard they sometimes were myopic in thinking about illnesses and used heavy-handed tactics to get what they wanted.

Before she could respond, he said, "I'm not sure I know what an epidemiologist does."

"Well, they analyze patterns of diseases among large numbers of people—as in epidemics. In Promissão, they were probably interviewing the families of the deceased children about illnesses in other family members, about exposures to insects and animals, about travel to other counties or to other regions of Brazil, about the food they ate—that kind of stuff. They're not medical doctors who diagnose and treat illnesses in individual people like I am."

"Okay. Ask Raven to give me a call."

She wished she had heard River wrong about the new death. She listened to the freezer compressor, to Eliot's booming voice from the far end of the lab. The children kept dying, a nonstop march of toddlers to the grave, and no one knew what was going on or how to stop it. Whatever the BPF strain turned out to be, it was wicked.

An idea budded and then bloomed to full flower in her head. Would it work? Could she pull it off? She had to do something. Even if it was unconventional. She got the phone number she needed from the chief hospital pharmacist and dialed it.

"Good afternoon. You've reached Hoechst Pharmaceuticals."

"This is Dr. Sidonie Royal. I'm trying to reach Dr. Lewis Hatton." This call had a low probability of success, but, to her, it was worth a try. After all, the probability of growing the BPF strain from Izabel's blood had also been low, but it had happened.

"He's on another line. He'll be with you in a moment."

While she waited, Sid listened to moody music, then to a nasal voice describing the newest drugs from Hoechst Pharmaceuticals. Cefotaxime was on the list, except that the recording called it by its brand name Claforan, easier to pronounce, easier to remember, easier to write on an order form. Then more music.

"This is Lewis Hatton. Good to hear from you, Sid. It's been awhile."

In fact, it had been five years since she'd last spoken to him on the day they graduated from medical school. She remembered him as the most social member of their class, handsome, cagey, and smart. "I hope Hoechst is treating you well."

"Working for the pharmaceutical industry has its benefits."

Indeed. A big salary would be one, she thought. "I'm interested in your company's new antibiotic, cefotaxime. I understand it has great promise for serious infections, particularly in children."

"We're pretty excited about Claforan." He paused for a moment, and before she could get to the reason for the call, he started talking again. "The clinical trials were even better than we expected."

She took a deep breath and began her pitch. "Well, I've stumbled upon several children with fatal infections in rural Brazil and am worried we may see more. I'm wondering if you could provide some of the drug for us?"

"What was the pathogen?"

"We don't know. We grew bacteria from the blood of only one of the kids; the sample was drawn as she was dying. We're not sure how reliable that culture is, and the organism—a Gram-negative rod—is strange. Any chance we could get several courses of cefotaxime?"

"Well..."

"I know this is an unusual request, but it's an unusual situation, Lew. All they have at the local clinic is ampicillin, and I understand that cefotaxime has a broader spectrum."

"Indeed, it does. It probably kills at least 25% more Gram-negative rods than ampicillin." He cleared his throat. "The problem is this: while it's licensed for adults, Claforan isn't licensed yet for children in Brazil. It'd be highly irregular to send it there for use in pediatric patients."

"You needn't send it to Brazil. My hope is that you would send it to me, and I'll do what I think is appropriate with it. You know, things like antibiotic susceptibility tests and animal protection studies, once we finish identifying the bacteria that caused the deaths. And possibly, we'd give it as emergency care to a dying child."

He sighed. "Okay. I'll get some to you. How much do you need?"

She did the math in her head. How many children could Dr. Alancar conceivably treat, considering that so far, he had treated none? Maybe eight. The amount of drug per dose, the number of doses per day, the number of days of treatment, times eight children. "Eighty two-gram vials should do it."

Lew said nothing but emitted a low whistle.

She heard papers rustle in the background. He said nothing. "We could start with half of that, and if we need more, I could let you know," she said.

He cleared his throat, again. "So, forty vials ..."

She adjusted her glasses and finally said, "That would work."

"It'll take at least a week for me to get it. Where should I send it?"

She gave him the lab address. "Thanks a lot. I really appreciate it. Let me know how I can repay the favor."

"You can treat me to a cocktail and a game of golf at our next med school reunion," he laughed. "Or better yet, a cocktail at the International Microbiology Society meeting. Will you be there, in Amsterdam?"

"As a matter of fact, yes. I'm presenting a paper."

14

1984 THE NETHERLANDS

The room was hazy from too many cigarettes, and with every breath, smoky bar air filled Sid's lungs. It prickled her skin and made her itchy. Her clothes would stink, and that thought made her squirm. Further, the bulbs in the wall lamps—they couldn't have been more than fifteen watts each—gave everyone around the crowded table a ghostly look, with eerie eyes, ashen cheeks, dull foreheads, and deeply blue—oxygen-starved blue—lips.

She took a sip of her beer. Raven, beside her, leaned into Doug. Sid hadn't met Eliot's old roommate before tonight, and she didn't think much of his loud mouth. Now, he stroked Raven's hair as if he were petting a cat.

Besides being dark and smelly, the bar was noisy. The

flood of conversation, mixed with the roar of Michael Jackson snarling "Beat it" from the sound system, filled the room. She had always thought of that song as mean-spirited, but tonight, as its wracking rhythm blasted past her, her foot tapped against the floor, and her fingertips drummed on the tabletop.

Eliot, across the table from her, emptied his beer glass. Something strange had happened to him. Earlier, he had pro-posed a toast—a thoughtful, erudite greeting to his old buddies and lab mates. It was a rugged-but-friendly Eliot who now set his glass on the table, not the grumpy, critical Eliot from the laboratory. With his wind-blown hair and plaid flannel shirt, tonight he reminded Sid of Robert Redford. She'd only dealt with him under the harsh, analytical fluorescent lights of the lab, never in the hazy glow of a smoky bar. That must be it, she thought. The lighting. And maybe the beer.

She glanced at her watch and yawned. They had arrived at Schiphol Airport at six in the morning, and her internal clock had gone haywire. Now, it was nine at night Dutch time. That would be three in the afternoon at home, and she had hardly slept at all since leaving Michigan yesterday. Was it yesterday? Yes, yesterday.

"What time does the meeting start tomorrow?" she asked.

"Who cares?" Doug called. The waitress set his fourth Grolsch before him. After laughing at his own words—which Sid didn't find funny—he planted a kiss on Raven's cheek and slurped another mouthful of beer.

"Hail to microbiology," Doug yelled. A hush fell over the room. People at other tables turned to stare at him. "Hail to Louis Pasteur." His booming voice bounced off the walls. "Do you know," he bent forward in front of Raven and hung his face four inches from Sid's nose, "that Louis Pasteur discovered the cause of bad beer? It was ... dum de dum dum ... *bad bacteria.*"

Sid leaned away from him. He took another swig from his Grolsch and continued, "Pasteur discovered that sour beer had bacteria in it instead of yeast. That was a triumph for microbiology. Hell, that was a triumph for beer." A loud hiccough gurgled from deep inside his chest.

"Shh, Doug," Raven whispered and pulled his arm from around her neck.

"Down with miasmas and foul humors and ptomaines," Doug roared. "Up with plasmids and pathogenicity islands."

"He's drunk," Sid mouthed to Eliot. She was exhausted and needed a break from the smoke and the dark and the noise. And from Doug. She finished her Heineken, stood up, and announced with another yawn, "I'm off to the hotel."

"We're just ... getting ... started," Doug yelled as he pointed a wobbly finger at her. "Sit back down."

"I'll leave the security latch unlocked," she said to Raven, who again leaned against Doug's shoulder.

The whites of Raven's eyes were crimson, and their lids puffy. She seemed to have trouble keeping them open. Sid paused for a moment. Could she make it back to their hotel safely? Especially in the hands of Doug? Sid headed toward the door. Raven, she decided, was old enough to take care of herself.

"Party hearty," she said over her shoulder. "I'm out of here."

Eliot followed her out of the bar. "Remember the way back to your hotel?" he asked.

She pulled a map from her purse. "Got it right here." She took a deep breath and drew the clean, refreshing outside air into her body.

"These streets can be confusing. My hotel is near yours, so I'm heading the same direction. Okay if I accompany you?"

The question was very out of character for Eliot. She smiled at him, unsure of his new temperament. "Sure," she finally said.

As they walked along the canal—Keizersgracht, Eliot called it—she listened to the water slap against the boats moored along the edge. Little slaps. Gentle slaps. She heard the tinkle of bells, one higher pitched than the other. Eliot pulled her toward the edge of the path, and two bicyclists weaved around them. When they approached the Leidsegracht Bridge, the dots of light that outlined its stone arches twinkled like fireflies as they reflected off the swells in the water.

She stopped. "This is really beautiful," she said. "So peaceful. So very simple." She struggled to find the right words to match her thoughts, words that would capture her awe of the scenery. "So old." She felt an odd shift or turn or whatever it was deep inside her. She couldn't name it. It felt as if a long-ago, pleasant memory had bubbled up to the top. But she'd never been to the Netherlands. She had, of course, visited her grandparents, aunts, and uncles in Belgium and had been enchanted with its old-world charm—the dormer windows on the roofs of the old buildings, the brick mosaic plazas. Maybe that was it.

They walked along the canal without speaking. The charms of Amsterdam were everywhere—the lace curtains on the windows of the canal boats, their creaks as they bobbed in the water, the smells of the ancient cobblestones splattered with diesel fuel, the classic Dutch bar.

"Doug acted like a jerk tonight," she finally said. "What got into him?"

"Too much beer."

"Well, yes. But he had a choice in that. What motivated his decision to get so drunk?"

"This conversation's getting a bit existential." Eliot kicked a pebble from the street into the oily water. It made a soft splat and then disappeared, leaving a circle of ever-widening ripples. "Your first trip to Holland?" he asked.

"Yes, and so far, it's lovely."

"It is. Tomorrow we should all go to the van Gogh museum. You must not miss that."

"You're very familiar with Amsterdam."

"I've been here a number of times. With my father." He rubbed his elbow, pulled at his sleeve. "My dad was in the diplomatic corps. I used to come with him on business trips. In fact, he was deployed here for a year when I was almost thirteen. We lived in an apartment about two kilometers to the west."

He pointed out the buildings—some well-lit, others dark—as they passed. "Here's a law office." He looked to the left, then nodded to the right. "And a dentist's office." Several steps forward, he pointed to a tall, slender structure that looked stern and scolding with empty, soulless windows. "That's an office full of psychologists." He laughed at the irony of the building's austere image and the shrinks that occupied it. So did she.

A block farther, his finger shot skyward. "There's the house with the heads." Looking up, she saw the white faces of ceramic gods that smiled down from high on the brick walls. "It's a music school. I took trumpet lessons there one summer."

It was hard to imagine Eliot and trumpet lessons. When she was growing up, the trumpet players were the cool, popular guys, not the science geeks. "Were you good at it?" she asked.

"No." Then he chuckled and shrugged.

"Your folks must have gone nuts during your practice sessions. Mine did with my piano lessons." She tried to imagine a young Eliot, red faced and earnest as he blew into his horn. "Must have been loud."

"My father was and still is an impatient person, but he tolerated the trumpet. In fact, he put up with a lot of nonsense from me. Everything considered, it was admirable of him." He paused a moment. "And Mother never had to listen to it. She was gone by that time." His voice had taken a downward dip.

Gone? Where'd his mother go? Dead? Ran away? How awful for Eliot. She wanted to hear more about her, but he quickly steered the conversation toward his father.

"Dad and I actually had a great time in Amsterdam. I used to sit in the back of conference rooms doing my homework while Dad met with Dutch diplomatic aides. And we had terrific meals here. The Dutch, in spite of being pathologically clean and regimented, can cook pretty well."

Considering that Eliot was a hard-core hermit in the lab, it was eerie to hear about his childhood and his family, especially about a mother who had disappeared for opaque reasons. Until tonight, Sid wouldn't have been able to imagine Eliot as a little kid. But now she could envision him tooting his trumpet and hanging around policy wonks with his dad. And being very sad.

The truth was, she didn't know much about his personal life, except that he was single. According to Raven, who kept up with all the lab gossip, he brought a different date to every departmental party. Raven said they all seemed to be smart women: liberal arts grad students or MBA or law students. Never scientists. And they all were beautiful.

After arriving at her hotel, Eliot and Sid sat outside on the stone steps and talked about the planning meeting earlier that afternoon. Someone had suggested Dr. Evans give a talk about antimicrobial resistance at the next world congress, and Eliot had insisted on another speaker.

"Why did you blackball Dr. Evans from giving that talk?" she asked.

"It would be boring." Eliot folded and then unfolded his hands. "And I didn't 'blackball' him. He's a horseshit speaker. You know that. I merely suggested an alternative."

It was true that Dr. Evans' speaking style was unidimensional, and he gave lifeless, disorganized lectures, yet she was stunned Eliot would say such a thing. Dr. Evans was his postdoc mentor. Eliot had a duty to speak well of him and to wholeheartedly support his giving an important talk at an important meeting. "Aren't you required to bolster Dr. Evans?" she asked.

"Required? By whom?" Eliot's left leg bounced on the lowest step of the staircase, and his voice had grown tense. "Evans is an excellent scientist, but he's a lousy speaker. It's our responsibility to identify the very best lecturers for the conference."

"I understand and respect your commitment to the conference." She could feel a dispute brewing between them but couldn't stop talking. "I also think you owe a measure of support to Dr. Evans." She wasn't going to let Eliot have the last word. She'd defend Dr. Evans forever. "He's been a terrific mentor to you, and to me, and to all of us, and he has earned your loyalty several times over."

Neither of them spoke. Finally, Eliot said, "I think we should agree to disagree."

Sid nodded. "Good idea."

She heard the hum of a boat moving along the canal and

breathed in the soft chill of the Dutch winter evening. A young man and woman, hand in hand, strolled past them on the sidewalk, babbling like crows in a language she didn't understand. They were clearly a couple in love, and whatever they were saying, its meaning was universal.

If the man beside her weren't Eliot, she, too, might have found the evening romantic. She could smell the earthy scent of his body. And tonight, he was funny, sweet, chatty, relaxed.

Suddenly he patted her shoulder, bolted to his feet, covered a yawn with his palm, and said, "Long day. Meeting starts early in the morning. Your talk is tomorrow, right? Where and when?"

"Room S203 in the convention center. At two in the afternoon." Part of her wanted to stay on the hotel steps with him a while longer. But she, too, was very tired. "Good night," she said. "I'll see you at my presentation."

Inside, at the end of the hallway, she unlocked the door to the little room she shared with Raven. Its six walls met at odd angles. The two twin beds—hers stood beneath the windowsill that sat level with the sidewalk—nearly filled the floor space. She watched several sets of feet and ankles scurry past and then closed the drapes. She brushed her teeth, pulled on her nightgown, set her travel alarm for seven in the morning, snuggled under the eiderdown quilt, and fell asleep.

Sometime in the middle of the night, a key twisted in the lock. The door creaked open, and Sid sensed a beam of light passing over her bed. Her body stiffened. "Raven?" she called. "Is that you?"

No answer. Now almost fully awake, she stared through the open door at the rectangle of dimly lit hallway. She saw no one. Who had opened the door? Who else, but Raven, would have a key? Maybe the manager. Why would he open the door at that time of night? What if it were an intruder? She could yell. Should she yell?

Her heart raced. She heard nothing from beyond the doorway, saw no shadows. Her only option was to get out of bed and check the hall, but that had no appeal. Still, what was the point in waiting? No matter who had made the noise, the door needed to be closed and locked. She pulled back the eiderdown quilt and set one foot on the floor.

Then she heard a giggle from the hallway. Sounded like Raven. Then, a woman's voice said, "Good night, big guy."

"How about I come in?" Doug's voice was slurred.

"Nope." The voice was, indeed, Raven's. "Sid's asleep in there."

"So what?" Doug yelled. "She won't care if I visit for a little while."

Sid stood up. His shouting would awaken everyone in the hotel. She took a step toward the door. Raven might need help getting rid of him.

"No, Doug," Raven said. "We'll see you tomorrow at Sid's talk. Good night."

Then the room darkened, and the door clicked shut. She heard Raven rumble across their room. It sounded as though she tripped over something. Probably her suitcase. She had left it open on the floor next to the bathroom.

"Raven?" she called again.

"Yes. Sorry to bother you. The door's locked. Go back to sleep."

Sid lay awake, running everything that happened that evening through her mind. Eliot was so different in Amsterdam.

Why? What had happened to his mother? A motherless little boy. Maybe that had made him so surly.

She thought of Raven and Doug. Of the way he smoothed her hair. And hugged her. And planted the kiss on her cheek.

She thought of past tender moments between her and Paul, and of the previously shiny stars that were going dim between them.

The next afternoon, Sid and Raven arrived early at Room S203 in the convention center. Sid handed her slides to the projectionist, saying, "I'm Dr. Royal, the third speaker," and then took a seat beside Raven in the second row. She smoothed the skirt of her new eggplant-colored suit so it wouldn't be wrinkled when she stood to give her talk, and tugged at her pearls, assuring herself the clasp was centered at the back of her neck.

She stared at her watch. Almost one thirty. Her presentation was from two o'clock to two-ten, and then she'd field questions from the audience until two-fifteen. She'd given the talk to the lab group and had the timing down pat. She'd remade a couple slides several times because she thought they didn't flow well. Eliot had suggested she add a table. "You need a visual to show all those chemical reactions; that string of verbiage is too cluttered for any mortal to follow," he'd said. Initially she'd resisted. She knew, after all, how to put data on a slide. But in the end, she'd added the table.

Raven squirmed beside her and then turned in her seat and stared toward the back of the room. "Where's Eliot?" she asked. "I don't see him."

"How should I know?" Sid folded and unfolded her hands and then folded them again. "I have enough to think about without keeping track of him."

"I don't see Doug, either."

"We're not taking attendance, Raven." Eliot would be there. She didn't doubt that.

By the time the moderator called the session to order, most of the chairs in the room were occupied. There must have been at least three hundred people.

"I still don't see Eliot. Nor Doug." Raven's whisper sounded desperate. Sid wished she'd be quiet.

As the applause faded following the first presentation, the second speaker, the one right before Sid, strolled to the podium. The moderator announced, "The next paper is titled 'Human T-lymphotropic Viruses Isolated from Men with Kaposi's Sarcoma.'"

Raven leaned toward Sid and muttered, "This should be interesting."

Sid nodded. She and Raven had talked about it on the plane—the new disease that afflicted young homosexual men that ruined their immune systems and left them to die of terrible, weird infections. Raven hadn't known much about AIDS. Sid had explained that some of the infected men developed Kaposi's sarcoma. "That's usually a slow-growing skin cancer in old men who live around the Mediterranean basin," she had said. "The homosexual men it affects, though, are in their twenties and thirties, and, in them, it spreads like hot butter."

Sid was tempted to turn away from the screen, but she needed to know about that disease. One of her patients might get it. The men in the photos were young, and skeletal, and peppered with puffy, almost black growths on their gaunt faces and sunken abdomens, their boney backs, arms, and legs. Someday River could be among them, and Raven, seated six inches to her left, had no idea about that.

At the conclusion of the AIDS presentation, four members of the audience lined up in the aisle behind the microphone to ask questions or make comments. The presenter readily answered the first one. Sid hoped the questions directed at her after her own presentation, if there were any, would be that easy. The speaker had more trouble with the second question. While he stammered at an answer, a man from the audience leaped to his feet and raced to the microphone. He introduced himself as the speaker's advisor and, as he proceeded to answer the question, he elaborated on the experimental details.

When it was Sid's turn, the moderator read the title of her paper, "An outbreak among infants in Brazil of fatal sepsis caused by an unknown Gram-negative Bacillus," and then announced her, by name, as the presenter. Only, he said it wrong—he pronounced it ROY-el rather than roy-AL. Common mistake. Many people made it. Still, it irritated her.

She rose from her seat, walked toward the platform, climbed its three steps, and set her notes on the lectern. Her hands quaked like aspen leaves. She glanced over the audience and tried to smile. Her face felt frozen. She spotted Doug leaning against the back wall. No Eliot.

She thanked the moderator and then launched into her talk. She described the infected children at the Promissão clinic by their ages and dates of their deaths, using the information Dr. Alancar had given her, and described the Gram-negative bacteria that grew from blood taken from patient five—she didn't use Izabel's name. The next slide showed the table of the biochemical tests from the BPF strain, the table Eliot had insisted she add. She pointed out that, despite careful study, the bacteria had not been identified yet and appeared to be something unusual.

She read the conclusions: "One. We report seven children with a fatal purpuric fever syndrome in Promissão, Brazil. Two. A Gram-negative bacillus was isolated from the blood of one child and may explain those deadly infections."

Then she was finished. She looked again over the audience and touched the bow of her glasses. Her hand was shaking less than earlier, but it still trembled. "Thank you," she said.

"Thank *you*, Dr. Royal, for the interesting presentation." The moderator mispronounced her name again. She took a deep breath.

"This paper is open for discussion," the moderator announced. Sid stepped back from the podium and scanned the audience one more time. Still no Eliot.

A man with a red bow tie headed for the microphone, introduced himself, and said he was from the Rockefeller Institute. He asked if the BPF bacteria outcompeted control bacteria.

"Excellent question," she replied. Her trembling fingers gripped the edges of the lectern as she tried to keep them still. "Those studies are planned."

Then a bulky fellow waddled down the center aisle. He leaned forward into the microphone, adjusted it slightly, and introduced himself. He spoke with an accent—Eastern European, maybe—and she didn't catch his name. She heard him say, though, that he was from the Global Health Alliance.

She stiffened. Was he the GHA guy that had nosed around Promissão? The one River had mentioned in his phone call?

The man cleared his throat with a theatrical flourish. "Interesting paper, Dr. Royal."

She nodded. He'd pronounced her name correctly. She appreciated the compliment.

Then he asked, "Did you have the Gram-negative bacteria tested at a reference laboratory?"

She didn't have the answer he wanted. Her heart raced. "We're in the process of identifying it, as I showed with the preliminary chemical reactions," was all she could say.

"Well, then, your report is incomplete. You definitely haven't proven that the strain caused any of the infections you have described, and you don't even know what kind of bacteria it is." His bushy handlebar mustache joggled as he spoke, and his brown corduroy jacket sagged at the shoulders.

"We're confident of the biochemical test results we've obtained so far," she said.

"You should consider sending it to a qualified laboratory for identification. The GHA will be happy to arrange that for you. As you know, tests performed by inexperienced technicians may not be accurate."

Inexperienced technicians? She was *not* inexperienced. She'd done the tests using standard protocols and had repeated each of them at least three times, and the controls always worked perfectly. She wanted to respond to the man's insulting questions with equally insulting answers, but her mind was blank.

He continued, his voice a growl. "I look forward to learning the identity of that microbe." With that, he waddled back to his seat.

Sid's eyes roamed the room. Where was Eliot? She desperately needed him to magically appear, to scramble to the microphone and corroborate that the tests she described were appropriate and had been accurately performed. She wanted him to tell the man that his offensive suggestion was stupid. But Eliot was AWOL.

How could he miss her talk? She tilted her chin upward, hoping to muster assurance from the ceiling tiles, and spoke slowly and quietly. "Thank you for that suggestion." She then gathered her notes, stepped back from the podium, descended the platform stairs, and took her seat beside Raven. By the time the audience had finished their respectful applause, she could feel the warm pink creeping up her neck.

"Where's Eliot?" Raven whispered.

Sid shook her head, swatted the question away with a sweep of her hand.

After the last talk in that session, Sid remained seated as the audience filed out of the room.

"Good job," Raven chirped.

Sid slowly shook her head. Didn't Raven recognize the belittling and embarrassing nature of the GHA man's remark? "Oh, quit it." She wanted to disappear into nothingness.

What now? She felt like a lost child, wandering alone in a dark forest, disassociated from everything she knew. What time was it? She could return to that tiny hotel room or stay seated in the auditorium, all by herself, for days after the maintenance crew shut off the lights. Or she could roam off into the lowlands between the dikes, never to return.

Instead, like a robot, she followed Raven and the convention crowd. They headed upstairs to the president's reception and its cash bar. Raven bought her a glass of white wine. "To celebrate. Congratulations, your talk is over," she said as she raised her goblet in a toast. The trays of shrimp and cocktail sauce emptied immediately, and the platters of cheese and crackers were barren soon after that. Sid spotted Lew Hatton across the room, surrounded by a bevy of men under a banner that said "Hoechst Pharmaceuticals." She didn't want to speak with him, or anyone else.

By now Sid was grounded enough to be furious with Eliot. She sipped her wine. It tasted flinty. How could he be so thoughtless? She had assumed he supported her, wanted to be proud of her. But no. She took another drink of the wine. She would ignore him, exclude him from all aspects of the BPF project, of everything else she did in the lab. For an instant, she considered ways to sabotage his experiments: add salt to his buffers, acid to his culture media.

With the next swallow of wine, her fury began to melt into worry. It started as a slow trickle of concern, then grew to an ever-larger wave of fear until it became raging terror. Had he had a stroke? Had he been mugged? Shot? Kidnapped? Maybe he was lying bruised and bleeding in a canal somewhere in Amsterdam. Now, she couldn't imagine anything other than tragedy that would explain his absence.

"Nice talk, Sidonie."

She spun around. It was Doug. "Thanks," she said.

"Hey Doug, Eliot's gone missing." Raven's voice had turned to sugar, and she smiled as if she were Cinderella and he the Prince. "Do you remember where he's staying?"

"Um ..." He stared at the ceiling. "I think it's something like the Rand Hotel. Or maybe the Tulip."

Raven pulled the program book from her meeting bag and paged through it until she found the list of the convention hotels. "Probably the Rand," she muttered. "Come. Let's find a phone booth." Raven grabbed Doug's arm. "I'm going to call him. Maybe he's sick or something."

"Yeah, maybe *katterig gevoel*," Doug laughed. "Last night

I learned the Dutch word for hangover." Sid watched them march through the masses, past luminaries in microbiology, past professors and graduate students, past science reporters and industry representatives toward the hallway.

She drained her wine glass and surveyed the faces in the crowd, frantic to spot Eliot, to be reassured he was all right. Her eyes jumped from person to person, but the gathering was huge. She couldn't see everyone.

Her head ached. Her pride smarted. All she wanted was to go to bed with the hope that Raven and Doug would track Eliot down. She set her empty wine glass on a tray of dirty dishes and moved through the horde.

As she neared the entrance to the foyer, she stopped. There he was. Not far from the door. At least he was alive. He was talking to an older guy and waving his arms like a flapping parrot. His left hand held a nearly empty goblet, and his right hand clutched a balled-up napkin. Probably he was describing some mechanism of bacterial pathogenesis. Eliot could get pretty exercised about his research.

She walked up behind him and said—he later asserted she had yelled—"Where were you this afternoon?"

He spun around. "Just a minute, Sidonie." He continued his fiery conversation with the older man.

She twisted her necklace into a knot, then untwisted it, then twisted it again. Even now he was ignoring her.

The other guy recognized the obvious—Eliot was in deep trouble—and quickly excused himself.

"That was very rude, Sidonie, interrupting us like that."

"Me, rude? You skipped my talk. What happened?"

"Nothing 'happened.' I had lunch with Jim Henry from

Minneapolis, and we started talking about a possible job for me when I finish in Evans's lab. They have a new Center for the Study of Bacterial Pathogens there, and the position of junior scientist is very appealing. The time got away from us." He raised his chin and seemed to stare down at her from beneath the lower rims of his glasses. "How'd the talk go? I assume you were your usual brilliant self."

How could he be so damn condescending? "Well, it was fine until some jerk from the GHA said I should have sent the strain to a reference laboratory before presenting the data on it." She didn't mention what the man said about lack of proof that the strain caused the infections. Eliot had claimed that all along.

His eyes studied hers. His lips narrowed. "That came during the questions after your talk?"

"Yes. He accused me of not knowing how to do the bio-chemical tests."

"He actually said that?"

"Basically, yes. You should have been there to back me up, to tell him I did the tests correctly. That's what senior postdocs do, Eliot."

He stepped back, away from her. "Look, Sidonie, you fought me tooth and nail when I tried to help with your talk, and now you're pissed off that I didn't bail you out during the questions? I can't babysit you forever. At some point, you'll have to stand up to the heat on your own. That's part of being a mature scientist."

"You're a ... bastard." She spun around and walked toward the door.

She heard a high-pitched laugh to her left and looked toward the noise. A blonde threw back her head and, as she chuckled, she reached out her arm and laid it on the sleeve of the man beside her. He was a big fellow with a black handlebar mustache. The GHA guy? Sid was sure of it. His eyes scanned the room and, after glancing past her, they shot right back. He nodded. She forced her mouth into a feeble smile and nodded back. Then she turned away from him and continued toward the door. The world was full of bastards.

15

1984 MICHIGAN

Sid couldn't make herself get out of bed. Yes, she had arrived home from Amsterdam after midnight and then bounced around her apartment for an hour before settling down. Yes, she'd then fidgeted nonstop before finally falling asleep sometime after four in the morning. Yes, she was tired. But mostly she didn't want to go to the lab.

That had never happened before. Every other morning, eager for an early start on the day's work, she had bolted out of bed before the alarm clock rang. But that morning, after hitting the snooze button the third time, she buried her head under her pillow to avoid the sunshine that streamed like molten crystal through her window. Those beams of light tried to nudge her awake, to prod her to lower her feet to the floor and hoist herself off the mattress, and she wanted none of it. Between the alarms, an extended, fractured dream—one of those "I-can't-move-my-legs-to-run-from-the-monster" nightmares—had scrolled through her restless mind. It had no plot. Rather, the dream was a series of ominous dinging bells, and orange and green blinking lights, and overwhelming flashes of badness: a naked sprint down a crowded street; a lost wallet; a puppy she'd forgotten to feed for a week; another child's funeral in Promissão.

Finally, her full bladder drove her to the bathroom. Her head throbbed. Her stomach roiled. At first, she thought she'd caught a virus. But she had no cough nor fever, no sore throat nor nausea, just a fluttery belly and aches from nose to toes. Mostly she felt depleted, engulfed in the free-floating foreboding that wrings life's sap from a person.

She tried to take charge of whatever had possessed her. She asked questions of herself and then tried to answer them. Why are you like this? Don't know. Is this good for you? No. What do you want to do rather than go to the lab? Nothing. Absolutely nothing.

She ran warm water into the bathtub, dumped in a splash of bath oil, and, when it was half full, climbed in. It felt good to lean her head against the back wall and let the silky liquid wash over her tingling skin and massage her crampy muscles.

The GHA fellow's stinging remarks lurked along the edges of her mind like vicious nettles. Should she cave to his comments and acknowledge that sending the BPF strain to a reference laboratory was a good idea? Maybe. Or should she ignore his comments and consider them nonsense? Also a maybe. The strain came from Brazil, so a US public health agency wouldn't touch it. She was certain the Brazil National Health Department wouldn't do as well as she would at identifying the bacteria.

What was wrong with her? She'd been disappointed before and had put it behind her. Ditto for disillusionment. She'd dodged embarrassing situations at all costs but had suffered through a few. Why was this one, the admonishment from the GHA guy, so awful? She swirled the water with her feet, dunked her head until she was completely submerged. When she resurfaced, she stared at the wrinkles in the ceiling paint for a long time.

The spirit of Dr. Bausch hovered in the corner high above her head. Had her long-ago hero ever been disappointed or embarrassed? Likely she had. But back in those college years, watching her on the stage, confident and poised, one would never have known it. How had Dr. Bausch dealt with disappointment? Or embarrassment? She'd probably evoke a bacterial mechanism to sort it out. She'd say something like, "When faced with stressful situations, such as high temperature or low humidity, bacteria produce heat shock proteins that wrap around important bacterial enzymes to protect them from thermal or chemical destruction. I think of it as a hug." That's what she, Sid, needed right now. A hug. From whom? Paul? He just wouldn't understand.

She rubbed the bar of soap over the washcloth and scrubbed her chest, belly, arms, and legs. As she rinsed the suds from her knees, she realized she was washing away Amsterdam dirt. When she finally climbed out of the tub, she watched the scummy water swirl down the drain. Gone.

Eliot arrived at the lab even later that morning than Sid did. His routine was to wander in after ten o'clock in the mornings because he stayed very late in the evenings—said he liked to work "in the peace of the night, when no one else is around to bother me." She didn't actually see him enter the lab but heard him talking from inside his cardboard nest. She didn't want to see him, would go to great lengths to avoid him that day.

Because she'd been away, there were no cultures in the incubator to examine. She thought about setting up the chemical tests on the BPF strain yet one more time to be absolutely sure they gave the same results as before, but there was no point. They would be no different. The voice of the bully from the GHA—his words about sending the strain off to a reference lab and inexperienced laboratory technicians—boomed through her mind. Now, as when he first said it, she found it sickening.

She opened her lab notebook but couldn't concentrate. She closed it again and stared out the window at the river in the distance. Last fall, when she first arrived in Michigan, she had enjoyed the pumpkin and persimmon colors of the maple leaves that peeked between the pines along the water's edge. Not today. The memory of the GHA man muddied the beauty of everything she cared about. Her neck muscles tightened. She shouldn't let herself be insulted by him, shouldn't give him the power to upset her so much. Her muscles slackened. Then they tensed again. What she "shouldn't let happen" didn't matter, because it was happening anyway. In truth, her pride had been kicked into a thousand pieces. If she were queen of the world, she would erase the whole Amsterdam incident. But she wasn't the queen of anything.

It had been a mistake to give the presentation. Maybe she should have waited until they were ready to publish the paper that described the work. But it was important for the world to know about the outbreak. Maybe she shouldn't have brought

Izabel's blood sample back from Brazil. But that blood could open the doors to knowing how to manage those awful cases in the future. Maybe ... maybe ...

"Sidonie." Eliot was nearby. His voice crashed against her reverie of "maybes." She turned on her lab stool—slowly because she didn't want to talk with him. Or see him. She wondered about the *real* reason he had missed her talk. Had time truly gotten away from him?

As he leaned against the end of the lab bench, his hip brushed the hazards cabinet. His hair was its usual tangle, and his glasses sat slightly askew on his nose. She expected him to be cynical or ridiculing. But his look was grim.

"I'm sorry I wasn't able to attend your talk."

The silence between them was leaden. She could hear the whir of a helicopter outside the window.

"Meeting with the chairman of microbiology from Minneapolis was important for my future. If I could get that job, I'd be surrounded by some of the best minds in microbiology. They have state-of-the-art facilities, promising students, plenty of money. I'm sure you understand."

No, she didn't understand. There were at least thirty elements to the issue: he could have taken control of his schedule; the man from Minneapolis would have excused him; Eliot could have met with him at any other time; lab mates supported each other; she'd needed him to counter the tormentor from the GHA; he had said he would be there. Now he expected a response. "I have nothing to say."

"Well," he continued, "I want to talk about the suggestions from that GHA fellow. By the way, who was he?"

She shook her head. "I didn't catch his name. He said it

quickly, with a foreign accent. I've never heard of him."

"Those folks can be very territorial, as you know. One of the postdocs in my Ph.D. program tangled with them over an outbreak of cholera in Pakistan. They stalled and told half-truths and picked a fight about the contact survey my friend had developed. In the end, she gave up and worked on a different project. I doubt that guy made those comments to further your work. He made them to make you look ineffective."

"Yeah, that's why I needed you to be there."

"Well, about the testing. I spoke with several colleagues in Amsterdam and have some ideas about additional tests you could do. Want to hear about them? We'll have to review a couple of papers to learn the protocols. Can't be too hard."

"I'll think about it." She turned away from him, picked up her wire loop, and ran it through the flame of the Bunsen burner to sterilize it. With the clean wire, she began picking bacterial colonies from an agar plate and inoculated them into new growth media. It seemed like an eternity before she heard his footsteps head away from her lab bench.

She was mixing a new batch of buffer when Eliot appeared at her bench again.

"I photocopied several of those methods papers from the library," he said. "Want to talk about them?"

She kept mixing. "I'm still thinking about it." She hoped he'd go away.

"Look, Sidonie. I know you're upset. You certainly yelled loud enough about it at the reception in Amsterdam. I understand that. But your work needs to move forward, even though I'm not completely convinced that germ you cultured actually caused all those infections in Brazil. I know that deep in your analytic heart, you are aware of that uncertainty, too. Still, you're interested in chasing that lead, and I'll support you in that."

He pulled a stool toward the lab bench and sat beside her. His shirt had the same spicy smell as in Amsterdam. Or maybe it was his hair. "What do you say?"

She held the beaker up to the light to check the clarity of the buffer, didn't want to talk to him.

Then he smiled. It was a nice smile, one that slowly dawned across the bottom of his face and spread to his eyes. They looked like favorite-uncle eyes, soft, warm, framed by dainty crow's feet. She had never noticed the tiny dimple in his right cheek when he smiled. Maybe that was because he didn't smile much.

He leaned closer to her. "Is that a yes?" The spicy smell was stronger.

Why was he trying, now, to be helpful? Maybe he truly regretted missing her presentation. Maybe he was trying to atone for that. Did he have something to gain in this? Of course he did. His name would be on all the papers that came from their work with the BPF strain. And although it was hard for her to admit, that would be appropriate.

Finally, she shrugged. "I suppose so."

Raven's voice trilled through the laboratory. "Sid." She'd strung out 'Sid' into two melodic syllables. "Phone."

"Can you take a message?" Sid was pipetting buffer into a 96-well microtiter plate and didn't want to risk skipping a well.

Raven held the phone's handset tight against the front of her shirt. "It's a woman with a foreign accent," she said, barely above a whisper. "Sounds important."

Who would that be? Not Cibele calling from Promissão; Raven would recognize her voice. Maybe a Russian or Chinese student looking for a postdoc position in an American lab. Sid set her pipettor on the lab bench and took the phone from Raven. "This is Dr. Royal."

"Hello. This is Dr. Karla Geiger. I'm the director of Global Infectious Disease Outbreaks at the GHA."

Sid's back stiffened, and her fingers tightened around the phone.

The woman continued. "The government of Brazil has asked the GHA to assist them in learning more about the disease outbreak in Promissão." She paused and then continued. "Our field representative, Dr. Wozniak, attended your excellent presentation at the recent International Microbiological Society meeting in Amsterdam. We think the strain you described in your talk would be very useful to us."

Why did they want the BPF strain? They were epidemiologists who surveyed people about risks of disease, not microbiologists who studied bacteria. First that representative—now she knew his name: Wozniak—claimed she hadn't proven that the BPF strain caused the infection, and now they wanted that very strain. "As Dr. Wozniak heard from my talk, our studies aren't complete yet," Sid said.

"It's not necessary for you to spend any more time characterizing the strain. Send it to us, and we'll arrange to have it identified. I'll give you a Federal Express shipping number." The woman's voice sounded scratchy, like a waterfall of gravel.

"The work is too premature to share the strain yet, but, as Dr. Wozniak heard, we have made excellent progress in identifying it."

"Dr. Royal ..."

"No, Dr. Geiger. I appreciate your interest in my work, but I can't share that strain yet. Goodbye." Sid hung up the phone.

She sat on the lab stool for a long time, rerunning the conversation with Dr. Geiger through her mind. Outside her window, the nearest tree had lost most of its leaves, and the bare branches, pushed by the wind, waved like witches' arms. Skinny arms on skinny witches. Dried leaves skittered on the sidewalks below. Dr. Geiger's request was absurd. She'd suggested Sid quit working on characterizing the strain and forfeit the project to the GHA. Yet Sid's knowledge of the circumstances surrounding the blood collection and the disease associated with it was critical to knowing the meaning of it all.

Near the top of the tree, one remaining leaf clung to its pitching twig, a lone survivor of the earlier storm. What about that leaf, she wondered, allowed it to stick? She knew that deciduous trees possess specific physiologic signals that tell their leaves to let go, as they do every autumn, but this one didn't follow the script. It persisted in hanging on. It must be missing one of the proteins that cause its stem to separate from the base. A separator mutant.

As she approached The Nest, she called Eliot's name.

"Yeah?"

"May I be admitted?"

"Yeah."

He leaned over a huge sheet of tag-board that was spread over the mess on his desk. "This's the poster I'm presenting in San Diego in a couple days. Looks good, huh?"

"Looks fine. Eliot, I just got a call from a Dr. Geiger at the GHA."

"Come in. Sit." He pointed to the stack of journals on the floor. "Was that the guy who skewered you in Amsterdam?"

"No. The caller was a woman. The director of Global Outbreaks. She asked about the BPF strain. Wants me to quit working on it and send it to them."

"And you said, 'Absolutely not.' Right? What nerve. You do all the work and GHA, who knows nothing about it, will claim all the credit for finding it. And will take a month of Sundays to do it. In the meanwhile, the epidemic will keep killing kids. That's how those folks operate. They're devious."

"I told her, 'No. We aren't through characterizing the strain.'"

"Perfect. You're totally correct. It would be irresponsible to send it to them until you know more about it. These are the folks who doubt it caused the infections, right? I'm telling you, they're slimy. They have been sinfully slow to jump on the AIDS bandwagon. It's all politics. Our rotten president won't utter the word AIDS, and GHA marches to his tune because the United States forks over most of the money to support their shoddy work."

She nodded.

"Have you thought about submitting an abstract to the meeting in Boston? The rat work and your results from my blood are interesting and would make a good presentation. And maybe someone there, a helpful person rather than a jerk, may have ideas about what makes the strain so deadly."

She nodded again. Yes, that was a good idea. She'd have the abstract written by the end of the day.

"Do you feel any better?" he asked.

She folded her arms across her chest and tapped her right fingers against her left elbow. Finally, she said, "Not really. I just want those goons at the GHA to leave me and my project alone."

"Hi, Paul. I'm exhausted. And mad."

"What happened?" His voice sounded like it came from the moon rather than from Oregon.

She told him about the call from Karla Geiger. He was sympathetic but didn't really understand the problem. She tried to explain it further. His understanding inched forward only a small notch. Eventually, she changed the subject and asked about his day.

Then his voice perked up. "Earlier, when I was at the grocery store, I watched a little kid pitch a tantrum in the checkout line. He wanted a candy bar. His mother picked him up and whispered into his ear for a while. The little guy nodded as she whispered. Finally, she stood him in the cart and let him set the groceries on the conveyor belt."

Sid wondered where that story was headed.

"I thought of you while I watched her. That's what you would do. No spanking. No yelling. No scene. Just creative distraction."

"What do you suppose she whispered to him?"

"I have no idea. But it worked. You'd be such a terrific mother, Sid. Just like Yvette."

They had been over this before. Paul and his older brother were lifelong competitors. Peter was born two years earlier than Paul, and Paul, despite nearly three decades of trying, had never caught up. Peter went to school first, learned to drive first, had his first date first, graduated from high school first, graduated from college first, married first, had a child first. Paul had always been behind and was now behind in the marriage and parenthood departments. He wanted Sid to help him with that problem.

"Yes, Yvette seemed a wonderful mother when I met her," Sid said. "Remember how she let Brian cut up celery for the turkey stuffing? That's the way to get kids to eat—let them cook." She paused a moment, swept her hair away from her face. "And I appreciate the nice compliment."

"What I remember about that Christmas was the way you read to Brian. He snuggled right up beside you on the couch and your voice was magic. Kind of musical as you read the rhymey words. Something about eggs and green ham."

"Yep," she laughed. She continued to quote from the book. That's all I can remember."

"That's pretty darn good. I think you read it to him at least four times. You're a natural."

"Well, I won't be a mother until I'm a wife."

"Easy fix to that. I'm in need of a wife."

"And, I'm in need of finishing my fellowship. That comes first."

Later that week, Raven wandered into Sid's lab bay. "Package for you." She held a large box in her arms. "Says it's from a Dr. Lewis Hatton, at something called Hoechst Pharmaceuticals. Sounds German."

"Terrific," Sid said. "It's the cefotaxime for Dr. Alancar. I'm going to take it to Brazil."

"Wow. That's exciting. You're going back? Will you stay with River again? I'm sure he'd be happy to have you. You're a pretty low-maintenance guest."

Sid called River in Promissão. He didn't answer. She tried later that day, and twice the next day. He still didn't answer.

"I can't reach River," she said to Raven. "Do you know when he'll be home?"

"No idea. Sometimes he makes field trips to farming areas around there. And sometimes he goes over to the coast. That's all I know about his comings and goings."

Sid sat on the sofa in her apartment sipping a Diet 7-Up and considered her options. She had put an Aaron Copland recording on the record player, and her leg bounced to the rhythm of the blaring horns and the pounding drums of "Fanfare for the Common Man." The music summoned her confidence. The fizz of the soda buoyed her. She swirled the bottle to tame the bubbles and stared out her apartment window. The full moon hung in the cloudless sky like a dull, lemon-gray balance ball and cast long shadows across the frozen ground. Where would the BPF strain have come from?

It might be a mutant of ordinary bacteria, a rogue strain that had acquired new traits, making it resistant to killing by immune factors in the blood. The results of her experiments with Eliot's blood and of the rat studies corroborated her theory. Bacteria acquired new traits through the power of evolution, that powerful, ethereal force that eliminated the weak and allowed the strong to survive.

She took another drink from the Diet 7-Up and put Copland's "Rodeo" on the record player. The music galloped, as did her thoughts. The beauty of genetic change was that it explained all biologic variation in living things: blue, green, gray, or brown eyes in people; fine, thick, blunt, or pointy beaks in finches; deadly or not deadly infections in bacteria.

The primordial BPF bacterium must have gained something to make it so deadly—maybe a whole gene, or a rascal piece of DNA, or even just a few new nucleotides, those As, Ts, Cs, and Gs of DNA that reminded Sid of pearls in a genetic necklace. Usually, a new "something" represented a fatal flaw, and the mutated bacterium died. But every once in a while, that new "something" gave the mutated bacterium an advantage over the other bacteria, and the mutant thrived. It had a fresh beginning, like one of Raven's second chances. What was that "something" in the BPF strain? A novel plasmid? Maybe. That's what Eliot thought. Or an altered endotoxin? That was her favorite theory.

The Diet 7-Up hit the spot. By now, her thinking was in overdrive. Maybe, when one bacterium that lived in a human somewhere in the interior of Brazil reproduced, its endotoxin gene made a mistake, a beneficial mistake, so that the mutated germ could withstand the onslaught of that human's white blood cells and serum immune factors. The mutant lived. Then it traveled to another human and, again, thrived against the killing factors in that human's blood. And it traveled again, and again, and occasionally landed in a young child who couldn't resist the attack at all. Thus, the deadly disease.

She took the last sip of her 7-Up. There was another possibility. Rather than gaining something, the mutant bacterium could have lost something. Maybe a regulatory factor, or an inhibitor that, when gone, allowed a previously silent toxic factor to bloom. That would be a beneficial loss. Beneficial, at least, for the bacteria. Benefit was not something people usually associated with losses. None of her losses had been beneficial.

So what had permitted the mutated bacteria to spread to other children so successfully? Possibly it was a two-step mutant, one with increased toxicity and also increased transmissibility. That would be unlikely, and really bad luck.

She wondered how it all would end. Would children continue to be infected with the BPF strain and die until the end of time? Probably not. Outbreaks of other scourges, such as the Plague of Athens, the Black Death, the 1918 Spanish flu, typhoid fever, and cholera, had dissipated, eventually. In time, those germs infected most people in the vicinity, leaving few people susceptible to the infection. Or the germs had been unable to travel to the next group of susceptible people, those in the next village or valley. Sometimes, the bad germs were overrun by less toxic ones whose toxin genes had themselves mutated.

By the middle of "Rodeo," she had come to a conclusion: she desperately needed more strains from Promissão. One wasn't enough to know if the BPF strain actually caused those deadly infections. As the closing notes of "Hoe-Down" bolted through her living room, it was settled. She'd take the antibiotics down to Dr. Alancar and bring back more specimens from wherever she could in Promissão.

She made a salad for her dinner and further contemplated how to transport the antibiotics to Brazil. And how to get more strains once she was there. She hoped River could accommodate her again. River. Knowing his secret while he didn't know she knew would complicate staying with him. She knew she was a terrible actress, but she'd have to try.

A junco had just landed on a branch of the oak tree outside the kitchen window when she heard the phone ring. She sighed and pulled herself away from the bird and the beautiful view of the setting sun.

It was Eliot. "Where are you?" she asked. "I thought you were in San Diego at that meeting."

"I am. In fact, I'm sitting in my hotel room, watching a Navy ship float by. And ... hey, there goes a seagull right outside my window, winging its way toward the bay."

Why would he call her from San Diego? Surely not to report a bird sighting. "Huh. At this moment, I'm watching a junco out my window. What's up?"

"While I was standing at our poster this afternoon, a woman walked up, read the information, and feverishly started taking notes. Her name was Karla Geiger."

She sank into her sofa. "Oh my God, Eliot. That's the woman from the GHA. The one who wanted me to send her the BPF strain."

"Yup. That's her, all right. She asked a lot of questions: which restriction enzymes did I use? What, exactly, were the conditions of the electrophoresis run? She also asked for clinical information about the dead child in Promissão and for details about how the strain was obtained."

"What did you tell her?" With her free hand, she tugged at a corner of a sofa pillow, tried to straighten a crooked seam.

"I told her, quote: 'The strain was collected by my colleague, Dr. Sidonie Royal, and I'm not a clinician, so I can't answer your questions,' closed quote."

Good, she thought. "No mention of how I brought it into the US?"

"Nope. Then she said they'd like to obtain your strain."

"I'll bet they would." That woman was very cagey, trying to use Eliot as an end-around to get the BPF strain. She picked, again, at the seam of the pillow.

"Don't worry. I agree we don't have enough data yet to share that strain with her. So I said, 'I'm not at liberty to send it to you.'"

"Good answer, but ..."

Before she could finish the sentence, Eliot interrupted. "She told me the National Laboratory of Brazil had asked the GHA to assist in analyzing the apparent outbreak. She said, quote: 'We are very interested in identifying factors associated with the deaths of those children in Promissão, and now in Serrana.'"

"What?" She tossed the pillow against the back of the couch. "What was that?" She moved toward the window, stretching the phone cord as far as it would go. "More cases? In a different place?"

"That was my reaction, too. I asked her about cases in Serrana. She wouldn't answer, said she wasn't able to discuss it any further. Clearly, she'd spilled the beans and was trying to cover her tracks. Do you know anything about Serrana?"

"Never heard of it. Is it in Brazil? I'll have to do a little investigating."

"Let me know what you learn."

"Will do." She settled back down on the sofa. "Eliot, I really appreciate your call."

Sid was already streaking bacteria onto agar dishes when Raven walked into the lab, hung her jacket on the coat rack, slid her purse into the bottom drawer of the file cabinet, kicked it shut, and asked, "Did Eliot reach you last night?" She pulled on her lab coat and started fastening the buttons. "He called me from San Diego to get your home number. The one listed in the new directory has a typo or something, because every time he dialed it, he got a U-Haul dealer. He was pretty wired up about meeting that lady from the GHA."

Sid flamed the tip of her wire loop and stuck it, butt end down, into a test tube rack to cool. "Yeah, he called me. Karla Geiger showed up at his poster and accidently mentioned more cases in Serrana." She carried the agar dishes to the incubator and set them on the top shelf. "Do you know where Serrana is? In Brazil? Is there such a place?"

"Hmm ... let me check." Raven pulled open the top drawer of her desk and rummaged through a pile of papers. "It's here somewhere," she muttered and opened a second drawer. "Here it is." She unfolded a map and spread it on the lab counter. "Let's see ..." She leaned closer, traced her finger along several roads. "Okay. Found it. It's in São Paulo state, about 250 kilometers, as the crow flies, northeast of Promissão. On the other side of that big reservoir."

"Thanks," Sid said. This could be her golden opportunity. Serrana may provide the strains she needed.

How would she pay for this trip? Dr. Evans had been generous in allowing her to use her fellowship money for supplies, but airfare to Brazil was expensive, and her fellowship funds were dwindling. Eliot had a grant for his plasmid research, but no one would be able to justify his grant paying for a trip to Brazil. Her personal bank account was nearly empty, and her savings account ... that was the answer: the money from her father.

Raven answered the lab phone, spoke for a few minutes, and then passed the receiver to Sid. "Here's my brother."

"Hi, River. Good to hear from you." She heard an echo from her voice. Bad connection.

"Greetings. I understand you're coming back to Brazil. Sorry I missed your calls. I was in São Paolo for a couple days. Needed to give the Department of Agriculture an update on the new variety of corn." His voice was energetic. "Sure, you can stay at my place again. No problem."

"Thanks so much. I have new antibiotics to bring to Dr. Alancar. And I'd like to collect additional samples if possible."

"Samples? More blood?"

"Yes, if Dr. Alancar can get some from a sick child. I have another idea, too. I'll tell you when I get there."

"I'll help you with whatever you need."

That was settled. "Another thing. I've learned about an outbreak of the Promissáo disease in Serrana. Know anything about that?"

"No."

"I heard it as a rumor from someone at the GHA. Anyway, I want to check it out. In Serrana. Any thoughts?"

"Okay." He paused, cleared his throat, then continued. "I have a friend who works at the Serrana branch of our agency. He's a good fellow."

The phone connection was even worse now; he sounded as if he were underwater.

"I'll give him a call," River said. "Greg ... that's his name ... will be a big help to you. His girlfriend works as a public health nurse, I think."

Sid passed the phone back to Raven.

"Hey River," Raven said with a playful smile. "Mom keeps asking me about your love life. She wonders if I met any eligible women hanging around you when I was down there. You need to get on that so she'll quit pestering me."

Sid looked away, toward the chemical bottles on the top shelf. She didn't want Raven to see her face, the look of alarm, of sadness, of unease. Poor Raven. Divinely ignorant of such an important aspect of her twin brother's being. She longed for the day his secret wouldn't be a secret from his sister anymore.

In most ways, she didn't care if anyone was gay. She kept telling herself it didn't matter at all. But River might end up like the gay people she had seen in the psychiatry clinic, tortured by crippling anxiety and neck-deep depression. She didn't want River and his buddies to experience self-hate like that. Or worse yet, she didn't want any of them to have AIDS.

While Raven continued to talk to River, Sid headed to her lab bench. She stared out her window at the tombstones in the cemetery, at the leafless trees scattered among them. She thought of the dead people buried in those graves, of dead people in general.

Her dad had set up an account for her before he died; it was those funds that would support the upcoming trip to Brazil. He told her it was for her wedding. She hadn't touched that money, and it was much more than the cost of any wedding she would have. Besides, the BPF project was more important than a wedding would ever be. Her dad might approve. Her mother wouldn't, so Mom didn't have to know.

16

1984 BRAZIL

Sid lay back against the plane's headrest, closed her eyes, and let her thoughts wander through the forest of her mind. For this trip there was no giddy anticipation, no sense of wild-eyed adventure. Rather, she was on a mission—deliver the cefotaxime to Dr. Alancar and collect more bacteria. The evidence that her BPF strain had killed those children in Promissão was not strong. Not at all. She had only one strain, an unknown bacterium at that, from only one child. That BPF strain might, after all, have lived peacefully in little Izabel's throat or intestines, oozed into her blood as she was dying, and had nothing to do with the ill-ness that caused her death. No matter how much Sid had tried to bury that worry, it had remained a recurrent, subterranean nag. She simply had to culture more blood from kids with that terrible illness. Or she had to find more strains of that bacteria wherever she could.

The ghosts of Dr. Karla Geiger's phone call and Dr. Wozniak's menacing comments at the Amsterdam meeting wouldn't go away, either. They were neither microbiologists nor physicians. They were epidemiologists, and their meddling might make it difficult to establish, once and for all, whether the BPF strain actually killed the children. Dr. Geiger made it clear they weren't interested in cooperating with her.

She ordered a glass of wine and flipped the pages of the airline magazine. She started to read an article about the beaches in Rio but then turned to a piece about a samba dance competition. Halfway through, she skipped to an article about a fish with purple and yellow horns on its head, and then paged to the back of the magazine to the crossword puzzle.

She was trying to think of a four-letter word for "defeat" that started with "l" and ended with "s," when a man five rows ahead rose from his seat and started down the aisle toward her. He was large and awkward. She wouldn't have paid him any attention except for his handlebar mustache. She leaned forward, tried to see his face more clearly. Dr. Wozniak had a mustache like that. It was possible she might encounter him, or some of his GHA buddies, in Promissão. But could he be on her plane? She tried to remember what he had looked like, but she'd been too rattled by his comments in Amsterdam to notice anything except his weird mustache and his foreign accent. And his dowdy brown jacket. This man wore a grassy green polo shirt.

When he reached her row, the plane lurched, and the man's body pitched toward her. She stared at the tarnished goose etched into his belt buckle, which now wobbled in front of her face. Then, she looked upward at his rheumy eyes and tousled dirt-colored hair, trying to remember.

"Excuse me," he said. He spoke in perfect American English. "We must have hit an air pocket. Sorry."

No accent. Not Wozniak. She sank back in her seat and waited for her wine.

When the flight attendant returned with the glass of pinot gris, Sid took a sip, savored its tang and its sweetness. Once there had been another glass of wine, beside a vineyard in Sonoma County, beneath a cloudless sky and the arching branches of a gigantic oak tree, with Paul. Among the grapes, the stakes, the wires, and the loamy dirt, he talked of his love for the earthiness of wine making. "All of it," he said, sweeping his arm toward the neat rows of neck-high plants. His eyes sparkled as he spoke. "From planting and grafting the vines, to nurturing the young fruit, to harvesting, to fermenting the juice into wine. It's like magic." Then he laughed. "In my next lifetime, maybe I'll be a vintner." She was charmed by his intelligence and attentiveness; she felt appreciated and completely alive. That was long ago. The thrill of that time had been replaced by misunderstanding and fanciful wishes. She sipped her wine again. Its tingle softened her muscles. She hoped it would chase away the worry. And the scratchy memories of Paul. She wished she could go back to those good times with him and then find some way to escape the impasse that currently divided them.

She returned to the crossword puzzle. With the next swallow of the wine, the answer sprang into her head. The four-letter word for "defeat" was "loss."

Sid waited beside the plane on the tarmac, fighting the wind that whipped her skirt against her calves until they stung. Off to the right, a jet raced down the runway and then nosed into the sky, spewing a cloud of gassy exhaust behind it. Obtaining the cefotaxime from Hoeschst had been easier than she expected. No pleading or bargaining, no shaming or cajoling. After her quick phone call to the company, Lew had sent it. For free.

She watched as the ground crew unloaded cargo from the plane's belly. Suitcases. A dog in a cage. A baby stroller. More suitcases. What's taking so long, she wondered? Maybe the boxes were still in São Paulo. Or JFK. Or worse yet, DTW. Her stomach wobbled at the thought.

After all the luggage had been unloaded, the men began to pile cartons labeled "Vegetable Oil," "Panasonic," "Forest Products," and "Schlumberger" onto a cart beside the plane. Finally, they stacked two white Styrofoam containers on top, each tied with a red rope, each labeled "FRAGILE—KEEP COOL." The antibiotics had made it.

Sid's next worry was that the cartons would sit on the tarmac too long. The sun beat down with unremitting intensity, and heat radiated off the concrete in quivery waves. The drugs needed to stay cold.

The airport waiting room was, as she expected, packed with people. Sid surveyed the crowd, searching for River. She appreciated his willingness to let her stay at his place. How could she repay him? For sure, she could buy some of the food and do some of the cooking. When she spotted him across the room, she waved. He waved back and then headed toward her.

In baggage claim, Sid tapped her foot against the floor tiles and checked her watch every three to four minutes. The cardboard carton and her suitcase had come immediately, and now she waited for the Styrofoam boxes. She assumed the ice packs were defrosted by now and imagined the vials warming more and more with each passing minute. At last, she spied the white boxes with their red ropes and pulled them off the carousel.

River picked one up. "Geez, this is heavy. What's in there? Gold bricks?"

She giggled. "No. Just ten vials of the antibiotic I told you about and ten vials of diluent to reconstitute the drug. And cold packs. That's what makes them so heavy."

"Well, what's that, then?" River pointed to the cardboard carton.

"Blood culture tubes. And supplies for my new idea."

They hauled the luggage, the carton, and the Styrofoam boxes to the parking lot. "The cold packs are melting in this heat," Sid said. "Any chance of stopping at an ice machine on the way to your house?"

"Ice machine?" He slowly shook his head. "Are you kidding? This is end-of-the-trail Brazil. No ice machines here."

His house was a two-hour drive away, and River's car felt like an incinerator. Where could she get ice? She studied the billboards on the side of the terminal: A TAM Airlines plane taking off. A Petrobras gas station lit up at night. A Lely harvester in the middle of a cornfield. A sweaty bottle of Brahma beer. Bingo, she thought. "How about a bar, River? Surely a bar would have ice to keep the beer cold. We can't let the drugs get too warm."

"Might work." He sounded skeptical. "We can ask."

They were only a few miles up the road from the airport when Sid heard a scraping sound from the rear of the car.

"What's that noise?" she asked. All they needed, as the antibiotics were getting warmer by the minute, was a breakdown.

"What noise?" River asked.

"That scraping sound. In the back."

"Oh, that's the tail pipe. It's loose."

"Is it safe to ride with it dragging?" Sid asked. "Will we make it to your place?"

"Of course. I'll fix it when we get home."

Just past the turnoff to a tattoo parlor, River pulled the Volvo to the curb in front of a squat building with an aluminum roof. The cracked stucco walls sported faded flowers of aqua, pink, peach, and purple paint, their grass-colored stems curving upward like Js when they reached the sidewalk. The door hung wide open. The sign in the dirty window blinked "Bar do Rodrigo." "They might have ice here," he said.

"I'll check." Sid opened the car door.

"No, ma'am. I'll check." River jumped out, started toward the building, and then turned back toward her. "You can come along if you'd like. It's not a good idea, though, for you to go in there alone."

She trailed him through the open door. The smoky, dimly lit room was nearly empty except for five wily-eyed guys seated at two tables, each topped with at least a dozen beer bottles, some capped, some open. At first, it reminded her of the bar in the fatal photo of River and Fernando, with the dark and the smoke. But it was too decrepit to be a gay hangout. The conversation stopped as Sid and River entered. She wished River had found a nicer bar.

He spoke to the bartender in rapid-fire Portuguese. The man looked at her, then back at River, and shook his head.

River kept talking. The man kept shaking his head. Finally, River pulled out his wallet and handed the guy several bills. The bartender pocketed the money, pried open the door of a refrigerator behind the him, and removed two aluminum ice cube trays from the freezer compartment. He yanked on the handles of the dividers, dumped the ice into four plastic beer cups, and shoved them across the bar toward River.

"Obrigado," River said.

From the tone of his voice and the set of his shoulders, Sid guessed River had thanked the man. "We really appreciate this," she added as she reached for two of the cups. The man's face was vacant.

Back at the car, Sid opened the Styrofoam boxes and dumped two cups of ice into each. She tucked the cubes around the antibiotic vials as if she were rearranging a delicate center-piece. It would have to do until they reached River's house. She hoped the drugs were okay. She really, really hoped they hadn't gotten too warm.

The road was as dusty and rut riddled as before. It wandered past the lake on the left and the stand of palm trees on the right, past the oyster-white church with the square bell tower, and then made a sharp right turn at the coffee shop with its red tile roof and iron lattice over the windows. River slowed when he reached the top of a rise, and on the downhill side, slowed even more when a squirrel-like animal, black as tar, scurried across the gravel ahead and into the grass that lined the ditch. The sights of Promissão were familiar and comfortable. She was glad to be back.

River pulled the Volvo into the parking space beside his

house. He hauled Sid's suitcase and cardboard carton into the back room while she carried the Styrofoam boxes to the kitchen. The cold packs inside were no longer frozen stiff but felt somewhat cool. So did the boxes of cefotaxime. And the boxes of the diluent. Her worry about ruined antibiotics floated off into the warm Brazilian air like dissipating morning fog.

"How's the ice holding up?" he called.

"Good," Sid answered. "The vials seem okay." She stowed the antibiotics and diluent in the fridge and slid the cold packs into the freezer compartment between a package of peas and a bottle of vodka.

"Can we tap the Absolut?" she called.

"Good idea," River answered and pulled two jelly glasses from the cupboard.

She studied River's face, the deliberate way he sipped his drink, the arch of his eyebrows. His features were less dainty than Raven's, but the two of them definitely were cut from the same bolt of silk. His eyes were smoky, full of mystery, and as he spoke, his lips moved in sultry turns. In a strange way, River's face reminded her of Paul's face. Paul's eyes were also smoky but no longer full of mystery. She now knew the thoughts behind his eyes; she knew his deepest wishes, his goals, his worries, and his dreams. And she knew hers.

Thinking of Paul released images of DNA that floated in the rarefied space of her imagination. All those molecules—the A, T, C, and G nucleotides—of the plus strand of DNA lined up perfectly with those of the negative strand. Every A reached out for its T, and every C for its G. And the bonds they formed were strong, resistant to alkaline salts, to heat, and to radioactivity. She pictured Paul's wishes, goals, worries, and dreams as nucleotides. How did they match with hers? Rather than smooth, wavy, tightly bonded strands, now the DNA she saw was jagged, with large gaps and dangling ends.

For dinner they made a stew. "This's Santa Inêz lamb from a ranch about five kilometers up the road," he said as he sliced into a slab of meat. He explained how they bred the sheep, fed them, kept parasites from infesting them. "I've been working with the rancher, helping him figure out how to market his meat. I hope you like it." She chopped apples and carrots and wept when she diced the onions.

"Sorry," she said through the tears. "I have trouble with onions."

"It's not trouble," he said. "It's nature."

After everything was in the pot, he added spices that she couldn't name but that smelled both sweet and zesty.

She had enjoyed cooking with Paul in Portland. They'd eaten smoked salmon from the Columbia River and experimented with kohlrabi, which they never learned to like. They'd baked a lemon chess pie from a recipe she'd clipped from *The Oregonian* and grilled chickens on the hibachi in his back yard. Like River, Paul was an inventive cook.

River reached into the cupboard and pulled out a bottle of red wine. "From Argentina," he explained. "The swill from Brazil it isn't worth drinking." He dumped a splash of wine into the stew and then poured some in his empty vodka glass.

Sid laughed. "'Swill from Brazil.' Hey. You're a poet."

He chuckled. "I don't think so," and offered to fill her glass with the wine.

While they ate, they talked about his work—how the farmers were finally willing to try his new seeds—and about Raven—how conscientious and careful she was in the lab.

"Speaking of Raven, she sent something for you." Sid dashed to the back room, opened her suitcase, and began to rummage through the folded clothes inside. Raven had been apologetic when she asked if Sid might have room for a gift for River. "I know you travel light, but could you tuck this into your bag?" she had asked. "For my brother?"

Back at the table, she handed the package to River.

He held the tan paper sack with outstretched arms for several seconds, then turned it over a couple times. He leaned toward her, a whimsical look on his face that asked if she knew what Raven had sent. He was like a three-year-old who was impatient with the wrapping paper around a Christmas present, eager to know what was inside, yet spellbound by the intrigue.

She shook her head. "You'll have to open it. Raven didn't tell me anything about it."

He uncrimped the top of the sack, peeked inside, looked up at her, and flashed a grin that would light up the evening sky. "Holy Hannah! What a great sister," he yelled. With a flourish, he dumped twelve Snickers bars on the table. "I love these things and can't get them down here." He tore open the wrapping of one of the bars, ran it under his nose, and took a deep breath. "Ooh, yeah."

The magic of siblings. Raven was to River what she, Sid, could have been to a sister if she still had one. She would send her sister perfumes and soaps and embroidered hankies from Brazil. And in return, her imaginary sister would send gifts that would mirror whoever she had grown up to be, maybe a musician, maybe a librarian. Sid shook her head at the sorrow of it all.

After he had finished his second helping of stew and emptied his wine glass, River set his spoon on the table and twirled it twice. "So, what, exactly, do you study with those bacteria?" he asked. It was a blunt question, with no gentle transition from the lighthearted conversation about candy bars to a discussion of deadly microbes. "Raven told me you found a germ in that blood you carried back to Michigan. Have you discovered, then, what's killing the children?"

"Not sure yet." Her answer felt inadequate. "We're limited by having the bacteria from only one child. We need more. That's why I'm here. To try to get more bacteria from Serrana."

"Greg's expecting you. You'll like him."

The dishes were washed, dried, and returned to the cupboard, and she curled in River's tattered easy chair to read a paperback she'd picked up at the Detroit airport. He sprawled on the couch, carving a fist-sized piece of wood.

"You never explained your work with those bacteria," he said.

"Do you want the long, technical version or a quickie summary? It's kind of complicated."

"Whatever you think is best." He chipped at the wood with a pocketknife, sending splinters to the floor. "We have nothing else to do tonight. Raven doesn't tell me much about her work. She thinks I won't understand it."

"That doesn't sound like something Raven would say."

"Yeah. But she thinks it. I'm not a science wizard like my brainy sister. I'm more like a science moron."

"Nonsense. It's not *that* hard."

She began with the simple version. "When Raven and I returned from Promissão after our visit, I put the little girl's blood on an agar plate to grow bacteria."

"Agar plate?" he asked. The piece of wood was beginning to look like an elongated ball.

She explained what that was and then said, "And, to my amazement, bacteria grew from that blood."

He listened intently. Even though his interest in her story surely lay in its connection to his sister and not in its scientific content, she kept explaining anyway. Finally, she said, "So we—Raven, Eliot, and I—are trying to figure out what kind of bacteria they are and what makes them so deadly. That way, we can know the best antibiotics to use for treatment if any of the children get to Dr. Alancar in time. In the meantime, I think the cefotaxime I brought will be a better treatment than the antibiotic they currently have in the clinic."

He scrunched his nose. "Eliot. I think Raven has mentioned him. He's the grumpy guy in the lab, right? The one you call 'The Ogre?'" Now the ball on the end of his piece of wood looked like it was a stubby bird beak.

Ogre? I said *ogre*, Sid thought? That must be what Raven had told her brother. Maybe that word had come up after the fiasco at the Amsterdam meeting. Eliot could be testy for sure. And sometimes downright nasty. "He expects excellent work," she said. "I guess that expectation looks like grumpy from time to time." What had Raven told River about *her*?

"Should I continue your microbiology lesson?" Sid asked.

"We can leave it at that. I wish you the best of luck." River's smile was warm and sincere. Still, there was a bit of reserve in his voice, a hint of stiffness to his face.

The morning sun was intense when River drove Sid and the two Styrofoam boxes, each filled with the antibiotics, diluent, and refrozen cold packs, to the clinic. They passed a woman walking beside the road with an armful of what looked like fat brown bananas. Sid tapped on the car's window beside her. "What's she carrying?"

"Cassava roots."

"What does a person do with them?"

"Sell them. Or eat them. They're kind of like potatoes."

The woman with the cassavas was about Cibele's age. "How's Cibele doing?" Sid asked.

He shrugged and turned into the clinic's driveway. "She's okay, I guess. A bit subdued. The whole town is quieter, what with seven new little graves in the Promissão cemetery. Everyone is mourning those dead babies and waiting to see who's next."

Dr. Alancar's nurse explained that he was stitching up a cut in a soccer player's chin. "The boy hit a goal post," she said. Then she asked, "Is he expecting you?"

"He'll be happy to see us. We've brought antibiotics from America." The nurse disappeared behind one of the doors.

Sid paced the waiting room and periodically stopped to read the posters on the wall: one was an advertisement for immunizations, and she couldn't tell what the other, a picture of a mother pinning a diaper on a baby, was about. She spotted a stack of the fliers she and Cibele had made. The most recent children to die hadn't gotten to the clinic early enough, just like all the others. She'd never know if their mothers had read the flier, if they'd been watchful enough.

When she tired of pacing, she took a seat beside River. Remote echoes of Cibele's screams and Ana's sobs seemed to bounce off the walls of the waiting room. "He went so fast," Ana had wailed that awful morning. "So fast, so fast." Yes, Gilberto, and all the rest, had gone so very fast.

The door creaked open, and Dr. Alancar greeted them with a smile. As he shook their hands, he nodded in his agreeable way.

"I understand two more children have died since I was here last," Sid said.

"Sim," he said. "Yes." His smile disappeared, replaced by a dusky gloom that darkened his whole face. He told her about the most recent cases. Same story of red eyes. Same fever. Same purpura.

She told him about the bacteria she had isolated from Izabel's blood. "We don't know yet the exact identity of that germ, but it's not one that commonly causes serious infections in children. I'm pretty sure, though, it caused her sepsis and her death."

She pointed to the two Styrofoam boxes. "I've brought you a gift from Hoechst Pharmaceuticals ..." Before she could finish, he flashed a puzzled look, and turned to River to translate. River shrugged. Neither knew what Hoechst Pharmaceuticals was. "That's a drug manufacturing company," she said. "Their new antibiotic, a drug called cefotaxime, has been successful in treating patients with serious infections. Even children did well with that treatment."

She went on to explain. "Cefotaxime should be better than ampicillin as it targets more bacteria." She spoke slowly to be sure he understood. His face brightened.

She opened one of the Styrofoam boxes and handed him a carton containing rows of cefotaxime vials. He pulled one out and studied the label.

"I brought enough to treat four children for ten days each. All the instructions are here on the package insert." She unfolded the paper that lay against the side of the carton and handed it to him. "The drug is given intravenously. You have IV tubing and butterfly needles as I recall."

He glanced at the paper. "Sim," he said. "This is good. I'll read more about it." He refolded the paper and slipped it into the pocket of his white coat.

They followed him to the storeroom and unloaded the cefotaxime and diluent into the refrigerator. Dr. Alancar rearranged vials of vaccines to make space for the new vials. It was a tight fit, but they were able to latch the fridge door securely.

"How do you handle all our electrical outages?" River asked. "Generator?"

Sid hadn't thought of that. If the power were out for a day in this heat, the vials would get too warm, and the potency of the antibiotic would drop. She looked to Dr. Alancar for his answer.

"Sim, we have a small generator. The gasoline is very expensive. But if the power fails when the refrigerator is fully packed, as it is now, it takes longer to warm up than when it's almost empty. The drugs should be fine." His smile was warm and reassuring. Sid hoped he was right.

"And here," Sid said, handing Dr. Alancar a box of blood culture tubes. "These are so you can get a blood culture if another child comes in sick while I'm here."

He stared at the box. "If I collect the blood, what do I do with it? We don't have a laboratory."

"Give it to me. I'll take it back to Michigan."

Sid warmed spaghetti and meatballs from a can for dinner and ripped lettuce leaves into bite-sized pieces for a salad while River fixed the Volvo's tail pipe. She was glad to be back in Promissão, glad to have the cefotaxime tucked in the security of Dr. Alancar's fridge, glad to start work on getting more strains.

While she was setting the table, River walked in the front door holding his outstretched hands, his fingers splayed, palms up. "Could you turn on the water, please?" he asked. "I'm a mess."

Indeed, oily dirt and chips of rust from the exhaust pipe coated his hands. She turned the spigot in the kitchen sink, squirted a dollop of dishwashing soap into his left palm, and said, "Just in time. Soup's on."

After dinner, she nestled in the bean bag chair and watched as he lay sprawled like a rag doll on the couch and continued to carve. Now, the wooden figure looked more like a bird, with a fully formed beak and the outline of a tail. His cozy little house was comfortable, as was the bean bag chair. She'd had one in her bedroom as a teenager. That one was peach-colored gingham while this one was well worn, navy blue corduroy.

"Ah, Sid," he said. There was a note of hesitation in his voice. "Since you're a doctor, you must know something about that new disease. Um ... it's called AIDS."

She sat up straight and stared at him. He kept his eyes on the bird, kept digging the knife into the wood.

"Well, as a matter of fact, yes, I do." Where will this lead, she wondered? Did she want to follow? "I've never had a patient with it, but I've read a lot about it." She took a deep breath. "It's a very scary and puzzling illness."

He nodded. "Sure is."

"Seems to be a particular problem in Haiti. I don't know anything about Brazil. Have you heard that it's a problem here?"

He shook his head. "Haven't heard. I was just wondering."

Then, a hank of black hair dangling on one eyebrow, he looked over to her, "Well ... see ..." He wiped the hair away from his face. "This is kind of hard to talk about."

She didn't move, didn't say anything.

"It'll be easier if I think of you as a doctor rather than as my sister's friend."

"That's fine." She still didn't move.

"Well, I'm not what my sister thinks I am. See ..." He paused and then spoke again. "See ... I've never been attracted to women." He took a deep breath. "I prefer men." Pink tinged his face, and his eyes returned to the bird carving.

The secret was out. Finally, out like an uncaged finch. "River, none of that matters to me. Are you worried you may have AIDS?"

"No." His answer snapped through the room as if he had slammed a door. "No, I don't. And I don't know anyone who does."

"Good. But it must be a worry."

"Well, I know it's caused by a virus, and I know how it's spread. I wonder, though, if there's any way to know if someone has the infection. You know, before they get really sick from it."

"Actually, just before I left Michigan, I learned that the FDA is testing a way to diagnose the infection from a blood sample."

He lay the wooden carving in his lap. "Interesting. So if our friends get the test, we can know if they are infected?"

"Right."

He kept on carving. Quiet filled the room. Finally, she said, "River, since we're into confessions, I have one." She could barely hear her own voice. "During my last visit, when you and Raven went fishing, I found a photo of you and someone, maybe named Fernando, tucked inside the pages of a book—*The Valley of the Horses*, I think. It fell out when I opened the cover. The photo looked like it was taken in a gay bar. So I suspected."

His gaze whipped away from the bird and landed on her face. Then he nodded and laughed. "So that's where that picture ended up." He suddenly stopped laughing. "Does Raven know?"

She shook her head. "I certainly didn't say anything about it to her. That's your story to tell."

"What'll she think if … or maybe I should say when … she finds out?"

She took a deep breath. "She feels very close to you. I think she'll be on your side no matter what."

"Are you worried you might get it from me?"

"AIDS? Me? From you? Absolutely not. We both know how it's spread, and none of that applies. Even if you had it, which you don't."

"Right. Still, do you want me to find another place for you to stay here in Promissão?"

She reached up and patted his hand. "No, no, no. I want to stay here if it's okay with you."

He lowered his head, stared at his knees. "The only thing I ask is that you don't tell Raven. I'm not ready for her, or our parents, to know yet. Has she expressed any suspicions to you?"

"None at all. She and your mother are eager for you to find a girlfriend."

He chuckled. "Well, that's not going to happen."

She smiled at him. "It's our secret, River, until you declare it no longer a secret."

17

1984 BRAZIL

As her bus pulled into a parking bay at the Serrana station, Sid eyed the rusty girders that lined the roof over the platform. A muddy bird's nest was wedged into one high corner. The bus jolted to a stop and a bird—looked like a barn swallow—darted away from the nest, the forks of its tail flickering with each wingbeat.

River said Greg, his friend from work, would meet her. How would she find him? What if she couldn't? She couldn't remember his last name; should have had River write it down.

She stepped off the bus and surveyed the people gathered outside the station. Most were elderly, many leaning on canes. On one end of the platform, however, a young man held a piece of cardboard against his chest. When she was close enough to read his sign, she saw the words "Dr. Sidonie Royal" neatly printed in blue Magic Marker. A woman with curly red hair clutched his arm.

Sid walked toward them. "Greg?" He was tall, very tall, with a serious look on his face.

"Sid?" He tucked the sign under his arm and smiled. "Welcome to Serrana. This is my girlfriend, Maria. Is this all the luggage you brought?"

She shook their hands. "I also checked a box—supplies to collect samples."

"Great. I've arranged for you to stay down the road from my office," he said. "The owner of the house, Senhora de Andrade, will take good care of you. Her daughter works as a typist at our agency."

"That's very kind of you. Do the folks here know about the horrible disease that has affected the children in Promissão? I understand it might be here in Serrana, too."

"You bet," Greg said, and Maria nodded. "It's all over the newspaper from Ribeirão Preto. I don't remember exactly how many children have died in this region—at least six or eight— and I think they're all from Serrana. It's very frightening."

He and Maria drove Sid to the rooming house. Serrana was similar to Promissão, but bigger. The dirt beside the road was as red as Promissão dirt, and the hills that swelled toward the horizon were a patchwork of fields. "The agency is in there." Greg pointed to a three-story adobe building.

Maria explained that she works for the State of São Paulo health services. "My job is to convince mothers to vaccinate their babies and to breastfeed them. Some think of formula milk as modern and breast milk as old-fashioned, and they want to be modern. But sometimes they mix it up wrong, or they try to save money by putting in too much water, and their babies starve." She scrunched her nose and shook her head. "Not good."

"Not good at all." Sid had seen that, too, in the United States.

"River asked me to take you to the clinic tomorrow," Maria said. "I'll be happy to do that."

"And here is Senhora de Andrade's place." He stopped the car in front of a house whose plaster walls were painted grapefruit yellow.

A plump middle-aged woman with a broad, gap-toothed smile stepped out the door. A large black and tan feather bobbed from the band of her orange hat. Greg introduced them, and Senhora de Andrade grabbed Sid's hand. Then she wrapped her arm around Sid's shoulders and pulled her into the house. "Bem-vindo," she said.

"That's 'welcome,'" Greg whispered. "I think you'll be very comfortable here." He said something in Portuguese to Senhora de Andrade, who nodded in reply. "Sorry, but Maria and I need to prepare for work tomorrow." They turned to leave. "Let us know if you need anything. Here's my phone number." He handed her a business card with his home number written by hand on the back.

"I'll come at nine tomorrow morning to take you to the clinic," Maria said.

Senhora de Andrade showed Sid to the parlor. Layers of lacy curtains hung at each window, and tatted doilies draped the arms of the overstuffed chairs. She smelled something sweet from the kitchen. In the dining room, the table was covered with a crocheted cloth, and more lace curtains hung on the windows.

Lots of lace, Sid thought, and she followed her hostess up the steps to the second floor.

The staircase was dark with dim sconces along the way. At the top, the senhora leaned against the door jamb of the guest room and asked in broken English if she needed a glass of water or another pillow. Sid shook her head and muttered, "Não." It was one of the few Portuguese words she knew.

She was tired from the bus ride from Promissão. The coach had swayed like a ship in a tempest as it made its way over the curvy, rutty roads through the rolling savannah. The woman in the seat beside her had peppered her with questions about America: What was her house like, did she have a car, was everybody really rich, did she have a husband? Sid was ready to be alone.

When the senhora finally left, Sid kicked off her shoes and lay on the bed. The pillow felt as if it were stuffed with balled-up socks. She rolled to her side, pulled the blanket—the green, blue, and gold flag of Brazil was printed on its fleece—over her shoulder, and closed her eyes. A cat cried from outside the window. The smell of jasmine wafted from the candle on the bedside table. In the morning, she would make her way to the Serrana clinic; she hoped to find someone who could update her on the children's deaths.

Like the clinic in Promissão, the health center in Serrana was small and simple. The porch's floor tilted to the left, and a crack bisected the glass in the front window. When Sid stepped on the bottom stair, the board squealed. She scrambled to the next step and then up to the porch. She wasn't sure, exactly, how she would get the specimens she needed. That would come after she understood the situation there at the clinic. Somehow, it would work out.

The door to the clinic stood slightly ajar. A sign nailed to the top of the door frame said "Clinica Serrana." She tried to peek through the door's narrow opening but couldn't see much inside. Maria knocked. No response. Inside, a light bulb glowed from the ceiling. Someone must be there, so Sid pushed the door open. "Hello?" she called. Again, no response.

She stepped into what was apparently a reception room and caught the smell of Pine-Sol. Three wooden chairs stood in a row in the middle of the floor. On the wall beside the window hung a poster likely meant to encourage mothers to vaccinate their babies—"vaccinar" and "bebês" it said along with other words she didn't recognize.

Maria pointed to the vaccine poster and then pointed to herself with a large grin.

Then Sid saw the boxes. Large cardboard cartons were stacked against the wall under the poster, and stenciled across their sides were the words: "Property of GHA."

Her heart galloped. They're here, she thought. Where? She surveyed the room and stepped around the corner. In the shadows ahead, a woman—the white cap perched on her head suggested she was a nurse—sat behind a large, wooden desk.

Maria began speaking, her Portuguese sounding like a rush of bubbly water. "Promissão" was the only word Sid understood. The clinic nurse tilted her head, and a blank expression washed over her face.

Sid stepped forward. "Senhora? Ah ... GHA?" The nurse's face lit up at the mention of the GHA. "Venha," she said, and waved Sid and Maria to follow her through an inner door.

More cartons labeled "Property of GHA" lined the hallway. On top were cardboard boxes from Becton Dickinson. Syringes,

Sid thought. Or needles. They must be planning to draw blood or give injections.

The nurse held open the rose-printed drape that covered the doorway into a long, well-lit chamber and nodded for her to enter. She tipped her head toward a woman seated at the far end of the room. "Doctora Geiger," she said.

Geiger? Could that be her? Never in a million years would she have guessed Karla Geiger herself would be there in Serrana.

She was younger than Sid expected and, in her navy-blue suit and crisp, white blouse, she had the starchy look of a Lufthansa stewardess. A beaded stick anchored her sand-colored hair into a tight knot. A class of young nurses surrounded Dr. Geiger. She was teaching them how to draw blood.

When Sid introduced herself, Dr. Geiger's eyes widened and, for a moment, she seemed to stop breathing. Then she stood up and thrust out her hand. "I'm very happy to meet you," she said with a rugged German accent. "We spoke on the phone several weeks ago."

"Yes." She was surprised at the woman's civility considering that she, Sid, had refused to send her the BPF strain.

"We can speak when I finish this lesson." Dr. Geiger smiled. Was it a sincere smile or an act? Sid couldn't be sure.

Sid found a chair in the hallway and thanked Maria for coming with her. "I can take it from here if you need to return to work."

Maria grasped Sid's hand in both of hers and said goodbye.

Sid and Karla Geiger sat across the table from each other in a small office. Stacks of papers littered the corner of the desk, and a German-Portuguese dictionary was propped on the windowsill. An opened carton, like the ones in the hallway, stood on the floor near the door. Sid could see plastic sleeves of agar dishes inside.

Dr. Geiger brewed tea, and Sid accepted a cup. "As you know, I, too, am interested in the bacteria that caused the fatal infections in the children of Promissão," Sid said. "I understand additional cases have been identified here in Serrana."

"Yes." Dr. Geiger clasped her hands together on the top of the table. Her voice was curt. "As far as we can tell, six children from here have had a similar infection. All were sent immediately to the Universidade de São Paulo Hospital in Ribeirão Preto. Four have died, and two—the ones who were started on antibiotics early in their illnesses—have survived. So far." Dr. Geiger's words were formal and matter-of-fact—nothing soft, no niceties. Her harsh eyes probed Sid's face for a reaction.

"Have you isolated bacteria from their blood?" Sid asked, staring back at Dr. Geiger, trying to be similarly severe.

"I'm not at liberty to discuss details of the patients." Dr. Geiger unfolded her hands, picked up a paper clip, tapped it on the table, dropped it, and refolded her hands. "Confidentiality, you know."

Nonsense, thought Sid. She wasn't asking for patient information; she had asked if any bacteria had been isolated from any of their blood cultures. Just raw numbers. There was nothing confidential about that. "I understand that patient names can't be divulged. I'm not interested in names. I'm interested in bacterial strains."

Dr. Geiger lifted her chin and gave an ever-so-slight nod. But she said nothing.

Sid leaned against the back of her chair and crossed her

arms. "It would be important to know whether the bacteria from the patients in Serrana are the same as those from the child in Promissão." She took a deep breath. "And important to know whether the bacteria possess the same virulence factors. We have the expertise to do those experiments."

Dr. Geiger's eyes narrowed. She nodded. "Yes, of course it's important to understand the bacteria causing these infections. Very important. That's why the GHA is interested in obtaining *your* strain." Her clipped words cut through the humid air like a knife.

Sid unfolded her arms and straightened her shoulders. "We are developing new assays to explore the virulence characteristics of our strain and would like to compare them to the strains isolated from the children in Serrana."

Dr. Geiger leaned forward. "The GHA is interested in your strain. We will be unable to share our strains with you."

"We haven't completed our studies yet." Sid took a deep breath, trying not to let that tough-as-gristle woman unnerve her. "And, as you can understand, we can't share the strain until all the experiments are finished, confirmed, and properly analyzed. We wouldn't want to mislead the GHA with preliminary and possibly imperfect data."

"Well, I guess we have nothing more to discuss." Dr. Geiger stood up. Her voice had the thud of finality. "I look forward to learning the results of your studies when they are complete." She led Sid out of the office, across the reception area, and out to the porch. "Have a safe trip back to America."

That evening, Sid had dinner with Greg and Maria at a café down the street from Senhora de Andrade's house. Greg, a pleasant idealist, was earnest about the future of agriculture around Serrana. "The farmers need to diversify their crops," he said. "They plant too many hectares in only sugar cane because prices are pretty high right now. But monoculture depletes the soil. The good news is that they're interested in learning about modern farming practices."

The waitress passed out menus. They were written in Portuguese. "Please order your favorite dish for me," Sid said.

"That'd be beans and pork," Greg said. "How are you with garlic?"

"There's no such thing as too much garlic," Sid laughed.

"I agree," Maria said. When she smiled, which she probably did often when speaking with her clients, the left side of her mouth lagged behind the right. Yet it was a beautiful smile, sincere and beguiling with a hint of the unusual.

Greg asked if the room in Senhora de Andrade's house was comfortable.

"Oh, yes. Very comfortable. The coffee, however, is a bit bitter."

Greg laughed. "Yes, that's the way they make it in this part of Brazil. Thick as varnish."

As she watched Greg and Maria, the way their hands touched, the way their eyes gleamed when they spoke to each other, she thought of Paul. He didn't even know she was back in Brazil. She hadn't spoken to him in two weeks. He'd left a message on her phone, but she was too busy packing to call him back.

"Well," Greg said, "I understand you and River's sister work with a germ that might be causing those mysterious deaths in the children."

She spoke in layman's terms, explained that the BPF strain

was not the usual kind of bacteria to cause fatal infections in otherwise healthy children. She had just taken the first bite of the dinner when Maria asked, "How did your visit with that doctor at the clinic go?"

Sid held up her spoon, pointed it to her mouth, smiled through closed lips, and kept chewing. Maria giggled.

While she gnawed on the tough piece of pork, she pondered the best answer to the question. She didn't know Maria, or Greg, at all. They had been kind to her, had gone out of their way to help her. Should she be honest with them? Should she unload her frustration with Dr. Geiger, who had essentially cut her off from any strains the GHA may have now or might acquire in the future? They wouldn't—couldn't—understand the microbiology of it all. Did she want to tell them of her failure to engage Dr. Geiger? She wasn't interested in broadcasting her disappointment. Finally, she swallowed the meat, set down her spoon, and said, "Well, I'd say it was a useful visit."

Sid tried to be quiet as she climbed the wooden steps at Senhora de Andrade's house. Her room sat near the back. Its ceiling hung low over her head, and the small window overlooked a hay field with a schoolyard far beyond. The air was stale, the bathroom muggy but clean. Large lime-green flowers dotted the wallpaper, and a path was worn into the carpet between the bed and the hallway.

In the quiet of the evening, she stared at the fringe on the lampshade beside the bed and thought of next steps. Outside the window, the moon hung low in the sky, a stark, snow-white-and-gray-speckled circle with a shallow divot in the upper right edge. It was an incomplete moon.

She couldn't force Dr. Geiger to share her strains any more than Dr. Geiger could force her to send the BPF strain to the GHA. That impasse was insurmountable. Now what? Should she take the bus to Ribeirão Preto and ask the bacteriologist at the hospital to give her subcultures of bacteria isolated from ill children from Serrana? Would the bacteriologist be willing to give them to her? Not likely. Not without permission from the GHA. Maybe she should contact the National Health Laboratory of Brazil to get the strains. Even if they had them, they surely wouldn't cooperate with a scientist Dr. Geiger had blackballed. These thoughts circled her head like rabid bats, darting in and out of her consciousness until she finally fell into an impatient sleep.

She awoke early, at least an hour before Senhora de Andrade would serve breakfast. She dressed and decided to go for a walk. The air in the courtyard was heavy with the morning mist, and the gate groaned when she pulled it open. The street was empty except for a truck loaded with vegetables that sprayed water on the sidewalk when it sped through a puddle. Up and down, on both sides of the street, colorful walls separated the houses from each other and from the sidewalk. She walked past the red brick wall that surrounded the next-door neighbor's yard and then the pale peach stucco wall around the next house. Pink blossoms lined the bottom of the stone wall around the third house and, behind it, the branches of a palm tree waved in the breeze. Overhead, webs of wires looped from utility pole to utility pole.

At the corner, she crossed the street to a park where several children kicked a beach ball while their mother, or nanny, or aunt, or whoever was supposed to be watching them, sat on a bench, smoking and reading a magazine. Sid took a seat on another bench and watched the kids scream with laughter as they chased each other through the patchy grass. One of the little girls wandered over to her and said something in Portuguese in a sweet, four-year-old voice. Sid smiled and shrugged her shoulders. The girl stared at her, probably wondering why that unkind stranger didn't respond to whatever she said. While the child stared, tiny flies swarmed around her head. The little girl wiped her arm across her eyes and dashed back across the open field toward her friends.

The flies. The child had nonchalantly brushed those nasty little gnats away from her face. They were everywhere, buzzing around the heads of the kids, crawling into their eyes and up their noses. She wondered if flies like that had crept over Gilberto's face when he played outside? The children who had died in Promissão had had conjunctivitis. Pink eye. Those flies could spread the BPF bacteria from one child's eye to another. She watched the children chase the ball across the park.

She stood up, straightened her shoulders, and stared at the treetops. That was it. The flies would be the target of her next studies. She would try to culture BPF from fly feet. Finding the bacteria there could explain how the germs were transmitted— from child to child by the flies. That was something the GHA would never consider even if they had noticed the flies. Their ossified thinking made that extremely unlikely.

As she walked away from the park and back toward Senhora de Andrade's house, she contemplated the next step. She'd return to Promissão and ask River and Cibele to help her collect flies.

After Greg dropped her off at the Serrana bus station, an exhaust-laden breeze danced through the open-air waiting room where old people, their luggage stacked at their feet, dozed in plastic chairs. A red and white bus pulled into a bay beside the platform, discharged three passengers, and left. She had an hour to wait before the bus to Promissão arrived.

She wandered toward the stall beside the ticket counter and nodded to the young woman inside. Candy bars and boxes of balloons were wedged on the stall's shelves between handkerchiefs, coloring books, and packages of Smurf stickers. She'd need a reward for the children of Promissão and decided against candy, as it was bad for the teeth, or balloons, as children could aspirate them when they tried to inflate them. She might have enough money for the stickers. She handed three packages to the clerk and spread the Brazilian coins across her palm. The clerk selected both a twenty-five and a fifty-centavo coin and slid the packages into a paper bag. Sid was set.

18

1984 BRAZIL

The unfinished business surrounding Cibele and her nephew's death was a three-ton sorrow that pulled at Sid always. She felt she had abandoned Cibele there in the clinic when Gilberto died; when she, Raven, and River walked out the door, Cibele had stayed behind, weeping with her sister in that tiny room full of cribs. During this trip, she hadn't seen Cibele before leaving for Serrana. Now, she hoped to complete that difficult business during dinner.

Sid settled into her seat in the front corner of the restaurant. River shared the bench with her while Cibele faced them on the other side of the table. "This's kind of a hole-in-the-wall place, but the *feijoada* is to die for," River said. "Are you up for kale and black beans? And any meat you want, but I like the pork. The whole mess is dumped on a pile of rice."

Cibele was elegant as ever in a copper-colored silk blouse and flowing black palazzo pants. Apricot and rust-tinted ribbons anchored her hair at the back of her neck. When she lifted her wine glass for River's toast—"To old friends"—Sid noticed her bracelet, strands of tiny cinnamon-tinted beads with ... Were those diamonds embedded in the gold clasp? Looked expensive.

Sid continued to stare at the bracelet, and Cibele raised her hand and flexed her wrist, showing off the jewelry. "A gift from an artist friend. Isn't it lovely?" she said. "The beads are made of sunstone."

Sid had never heard of sunstone and wondered about the name. The color of the beads didn't relate to the sun at all but rather resembled copper pipes instead of lemon skins. Nonetheless, the bracelet was stunning.

Over dinner, the conversation wandered from the history of the Portuguese colonization of Brazil and the economic base of Promissão to the murder of Indira Gandhi and the insufferable election of President Reagan. "The man's a jackass," River said without listing specifics. The talk then moved to their favorite books and how River got his job with the agriculture aid organization. "Pure luck," he said.

Sid became edgy. Finally, she couldn't stand it any longer and, at a break in the discussion—they questioned the wisdom of holding the Olympics in Sarajevo—she said, "Cibele, I've thought a lot about you and your sister since little Gilberto's death."

Cibele bowed her head and dabbed her eyes with her napkin. Her shoulders trembled as she quietly sobbed. "So sorry," she muttered.

"It was unimaginable," Sid said. "Crying is fine."

Slowly at first, Cibele began to speak about her nephew and Ana. "My sister ... she longs to feel the chamois skin of his cheek against her cheek, to smell the daylight on his hair." She started to weep again, then added, "He was a beautiful baby, soft and warm and cuddly."

The waiter set a bowl of *feijoada* before each of them, and Cibele kept talking. "Everyone cries, all the time. Ana and the other parents visit the cemetery every single day—sometimes several times a day. The candle lady at the church had to order three more cases of long tapers because they are being burned so fast."

Sid shook her head. It was hard to listen to.

"The whole town is terrified whenever a child becomes sick with anything. Every sniffle, every cough, the parents panic," Cibele said. "They're so scared that death will carry their son or daughter away from them, too."

Sid patted Cibele's hand. "I really wish you didn't have to go through any of this."

Cibele wiped her eyes again.

"You may not know that I took a sample of Izabel's blood back to my laboratory in Michigan," Sid said. "We found the germ that we think caused those infections. Hopefully after we study the germ more, we will learn how best to treat the infection. In the meanwhile, I brought a new antibiotic for Dr. Alancar to use if another child comes to the clinic with that sickness."

"The last one was less than two weeks ago," Cibele said, trying to smile through her tears. "They just don't stop."

"Sid has a new idea for learning more about the sickness," River said. "Tell her, Sid."

"Well, I wonder about those tiny flies that crawl all over the children's faces."

Cibele closed her eyes, wrinkled her nose, opened her eyes again, and ran her spoon through her *feijoada*.

Sid continued. "I wonder if the gnats might be spreading the infection—or at least the bacteria that cause the infection—from one child to the next."

"Maybe." Cibele shrugged. "Those flies are nasty."

"Right. And they don't travel very far. So I'd like to trap some of the flies near the homes of several of the children who have died. And to swab the eyes of neighbor kids. We need to study more of those bacteria, the same germs that Izabel had."

Cibele nodded. "I'll help with whatever you need."

"Why just kids?" River asked. "Don't the flies crawl into adult's eyes?"

"I don't know," Cibele said. "But they don't bother grown-ups nearly as much as children."

"I don't know, either," Sid said. "Maybe it has something to do with moist eyes. The mucus and tears of kids may be different from adults and more attractive to the little gnats. Another mystery."

The next evening, River stood at his stove, stirring tomatoes into the stew that bubbled in his stock pot while Sid, seated at the table, snapped the ends off green beans.

"Those gnats are the key to understanding the whole picture of this awful infection. At least I think that's the key." She snapped the stem off another bean. "I appreciate your help, River. I really, really do."

He nodded and tipped a shake of salt into the stew. He stirred again. "Okay."

It was an unconvincing "okay." Was he getting testy? She must be pushing him too hard. Better back off.

"So here's the deal," she said. "I brought most of the stuff I need to collect the eye samples and gnats, but I forgot to bring a bug net. I'll need a coat hanger, some cheese cloth, and a needle and thread. Could you round up those things?"

"No problem. Coat hanger from my closet, needle and thread from my sewing kit. I'm sure my neighbor has some cheese cloth because she makes a lot of guava paste."

While Sid washed the dinner dishes, River ran next door and returned with an armful of cheese cloth. "Enough?" he asked.

"Oh, my gosh, yes. Plenty. Enough that I can sterilize some for net liners."

"Sterilize?"

"Yeah, in boiling water on your stove."

"Right," he said, laughing and tapping his temple with his finger.

He bent a wire coat hanger into a circle, and Sid stitched together a cone of cheesecloth. Then she sewed the open end of the cone to the bent hanger. "Perfect," she said, waving it through the air.

"It needs a longer handle." River fished a roll of duct tape from his junk drawer and bound the net's wire handle to a stick from the broad-leaved tree in his front yard.

"Oh, and we'll need control flies from a place far away from kids, a spot where the gnats are very unlikely to pick up the bacteria from a child's eye, she said. "Any ideas?"

"There's an area along the reservoir where the gnats convene by the thousands. Makes it a great fishing hole."

As they walked up the path to Ana's house, Sid smelled braised onions. She climbed the steps to the porch. A tarp was draped over a three-legged chair beside the door. A broken broom lay in the flowerbed, and a panel of corroded sheet metal hung off the shed beside an old car.

Sid knocked on the door. The screen door swung open, and Ana stepped out, dressed in a loose black shift, followed by Cibele. Sid gave Ana a hug, felt the quiver of her new friend's shoulders as she quietly sobbed. River and Cibele and Ana spoke in Portuguese. Cibele waved her hands to the rhythm of her words, while Ana remained somber, her arms at her side.

Finally, River turned to Sid and said, "It's all set. The children should be here shortly."

"Sim," Cibele nodded. "I told them a lady from America wanted to meet them. I said they could help the lady with a scientific experiment. They're pretty excited about meeting someone from America. They wonder if you know Spider-Man."

Ana clasped Sid's hand, and tears streamed down her cheeks. She said, "Thank you for coming back to Promissão and for everything you are trying to do to stop this awful disease. I'll wait in the house while you do your work."

Within a half hour, twelve little kids crowded into Ana's yard. They looked as if they were two to five years old or so. Some were girls, most were boys. They fidgeted while they waited, shifting from one sandaled foot to the other. Their skinny brown legs bore the bruises of recent mishaps, and their T-shirts advertised Mickey Mouse, GI Joe, Charlie Brown, and Road Runner. Sid lined up her equipment—swabs, gnat net, sterilized envelopes, and the Smurf stickers—on top of her cardboard carton.

The sky was clear and the sun warm, so Sid slipped off her

jacket, hung it on one of the pickets of the garden fence, and went to work. Cibele explained to each child that Dr. Royal would rub a little piece of cotton on their eyelids. She told them it would feel kind of funny, which made it fun, and it would last only a moment. "Quick as the flick of a squirrel's tail," she said with a toss of her hand. "And then it's over."

Cibele held each child's head against the side of her chest with her right hand and grasped their wrists with her left hand, saying, "This is a special kind of cuddle, a germ-catching cuddle."

In one sweep, Sid pulled down a lower eyelid from each child and dabbed a moist cotton-tipped swab across the pink part. She then put each germy swab into a glassine envelope, sealed it, labeled it with the child's name, pressed a Smurf sticker onto the front of each volunteer's shirt, and moved on to the next child in line.

Almost all the children, at first confused by the procedure, rubbed their eye after Sid finished obtaining her sample and then danced around the yard, laughing. The way they gurgled and twisted was pure theater, each trying to outperform the other. Each child then skipped back to the circle of other kids to watch Sid stick a swab into the next eye.

Gnats darted around the heads of three boys with gooey eyes, and she swept them into her net. One of the boys wanted to work the net. She let him touch the handle, and then the rest of the kids begged for a touch. By the middle of the afternoon, she had collected samples from all the original children as well as from curious add-ons who had straggled into Ana's yard to see what was happening. They peered at the gnats and swabs in the glassine envelopes and laughed. They slapped the flies from each other's faces.

"Dona and Marcelo are expecting us," Cibele said. "This will be as hard on them as it was for Ana. Cruel memories."

They were waiting on their porch when River pulled the Volvo into their yard beside the cornfield. Marcelo's arm was wrapped around Dona's shoulders, and Dona folded her hands over her very pregnant belly. Sid had forgotten about the pregnancy. Dona's face, drawn and gray with a forced smile, reflected the complicated joy and heartache of bringing a new baby into the world so shortly after losing their other child. Cibele introduced Sid to the couple. Marcelo shook her hand, and Dona, sobbing, grasped Sid's cheeks between her palms and kissed her forehead. Sid, struggling against her own tears, hugged the grieving mother.

Over Dona's shoulder, Sid glanced through the screen door into the house. Straight ahead, a memorial to Mariana stood on the table: pictures of her as a baby and with her grandmother, a stuffed kitten, a sippy cup, a folded flannel blanket. Even in the daylight, candlelight flickered against the dreary wall.

Ten neighborhood children lined up at the foot of the porch. Dona and Marcelo retreated into the house, and Sid and Cibele repeated the routine they had established at Ana's house. These kids also hopped around the yard after having their eyes sampled. Sid decided all the children of Promissão were natural thespians.

The next afternoon, Sid crouched beside a murky stream where it dumped into the reservoir, her head buried in a swarm of gnats. The squawky calls of jays echoed through the trees above her head. Her shoes were slathered in mud the color of rusty fenders, and she was hot. Very hot. And sweaty.

Wretched bugs, she thought. Cibele was right. They were

nasty. A cloud of the tiny flies hummed around her ears. She swatted at them, but they kept swirling into her mouth, into her eyes. "Leave me alone," she muttered, "while I get the net ready."

If someone had told her five years earlier that she would travel all the way to backwater Brazil to gather *Hippelates* flies, she would have considered that person to be wildly crazy. But there she was. River sat on a boulder on the bank, downstream. He yawned, swatted flies away from his face, and then flipped a stick into the cloudy water. Then another. As he had predicted, the place was loaded with gnats. He tossed yet another stick into the lake. "Remind me why you need to collect the bugs?" he called.

"I'm going to culture them to see if they're carrying the BPF bacteria," she called back. She'd explained that last night when she asked where to find the flies. Why did he ask now? She stared hard at him. He batted at the flies, kicked at a stump beside his rocky perch, and turned his head toward her. The impassive look on his face told her he remembered perfectly well what she had said about culturing the flies. He was being sarcastic. It was her punishment for dragging them to that miserable, fly-infested riverbank.

"Are we done now?" He pitched a moss-covered stone into the water. "I'm hungry."

She watched the ripples radiate away from where his stone had landed, watched them fade to nothingness in the still water. He was at the end of his unraveling rope with the bugs. And maybe with her. "Please be patient. It won't take much longer."

She shook the wrinkles out of the homemade net. It was simple but serviceable. Carefully she lined it with another piece of sterilized cheese cloth and swung the net through the buggy cloud. Then she emptied the trapped flies into one of the sterile envelopes, sealed it, labeled it, and dumped it into her cardboard box.

"How many do you need, anyway?" he asked.

"More than this. The more I catch, the higher the probability we'll find the bacteria. Assuming they are on these little critters. Do you have something else to do this afternoon?"

"No. This is a little boring is all."

"Yeah, for you I guess it is. Sorry. But seeing whether the BPF bacteria live on the fly feet is important. That could be the way they spread from child to child."

After removing the used net liner, she inserted a new, sterile one, swung the net again, and emptied the contents into an envelope. She swung and emptied, swung and emptied, over and over. The jay continued to squawk in the treetops, and now she heard another one answer from across the stream.

When she'd gathered enough gnats, she called to River. "I'm done. We can leave now." He jumped up from the boulder, brushed the dirt from the seat of his pants, and scurried over to her. "Let me help," he said and carried the cardboard box to his car.

"As soon as we get back to your place, I'll put the envelopes in your fridge until I leave."

"My fridge?" He stared at her as if he was looking at a ghoul. "You're going to put those gnats and the killer bacteria in the fridge next to my food?"

He'd been a very good sport. She made her voice as gentle as possible. "It's okay. The envelopes are sealed tight. I'll even double bag them. I'll stick the envelopes down in the empty vegetable bin. All by themselves. They won't touch any food.

I'll scrub it down before I leave. And I'll be the first to eat something from the fridge after I put them in there." She waited for his reaction, studied his down-turned eyes.

He rubbed his foot into the earth beside the car and shoved his hands into the pockets of his jeans. "That's all right, I guess. If I get sick, you have to tell my sister it's your fault." Then he smiled and climbed in the driver's seat.

19

1984 MICHIGAN

Sid was smearing the dead flies on agar plates when she saw Eliot walking toward her bench. He perched on a stool, hooked his heels on the cross bar, and folded his hands in his lap.

"Welcome back," he said.

She told him about meeting the frosty Karla Geiger in Serrana and described Karla's refusal to share the Serrana strains with her. Eliot nodded in agreement at her description of Karla as solid ice. She explained her newest idea for obtaining additional BPF strains and her decision to return to Promissão to collect the tiny flies that swarmed around the children's eyes. As she spoke, she continued to spread dead gnats across the agar with her sterile wire loop. She needed to process them before they dried any further.

Eliot listened without interrupting. She couldn't read his deadpan face.

When she finished her story, he slowly shook his head. "What were you thinking, Sidonie?" He stood up and began to pace between the window and her lab bench. "Even if the BPF bacteria are carried from one child to the next by a few gnats, what is the probability you'll find those bacteria on the minuscule number of insects you sampled? Consider the gazillions of little flies that live in Promissão."

Would his criticism of her never end? She took a deep breath, but before she could speak, he added, "The probability is a hair—a very slim, microscopically thin hair—this side of zero."

"It's true the likelihood is small," she said, "but if I find our bacteria, that's important. A negative result means nothing, but a positive result—if I show the gnats have BPF on them—means a lot."

"What?" he asked. "What, exactly, would it mean?"

Her ire was growing, blocks of irritation with him were piling, one after the next, on top of each other. "I'll see if the gnat bacteria are identical to the BPF strain. If that's the case, then we have additional bacteria to study."

He shook his head. "Now you're really making no sense, Sidonie."

She was tired. And frustrated by the BPF project in general. And angry with Karla Geiger for standing in her way. And furious with Eliot for being such a know-it-all. "That's your opinion. I have work to do. You may be excused." She turned away from him and dropped another dead fly onto another agar plate.

It was late in the afternoon when Sid put on her coat and mittens and headed for the river. She sometimes went there to empty her mind of troubling, confusing clutter. She hadn't been able to concentrate on writing the abstract to submit for the meeting in Boston. The words wouldn't come out right, and her ideas tangled together into a meaningless mess. The river's edge was a good place to sort things out.

As she wandered the path between the lab and the park, she watched the sun hover above the treetops until it was swallowed by a passing cloud. Several steps later, after the cloud had moved on, the sun once again glimmered in her eyes.

The path led to a bridge that led to an island. She rested her elbows on the wooden rail and watched the usually silvery swells, now dull in the fading sunlight, flow far beneath her feet. An empty Vernors can floated past. Then a plastic bag that billowed like a jellyfish. A gray feather. A pine twig. A bigger twig. The water and all the flotsam it carried were relentless in their rush to Lake Erie. Relentless. It was a strong, determined word. Like the GHA in their pursuit of her strain. Like Eliot's insistence that a plasmid, but not endotoxin, explained the BPF toxicity. Paul would say her ambition bordered on relentless.

Would other scientists, or Eliot for that matter, view her as relentless? She didn't see herself that way. She was committed to her work but that was different from relentless. She saw herself as motivated by curiosity—she simply, fervently, passionately wanted to understand how bacteria made people sick and, particularly now, why the BPF strain was so deadly. They—all bacteria—were so very clever. They'd figured out how to live in the most inhospitable places on the earth: high temperature, low temperature, high acidity, high alkalinity, no oxygen, inside people's guts and vaginas, under people's toenails. They lived in the river below. Even in the late fall. Their ability to live anywhere was the fruit of their relentless determination to survive.

Ever since she first learned about bacteria, she'd been fascinated by the ways they maneuvered around every immune assault a body could mount. That's what had happened to Mariana, Luiza, Gilberto, Izabel, and the other dead children in Promissão. Their bodies had labored hard to fend off the bacteria but, in the end, the children lost the fight. Why had it been impossible for those healthy kids with their healthy immune systems to conquer the BPF strain?

The answer might be in bacteria's ability to change the faces they presented to the world as quickly, and as dramatically, as an actress could change her costume between scenes. Dr. Bausch's lecture, so many years ago, had taught her that bacteria were able to add a protein here, remove a carbohydrate there, turn a gene off, turn one on, and each change could alter the topography of the bacterial surface. She was fascinated with the way bacteria could shuffle the chromosomal deck into many combinations of genes, ultimately yielding a large army of bacterial factors, which were sometimes killer proteins, made by killer genes. That's what had likely happened to the BPF strain. One bacterium picked up a killer gene, or changed an ordinary gene into a killer gene, and then that bacterium multiplied and spread among the children in Promissão. She lifted a leafless stick from the floor of the bridge and tossed it into the water. It landed in an eddy and spun three times. Then it headed downriver. Relentlessly.

Now that the sun had plunged behind the trees, she was cold. The color of the river had turned from muddy coffee to lead. She huddled on the bridge and watched the water surge beneath the wooden planks.

She tied her scarf tighter around her neck. The wind had kicked up the water, and the ripples slapped against the bridge posts. Over and over. The rhythm of the waves. The chilly evening air. The memories in her head. All that, too, seemed relentless. And powerful. She turned away from the river and wandered home to once again work on the abstract for the Boston meeting.

After she changed from her work clothes to her relaxing clothes, she brewed a cup of tea and tackled the day's mail. At the bottom of the stack was a letter from Cibele.

My dear Sidonie,

Greetings, again, from Promissão. We all enjoyed seeing you again and hope your experiments with the samples you took from the children here were successful. The kids still talk about the lady from America who put cotton sticks in their eyes. Most of them thought it was fun.

Ana sends greetings; so do Marcelo and Dona. Their baby will come any time now. They are so very worried about that little one; worried he or she will get sick, too. Dona can't sleep and doesn't eat much. Marcelo is as worried about her as about the baby. He tries to tell her that the baby can't be healthy if she doesn't eat, but she can't seem to hear him.

Shortly after you left, another little one died here. Same as the rest of them. Red eye followed by fever and purple patches and then they die. It just doesn't end.

We all hope to see you again in Brazil, soon.

My warmest blessings,

Cibele

"Say, what did you find on those flies?" Eliot asked.

"Nothing," Sid said.

"Nothing?"

"Right. No additional BPF strains."

"Too bad." he said. His eyes were soft, his voice gentle. "So goes another great scientific hypothesis."

He started to leave, then turned back to her. "Say, where's Raven? I need to borrow that huge pipettor of hers."

"She and Doug are in Monterey for a few days. A gift from his parents. They must be rich."

"Yeah, they are." Eliot chuckled. "The first time I met his folks, I was caught completely off guard. We students lived the lives of paupers in our hovel above a professor's garage, yet Doug's parents showed up in a rented Bentley and drove us all to dinner at the priciest restaurant in Palo Alto. They are very rich. His dad is a financial guy. From New York. Doug doesn't give a rat's ass about money, which suits him well as a starving microbiologist."

"Interesting. Go ahead and borrow the pipettor. It's in her top drawer, and the big tips are on the shelf above the Bunsen burner."

Sid still had trouble imagining Raven and Doug as a couple—Raven, a California girl who was comfortable with her backwoods ways, and Doug, an East Coast elite trying hard to shed his elite-ness. But then, reason didn't always apply to love.

"What are you doing next weekend?" Paul asked over the phone.

"Hmm. I really haven't thought much about it," Sid said. "Probably work."

"Want some company?"

"Huh?"

"I was thinking of a visit to Michigan. How about it?"

So sudden. So unexpected. She hadn't seen him since her last visit to Portland last August. Four months ago. So much had happened since then. Her trips to Brazil, the discovery of the BPF strain and everything that entailed, the GHA mess.

During that visit to Oregon, they had gone to a play called *Two Gals and a Guy*. She laughed at the two old maid sisters who shared an ancient house and the bachelor who lived in the upstairs apartment. Toward the end of the first act, Paul had wrapped his fingers around her hand. She edged toward him. She had treasured the warmth and strength of his hand. He was so solid, so reliable.

But the next day, he started lobbying for her to return to Portland. She had chatted on and on about the lab and the results of the experiments, but when she mentioned a problem with an experiment, he said, "See, it isn't all perfect."

"Of course it isn't all perfect. Nothing is," she had said. And the lobbying had continued through all those phone calls.

"Sid, are you still there?" Paul said now. His voice sounded worried.

"Yes, I'm here." She had been thinking. Next weekend he might come. She had nothing planned. Did she want to face the inevitable? No, but that had to happen sometime. "Sure. A visit would be great. Bring a heavy coat. It's winter here."

The morning sun was bright as fire behind the dark tree branches outside the window. She was working alone in the lab. Eliot, cloistered in his cardboard cave to write yet another grant application, had issued an edict that no one should pester him unless a tornado was headed their way. After the trip to Monterey with Doug, Raven had gone to Santa Rosa to spend a three-day holiday with her mother. She had planned to return to Michigan last night and was probably sleeping in this morning. As Sid gazed out the window at the cemetery, a thick cloud shaded the sun, and the lab turned dreary.

She was working on her slides for the upcoming meeting in Boston when she heard Raven's desk drawer slam shut. "You're back," she called.

Raven's answer sounded muffled.

Sid walked around the corner. Raven, seated at her desk, was bent over, her head buried in her folded arms that rested on top of a pile of papers. Her shoulders quivered beneath her sweater. Quiet, stuttering noises dotted the air.

"What's wrong?" Sid crept toward her. "Are you okay?"

Raven shook her head and continued sobbing into her arms.

"When you're ready to talk, I'm ready to listen." She rubbed Raven's trembling back. Raven nodded.

Sid returned to her bench. What could be wrong? Had Raven and her mother gotten into a fight? Was it about Raven's father? Sid didn't know much about him except that he was an impoverished artist, a dreamer who wandered from one failed adventure to another. Boyfriend trouble? Not likely. There was never trouble between Raven and Doug. She didn't understand how two highly independent and different people could be so compatible. They seemed to draw sustenance from each other, and when one stumbled, the other was able to break the fall. River? Must be about River.

Just outside the lab window, a chickadee perched on a swaying twig of the sycamore tree. His little feet curled around the thin wood in such a tenuous way that she worried he would fall. His beak was like a wedge in the wind. Yet he didn't leave. And he didn't fall. He just clung to the twig. And swayed.

"Sid?" Raven wandered toward Sid's lab bench and stopped. Her voice was one notch above a whisper. Her bloodshot eyes glistened behind the tears.

"Sit down," Sid said. "What happened?" Raven looked depleted, like an old woman, broken from despair.

"River made a surprise visit to Santa Rosa."

"How wonderful ..."

Raven shook her head and held up her hand to stop her. "No, no. It wasn't wonderful. It was terrible. When you were in Promissão, did River say anything about coming home for a visit?"

"Not a word." Instantly, Sid knew the problem. She could have written the script of what was to follow.

Raven explained that River had shown up unannounced in California. He was irritable and didn't eat anything, not even the ham their mother had baked. They had never seen him that way. She paused. "I don't know how to tell you what happened."

Sid knew what had happened. But she couldn't tell Raven that she knew or how she knew it. "Take your time," she said.

Raven drew a deep breath. "I couldn't stand it any longer and asked him what was up. He didn't answer, so I asked if he had the flu or something. When he said 'no,' I asked, 'What kind of trouble are you in, anyway? The law? Drugs? A wicked woman?'"

Sid shook her head. Poor Raven.

"He said not the law and not drugs. And definitely not a woman. Then he said, 'See, I don't go for women, Raven.'" She choked up and then, gulping for air, continued. "He told me he could keep secrets from the world but not from me. Then, he said, 'I'm gay.'" A sob burbled from her chest. "He said he couldn't hide himself from us any longer."

Somehow, listening to Raven talk about her brother's sexuality made it even more real and more difficult. The repercussions would extend beyond River's life in Brazil and would deeply touch his sister and their mother. So much heartache over one person simply loving another.

"The thing is, he's my twin brother, and I was oblivious to the real him. I teased him about finding girlfriends, didn't even consider he might be gay. There were plenty of clues, but I didn't tune in to them. Poor River had to play along with my naïve, fairytale picture of him for years. Heck, I wouldn't care if he were making love to a wolf, but I can't stand to have been so stupid about him. So obtuse."

Sid shook her head again. It was all so complicated. "Raven, you've been the best possible sister for River. Please don't be so hard on yourself."

"And when he was finished telling us, he said to me, 'Don't worry. I'm always aware of the octopuses, Raven.' What a guy. I'm so lucky to have a brother as great as River."

Sid squirmed in her chair. Which octopuses did he mean? The risk of living in the world as a gay man, in general? Something else? Raven didn't mention AIDS. Neither did she. It was like the thousand-pound, smelly, sweaty goon in the room that everyone refused to acknowledge. AIDS was always a coda to any discussion of being a gay man.

20

1984 MICHIGAN

Sid stood at the gate, waiting for Paul's plane. One part of her looked forward to his visit, to spending time with him and hearing his laugh. In some ways, she missed the comfort of his easy presence, missed the walks along the riverfront and the movies on the weekends while she lived in Portland. He would listen to her complaints and worries, offer advice for getting through the rough stretches.

Yet another part of her dreaded his visit. Was she prepared for the reality of it? For the pressure on her to match his kindness with some of her own, to find the right niche for him in her complicated life?

Something different had to happen between them, and

this visit would settle that. She could feel it in the squirm of her bones, in the itch in her nerves. She wasn't sure, however, exactly what that change would be.

An hour earlier, she sat on the edge of her bed, pulling her lacy black hose up over first one leg and then the other, and worrying. The stockings gave her body the illusion of style and a tiny hint of naughtiness. But would they be too fancy? Would they send the wrong message? No, she decided, they would not. Paul probably wouldn't even notice. He'd never cared what she looked like, even when she hadn't washed her hair for three days or wore a holey T-shirt because it was the only clean one in the drawer. She slipped her crepe dress over her head and eyed herself in the mirror. She turned to the side. She patted her abdomen. Her mother had taught her that dark clothing hid many imperfections, and Sid counted on that to de-emphasize her midriff. It wasn't a terrible tummy, just not the perfectly flat one she wished for.

How about jewelry? Pearls? Her coral necklace? The pink and green stone necklace she had bought at the market in Promissão? She draped each of them across her neck and studied each in the mirror. She decided on the one from Brazil. The muted colors of the stones shimmered against the black crepe, and the gold sticks—the little brass bars that, according to Raven, looked like baby French fries—reminded Sid of museum gems laid against thick velvet. Where were her gold hoop earrings? They'd look good with that necklace. She rummaged through her drawer and found them hidden beneath the ropes of purple, gold, and green beads from Mardi Gras.

Mardi Gras. That long-ago weekend in New Orleans just before she left for Michigan. Eggs Benedict at Brennan's, the walk along the levee in the French Quarter, the beat of the music, the verve in the air, the silky sheets at their hotel. She let the carnival beads spill between her fingers back to the bottom of the drawer with a sigh.

Maybe she was overdressed for the airport. But she wanted to look nice for Paul, to at least start out on a positive note.

His plane was late. She stared out the big windows at the traffic on the tarmac. This visit had been his idea. He said their phone calls were inadequate—"too sterile" had been his words—and he needed to look into her eyes. Finally, she watched the Delta 727 edge up to the jet bridge.

The first-class passengers emerged first. He wouldn't be among them. She studied every person that walked through the door from the plane, some angry looking, some rumpled, others yawning.

Finally, she saw him, his schoolboy-cut brown hair, his black rimmed glasses, his green plaid shirt and khaki pants, his parka slung over his arm. His head swung from side to side, looking for her. His face lit up with a smile when he finally spotted her.

She put her arms around him, and he squeezed her tight. "Hey, you're squashing me," she laughed.

"That's okay," he whispered into her hair.

"But I have to breathe," she gasped.

Neither of them wanted to eat dinner at a restaurant, too many people, too noisy. Paul suggested they stop at Kroger for steaks and vegetables.

"How about a T-bone?" he said as he peered into the meat case.

"The ribeyes look good," she said.

"Two ribeye steaks," he told the butcher. He pointed his finger at the glass. "We'll take the two closest to you."

She wandered over to the stack of potatoes. "We need spuds," she said and tossed a bag of small redskins into the cart.

"Ah, those are kind of small." He picked up an Idaho. "I'm hungry for a big baked potato with sour cream and chopped chives."

"That thing's the size of your shoe," she said, pointing to his left loafer. She returned the bag of reds to the display pile and set two giant Idaho's in the cart. "We'll need to get sour cream and chives, then, too."

So is this the way the visit is going to be, she wondered?

"Let's walk over to the river," Paul said. "Do we have time for a stroll before dinner?"

"Sure," Sid said. The peace of the river would be good.

They took the path that wound to the left, the one through the thatch of dried weeds that spread over the ground like a golden quilt. Overhead, the naked tree branches swayed in slow motion. She pointed to a white spot in the mat of brown dead leaves under a huge oak tree. At first, she thought it might be a late fall flower, but when she stooped toward it, she saw that it was a discarded wad of Kleenex.

They wandered along the edge of the river until they reached the bridge to one of the islands. Halfway across, they gazed down at the steely water through the spaces between the boards, and when they reached the other side, they started down a path that led along the shore. At the rim of an open meadow, he suddenly stopped. "Hey, hear that?" His voice was bright, joyful.

She listened. The water lapped against the rocks at the river's edge. A jet plane rumbled high overhead, a voice called from far away "Brian, where the hell are you?" Then she heard a staccato whistle. "That?" she asked. "A bird?"

"Yeah. A cardinal. See him?" He pointed to a bush behind a fallen tree.

It was, indeed, a cardinal, a large, nervous-looking bird whose feathers were a deeper, richer red than usual cardinals. The bird flew to the ground and hopped in a straight line through the dried grass. He stopped, looked back at them with his beady black eyes, then flew up over the bush and across the river. Paul was chuckling.

"What's so funny?" she asked.

"When I was a kid, the birds in our town used to eat fermented honeysuckle berries until they were three sheets to the wind. They'd stagger around the lawn like Saturday night drunks."

She smiled. Other than the competition with his older brother, he'd always spoken fondly of his glorious childhood. And she'd felt that his gentle, good-natured spirit spoke of an inspired upbringing. He'd told her how he, his brothers, and his cousins built a tree house in the woods behind their house, how they threw stones at the trains that roared down the tracks beside their garage.

She swept the dried leaves off a log. "Let's sit," she said.

They settled side by side on the fallen tree trunk, its bark thick and scabby. "So, what's happening with your research?" he asked.

How much detail did she want to share with him? How much did he really want to know? The specifics were complex, and the whole story so very sad. "Let's just say my recent results have been disappointing."

"Well, that's a bummer," he said, his face sincere, his eyes kind.

In her world of research, he wasn't a threat. He wouldn't make harsh judgments about her experimental priorities or her scientific reasoning. He wouldn't have endless suggestions about how she should have done the experiments as opposed to the way she did them. But she didn't want to mislead him into thinking she would give up on the research.

"I think I mentioned that more Brazilian children were dying in a little town called Serrana. So that's two places with the infection, Serrana and Promissão. When I arrived in Serrana to collect additional bacterial specimens, I bumped into a representative of the Global Health Alliance." She described Karla Geiger, told him how she and the GHA had stonewalled her. "We may never be able to figure out exactly why those bacteria are killing those little children."

"Ouch. Sounds ugly."

"It is." She spoke softly. "So, on my most recent trip to Promissão I tried to find more of the BPF strains from the gnats that swarm all over the kids' eyes." He leaned toward her as if to hear her words more clearly. She waved her open palms in the air and blurted it out. "But I found nothing."

"Nothing?"

"No bacteria from all those gnats."

"A bigger bummer."

"Yeah, and a waste of Dr. Evans's money." She stared at her lap.

"Sounds like a wall not worth banging your head against."

She straightened her back. "No, Paul. The challenge is worth every bit of it. I plan to submit a grant to the NIH to fund the upcoming experiments on the BPF strain. We need to know what about them makes them so deadly. The review committee might laugh themselves silly at a proposal that depends on only one bacterial strain. But I have to try."

He picked up a broken stick and stirred the dried leaves that lay scattered on the ground. "Good for you for trying. I admire your tenacity. At some point, you need to calculate the cost-benefit ratio."

"I already have." What was he doing? Trying to sway her against her research? She studied his resolute face, pursed her lips to match his decisiveness. "In a couple weeks, I'm going to present the studies of the one strain we have at a meeting in Boston." She looked ahead at the river, then turned to face him. "It's a mean microbe, that BPF strain. It kills both children and baby laboratory rats, and we need to figure out how to control it. That is definitely a battle worth fighting."

His eyes were stone. She kept talking. "My long-term hope is that we can develop a vaccine to prevent the infection, or at least a way to neutralize its toxicity."

He reached for her hand. She leaned into the warmth of his closeness. The kindness of his listening. The tenderness of his being. Why did life have to conspire against them? Why couldn't a miracle appear that would glue them together? They walked the path back off the island and through the park toward her apartment.

After dinner, Paul emptied the rest of the zinfandel into their glasses, and they moved to the living room. "That plant has really grown," Paul said of the rubber tree beside the sofa. "Do you feed it vitamins or something?"

From the tone of his voice she knew his comment wasn't sincere. He didn't care a bit about the health of her plant. What did he really mean to say?

They talked about his work—challenging and satisfying—and the idiocy of Portland politics, about his fishing trip last weekend and his irritating next-door neighbor. He started to talk about his nephew—"he's really smart for a three-year-old"—and then suddenly Paul was quiet. He sipped his wine.

The silence hung in the air like heavy water. She'd better hit it straight on, or not hit it at all. "Paul, we both know where this is heading. You have the itch to get married and start a family."

"Well, yes. And you'd be the perfect partner in that venture."

"I'm not sure about that. I suspect you have decided you want to be a father, and I'm the woman who's hanging around right now. Many women could serve as a good companion in your parenting venture."

The words seemed so crass, a "parenting venture." Sounded more like a business deal than what she imagined having a child would be. Shouldn't that grow out of love between two adults, and from that, the desire to create a new life together? To build a shared future that goes on and on and on for generations? After all, speaking biologically, to have children was to assure the continuity of the species. But put that way, "continuity of the species" sounded almost as vapid and harsh as a "parenting venture."

"But I haven't met any of those women yet, except you."

"It's all about the timing, Paul. Earlier, when you were dating other women, you weren't ready for parenthood. Now you are, and I'm the closest woman. Which is a problem, because in fact I'm not close. I'm in Michigan, and you're in Oregon."

"You are so damned analytical, Sid. Maybe you could stow

your logical hat for a while and be ..." He scratched his head. "... be more unscientific. Let your mind roam into the fields of romance."

She smiled and shook her head. "I like romance as much as the next gal, but eventually romance meets a Y in the road. I think we've encountered that fork."

"Fork?"

She looked away from the glum look on his face and the slump of his shoulders and then looked back again. "It boils down to this: I can't leave Michigan, and you can't leave Oregon." She took a deep breath. "How long should we continue to torture ourselves? And each other? I want you to be free."

"Free of you?"

"Free to meet other women. Free to be the father you want to be. And I want to be free to pursue my research without feeling guilty about stringing you along or, worse yet, betraying you."

He laid his head on her shoulder. "That's not what I want to hear."

She could feel his breath, irregular little spurts of warm air, on her neck. He wanted to hear that she would be back in Portland soon. That she would marry him. That they would start a family right away. "I know it's not." Why did this have to be so hard? "I wish my words could match your wishes." It was like jagged strings of DNA, full of mismatched As, Cs, Ts, and Gs, struggling to find the right partner but never succeeding.

He sat up straight, rubbed his hands together between his knees. "When I look ahead, I see us together. I can't imagine it any other way. I want us to live together, to build a comfortable home together, to share the deepest, most rewarding kind of love together. And yes, to grapple with the dark things married people have to grapple with. Together."

"Paul, it's a beautiful fantasy, but I don't fit into it. When I look ahead, I see working very hard to figure out the mystery of the BPF strain. That's my immediate priority, and I have to be successful in that before I can look at any other kind of future."

"How long would that take?"

"I don't know."

"You don't know." His voice grew louder. "Five years? Twenty-five years? That's too long."

"I know that. That's why you have to be free of me. Now."

He stood up and shouted, "I don't want to be free of you. I want you to be free of that damned ambition of yours. It's strangling us."

"You want to proceed on your terms, and your terms only, with marriage and children. I can't do that. Not now."

Paul paced across her living room from the front entryway to the hall that led to the bedrooms and back. Twice. Three times. He said nothing. Neither did she.

He stood in front of her with his palms covering his face. Was he crying? She couldn't stand to watch him cry. She rose from the sofa.

"Paul, I'm sorry." Her voice was a whisper. "I wish this had turned out differently."

21

1984 OREGON

Overhead, the white and pink gingham canopy of her childhood bed drooped from its wooden frame. She lay beneath the quilt, listened to the rain on the roof, and surveyed her old room, now aglow with dawn's first light. Hanging beside the mirror across the room, the once dewy, cream-tinted corsages from long ago proms and homecoming dances had dried to the color of swamp water. A nearly empty bottle of Wind Song perfume sat on the bedside stand, and *The Night They Burned the Mountain*, by her first idol, Dr. Tom Dooley, lay on the bookcase. Dr. Bausch was her second idol, the inspiration to become a microbiologist; Dr. Dooley was the inspiration to become a physician. She was heartbroken when he died of cancer—so young, only

247

thirty-four—and even more heartbroken when she learned of his life as a CIA spy and of the falsehoods in his books about the Viet Nam war, the books she'd admired so much. They remained on her shelf because she had buried the true version of him in the depths of her subconscious and retained her focus on the humanitarian version of him.

The butterscotch light of morning bounced off the glass cover of her old insect collection that stood on the dresser. She had fun gathering all those bugs—she had trapped some along the floorboards and windowsills of this very room—and enjoyed the challenge of figuring out their names. Beside the insect box sat the *Student's Guide to Insect Taxonomy*. In it, she'd read about arthropods' life stages and what they ate, and had learned how butterflies spin cocoons, how beetles have six legs and spiders have eight. Her goal had been to assemble the largest collection of the seventh-grade class, and she'd succeeded. One hundred forty-three specimens. For that, she'd won a science award at the end of the school year.

Sid's mother had disapproved of her daughter collecting insects. Creepy crawlies, she called them as she wrinkled her nose and said that nice girls didn't touch things like that. While Sid was wildly excited about the bug project, her mother's preference was the alternative assignment—writing an essay about how plants grow. Sid won that battle.

Today was her mother's birthday. Number sixty. What would it be like to be age sixty? It seemed old, two-thirds of a lifetime at best. The most fruitful part of life had passed by at that age, while the lonely part lay ahead. Yet there was something special about decade birthdays; sixty seemed very different from fifty-nine or sixty-one. Thirty, forty, fifty, sixty: simple even numbers divisible by ten. They were all two-syllable words, crisp and rhythmic as a trotting horse. And lively. That's how her mother should be. But she wasn't.

She wandered to the bathroom and washed her face. In the mirror, she saw reminders of her mother, and her mother's mother: the nose with the knobby tip, the way her hair turned away from its part. That grandmother, a sweet Belgian lady who spoke only French, had given Sid her name. "Ma chérie," she had sung as they rocked together in the glider chair, "Ma petite chérie, Sidonie ...." Grand-mère made up songs that rhymed with "Sidonie" and chanted in warbly tones that reminded Sid of a circus parade.

Grand-mère had a niece called Sidonie, another sweet Belgian lady who was very smart. Sid had met that Sidonie twice while visiting Brussels as a child. Aunt Sidonie was a chemist who knew how to crochet lace tablecloths.

"It's an icky name," Sid had said the day after her sixth birthday. "I want to be Jennifer or Karen, like the other girls." That had made Grand-mère cry. And then Sid felt bad. Years later, when she no longer needed to be exactly like the other girls, Sid grew fonder of her name. The greatly admired Dr. Bausch's first name, after all, was Louiselle, also uncommon, also French.

Back in the bedroom, she began to unpack her suitcase. She set her good pumps, the ones she'd wear to her mother's birthday dinner, on the floor beside the dresser, then piled her shirts on the desk and opened the closet door, looking for a hanger for her new skirt.

As a little girl, she used to sit there on the closet floor, down among the slippers and boots and stuffed animals, and squeeze her eyes shut. When that didn't work, she'd squint harder. And sometimes, if she squinted really tight, Evelien would appear. Against the black insides of her eyelids, her little sister's wispy hair sparkled in the sunlight like threads of gold. Her eyes were the blue of the sea—dusty and gray, but still blue.

Sid had tried to scrub away the salmon-colored blotch on the back of her sister's little neck. Their mother called it a stork bite, said it was where the stork's beak had picked up baby Evelien to carry her to their house, said to quit bothering it because it wouldn't wash away. Alone in the dark of the closet, Sid had watched the image of her little sister walk in her wobbly way and heard her toddler voice say "cookie" and "no" and "mine" and "Siddy"—her name for Sidonie. Evie never grew up.

Now, she pulled the desk chair to the bedroom window and, sitting, stared at the house next door. Rain that spilled over the eaves dripped like a metronome onto the bushes below.

In the silence of the room, the sounds of their mother's screams were as vivid as the day her sister died. They ripped at the air, tore through the walls. "Holy Mary, Mother of God," their mother shrieked, over and over, as she lifted Evelien from her crib and ran out the front door. That was the last time Sid saw her sister, whimpering like a wounded rabbit, pale and limp in their mother's arms.

Now the windows of the house next door were lifeless, and its stucco stained with rust streaks from the sprinkler.

Their neighbor had driven Evelien and their mother to the hospital. His wife took Sid by the hand, led her to that house out the window. She called Sid's father and gave her a glass of milk. It seemed like a grand adventure except for her mother's screams. Why was her mother screaming?

Sid moved away from the window, pulled on her jeans and

a long-sleeved shirt, and found her mother seated at the kitchen table. Her hands, bony now with age, cradled a mug.

"Tea?" her mother asked.

"I'll get it." Sid poured water from the steaming kettle into a cup and steeped a bag of Red Rose tea. Only Red Rose. No other kind for her mother. She settled into a chair beside the kitchen window. Outside, raindrops pattered on the dark green leaves of the camellia bush at the edge of the patio. Several of the buds had opened, and the blossoms, pink as strawberry ice cream, bobbed in the wind. Flowers in November. Pretty, delicate flowers at that house of unease.

"We need to celebrate your birthday. Is there anything special you'd like to do?"

"I don't like birthdays. Having you here is special enough, my dear." Her mother sipped her tea and ran her fingers through her greasy salt-and-pepper hair. The dark circles under her eyes looked like bruises. Would Sid look like that at age sixty?

"Did you hear that Becky is pregnant with twins?" her mother asked.

"No." Sid knew what was next: the comparison of the cousins. One fertile. One barren. One married. One not. One a wife and mother-to-be, the other a scientist and a doctor.

"Becky will be such a good mother. Twins are a lot of work but also a great joy." Her mother sighed and stared at Sid. "When are *you* going to be a mother? And me a grandmother?"

"Motherhood has to wait until after I get married. And that isn't in the cards anytime soon."

"Do you ever hear from Paul?"

Those words stung. "No." Before her mother could respond, Sid added, "Paul and I decided to go separate ways. You know that. Stop asking about him."

"I'm sixty. You're twenty-eight. Time for you to be married."

"You want me to get married so you can be a grandmother. That's not a reason for me to wed right now." She closed her eyes and leaned against the back of her chair. When she opened her eyes, she said, "Sometimes I wonder if you want me to have a baby to fill the emptiness in our family that emerged after Evie's death."

Her mother set her teacup on the table and stared out the kitchen window. "That's an evil thought, Sidonie."

Sid glared at the back of her mother's head, at the swirl flattened from her pillow, at the gray hairs that peppered her otherwise auburn hair. Evil thought? Another way to describe it would be an honest thought. "Where should we go for dinner?" Sid asked. "How about that new place on Hanover Road?"

Her mother, shoulders slumped like a wounded bird and head bowed with self-pity, stared past the raindrops on the window glass, past the end of the patio and the bobbing camellias, on to the far reaches of the back yard. "No, I'd rather eat at home where it's quiet."

Sid should have expected such an answer. Her mother had never liked dining out. Maybe another kind of gift. A plant? A piece of jewelry? A box of chocolates? She watched her mother tap the side of her mug with her knobby fingers and take deep, gulping breaths. The truth was that nothing—certainly no physical object—could bring happiness to her mother. Two years might be enough grieving for some widows, but not for her mom, whose losses were layered—black frosting over black cake on a black plate. First her baby daughter long ago and more recently her husband, but those two fields of grief had merged into an anguished, pervasive whole.

She wanted her mom to move on but knew she couldn't. Or wouldn't. And certainly not at her daughter's insistence. She'd tried that. How many times she had begged, reasoned, bribed, and wheedled to instill a note of joyfulness into her mother's dark world? Nothing had worked in the past, and nothing would work now. Her mother was committed to a life of mourning.

What if she also carried the gene for that debilitating affliction? If she experienced an overwhelming loss would she, too, sink into a dark hole, unable to climb out? The parting with Paul had been difficult, but she had remained functional; she continued to work, was good at her work. Now, a life of loose attachments seemed worth the price of being alone.

"Okay, I'll go to the store on my way home from Laurie's and get something for dinner. I'll cook. I insist."

Her mother smiled and nodded. "Oh, all right." Her voice was a quiet, hymn-like intonation. "Laurie? Your college roommate? Does she have any children?" Her eyes grew dull when Sid simply said no.

As Sid drove her mother's car through the streets of Pendleton, the neighborhoods looked familiar but strangely different, as they had after her little sister died. Everything then became instantly different.

Most of all, her parents, the anchors of her life, had changed. Particularly her mother. Sometimes she stayed in bed for days. Said she had a "sick headache." Said she'd eat later. Sid used to climb onto her parents' bed and snuggle against her mother's back.

"Let's play, Mama," she whispered.

"Later, sweetheart. When Mama feels better."

Sometimes she pounded on her mother's shoulders and yelled, "Get up." Other times she pulled at her mother's hair or poked her finger in her mother's ear. Then her mother would begin weeping and, in one smooth motion, shove Sidonie off the bed.

"You're mean," Sid would scream as she raced from the room.

She parked her mother's car in front of Ted and Laurie's house. Roses—these were mere sticks—were planted beside their front door. In Pendleton in November, the roses were hibernating.

Laurie gave her a hug and ushered her into the living room. Except for a different hair-do—this one was shorter, curlier—Laurie looked the same—pert, doe-eyed, calm—as when they were in college. And she seemed to have come to terms with the loss of her pregnancy. "We're still trying. Someday it'll work."

They talked about Laurie's search for a new job. "Too much politics at the old agency," she explained. "I've applied for a social work position in the Umatilla County School District. Better fit for me, I think, than hunting for nursing home beds for senile old folks." They talked about Michigan. Sid explained her research project in simple terms and told her about the lab crew.

"Eliot sounds like a creep," Laurie said.

"He is." She described the trips to Brazil, mentioned the dead babies of Promissão and Serrana and her search for the cause.

Laurie asked about Sid's mother.

"Oh, she's pretty much the same."

"I remember her as beautiful, in a dark, broody way. She had so much trouble with your little sister's death. Do you think of that much?"

Laurie's question nudged open a door to things Sid hadn't spoken of for a long time. "You know, what I remember most vividly was the neighbors' bathtub."

Fever

The night Evie died, the neighbor lady had guided little Sid up the wooden staircase to a dark hallway and then into a bedroom with filigree curtains on the windows that faced Sid's house. The ivory-colored lace bedspread was even prettier than the spread in her parents' room. "You can sleep here until your mom comes back," the neighbor lady said.

Before going to bed, Sid took a bath in the only turquoise tub she had ever seen. She thought all tubs, toilets, and bathroom sinks had to be white. In this bathroom, they were different. Funny, but pretty. The bar of soap floated in the bath water like a boat, and when Sid made waves in the silky suds with her arms, soap foam bubbled against the tub's aqua walls.

The neighbor lady helped her dry off with a towel and then slipped one of her husband's T-shirts over Sid's head. "This will work as pajamas," she said.

"I bet you were cute, with that T-shirt dangling around your ankles," Laurie said.

Sid laughed. "Maybe. Funny, the little things that stick in one's memory. The sheets on the neighbor's bed smelled like flowers, and the pillow was soft as a cloud."

But it was bedtime, and her mother wasn't there. The grand adventure had turned into something wrong. "Where's my mommy and my sister?" she had sobbed while the neighbor stroked her hair. She wanted to go home.

"They're at the hospital. The doctors there will help Evelien get better. You can stay here at my house until they come back."

"Where's my daddy?"

"He's also at the hospital. Go to sleep, now. We'll have pancakes for breakfast."

"Oh, Sid. That sounds awful." Laurie shook her head slowly.

255

"I've never heard that story before."

"It was a long time ago. I was pretty little."

"That makes it even rougher. You had no way to reconcile it all."

"It's odd that I have no memory of waking up in the neighbor's house the next morning. Nor of my parents coming home. Nor of the funeral. According to family lore, my grandparents—all four of them—came from Belgium, and aunts and uncles and cousins came from various other faraway places. I didn't go."

"That's probably appropriate. How old were you?"

"Four. Strange that all I can remember is staying at the neighbor lady's house—the bed and, particularly, her turquoise bathtub."

And she remembered her family's home. Suddenly it had become a different, and eerie, place. No more baby cries and giggles. Evie's crib and her toys, including the terry cloth stuffed kitten she called "Kiki," disappeared, and eventually her sister's bedroom had turned into a storeroom.

On the way back from Laurie's house, the dull light of the overcast afternoon filled the sky. The ominous clouds roiled behind the trees that lined the street, just as they had the day they buried her father two years ago.

Memories of the smell of her father's Aqua Velva filled the car, as did those of the coarse scratch of his tweed jackets and the silky touch of his ties when they caressed her cheek. Memories of the way he sang "Poor Jud is Dead" in the shower, his basso profundo voice piercing the bathroom door. Of their trips to the swimming pool, and the skating rink, and the toboggan slide, and then later to concerts in the park, and to the farms along the river.

He had worried about her, didn't understand why she wanted

to go to medical school. "Don't you want to be a wife?" he asked, his gentle voice almost breaking with concern. He had even set up that bank account for her wedding. "When you find the right man, you need to have a lovely wedding," he said. "A beautiful dress, lots of flowers, a band, a huge cake—the whole works."

Dreams of an expensive wedding did not fill her mind. Ever. Not even when she was dating Paul. She had wondered then, vaguely, about marriage—a small and simple ceremony, maybe—but those thoughts dissipated when she moved to Michigan. And subsequently, she never thought of weddings of any kind. Visions of her future centered on completing her fellowship training and then working as a physician and a scientist.

The twenty thousand dollars in the wedding account was a lot of money. She planned to leave it—what was left after that second trip to Brazil—in the bank and let it grow. Maybe someday she'd use it to take a tour around the world or give it to her medical school for a student scholarship.

She pulled the car to a stop in front of the grocery store. This was the hour to think of birthdays, not weddings.

While the potato gratin and the ginger-and-orange-smothered chicken baked in the oven, and her mother napped, Sid lay on her bed and stared, once again, at the pink gingham canopy overhead. She tried to think pleasant thoughts: the camellia blossoms, the Red Rose tea, the meal ahead. But her thoughts kept drifting to Brazil. To the dead children. And their parents. And Cibele. And River.

She wondered what was happening in the lab. Raven would be worrying about her Ph.D. thesis, and Eliot would be bossing everyone around.

"Go," Raven had said when Sid hesitated about the trip to Oregon. "Your mother will appreciate your visit. Sixty is a landmark." At first, Sid thought Raven had said sixty is a land mine. It's that, too, she decided.

She phoned Raven.

"Is it warm there?" Raven asked. "It's ice-cube cold and blustery here."

Sid stared out the window. "Chilly and rainy. But the camellias are blooming." She told her about the birthday dinner she was cooking. "We'll have Willamette Valley pinot noir. From a vineyard about seventy miles from Portland."

"Cake?"

"Of course. It's a birthday. I bought a chocolate cake from the bakery. I had them put six candles on it. One candle equals ten years. Sixty candles would bring out the fire department."

"Sounds yummy. I'll be right over," Raven laughed. "Should I bring Eliot?"

"No."

A pan rattled in the kitchen. Her mother was up from her nap. Time to finish the dinner. She said goodbye to Raven and headed out her bedroom door, hoping her gloom would stay stuffed in the corner of the room or, even better, disappear altogether.

"I should tell you about Brazil," Sid said. She poured herself a cup of tea and sat at the kitchen table.

Her mother lowered herself into the chair opposite Sid. "How was it?"

"It's a beautiful country. Full of beautiful people." Sid didn't explain that the recent trip to Brazil was actually her second. All that was too complicated.

"It's so far away." Her mother sipped her tea.

She didn't tell her mother about the dying kids in Promissão and Serrana, either. That would set off memories of Evie and send her into another downward spiral.

"It's spring down there. Balmy. We stayed with Raven's brother." Enough about that.

Her mother nodded. It was an absentminded nod. "Sometimes, I wonder what drives you so hard."

"It doesn't feel like I'm driving hard. It feels like I'm solving mysteries—scientific mysteries." It was that old ambition thing again. Its gray shadow of accusation seemed to follow her wherever she went.

"Are you trying to prove something to someone? Your father and I were proud of you no matter what. You've always been like that. Racing like a madman toward whatever goal you were chasing."

"To me it feels like working to succeed. Nothing wrong with that."

"I guess not. I just hope you're happy while running that race." Her mother became silent. Then she said, "The chicken must be done."

After dinner, her mother read the day's *Pendleton Record* while Sid paged through an outdated copy of *Time* magazine. Across the room, an old family photo stood on the fireplace mantle. In it, Sid's mother wore a pillbox hat with a net across her face that almost covered her smile, and Sid was perched on her grinning father's lap, her Mary-Jane shoes dangling between his calves. Evelien, wrapped in a baby blanket, lay in their mother's arms.

As a little girl, Sid had asked about the sickness that took

Evie to live with the angels. About the shaking and the purple patches on her legs.

"It was caused by a bad germ," her father had explained. "The germ got inside Evelien and made her very, very sick. So sick the doctors couldn't make her better."

"Will that happen to me?" she asked.

Her father's face slumped, and his eyes grew misty. "Oh, my little darling ..." He rubbed his cheeks with his big, thick hands and said, "No, Sidonie, that won't happen to you." Still, she kept inspecting her legs, waiting for the purple spots to appear.

What did the bad germs look like? Where did they come from? Why did they get inside her little sister? And how? In third grade, she looked up the word "germ" in the dictionary at school and sounded out the strange words as she read them: "a small mass of living substance capable of developing into an organism or one of its parts."

She set her finger against the word "substance." "What's this?" she asked her teacher.

Her teacher looked confused and then smiled. "Well, it means matter. Something you can feel or smell or see. You're looking up the meaning of "germ?"

Sid nodded.

Her teacher knelt down and took her hand. "Sidonie, a germ is a tiny, tiny creature that we can't see, and sometimes it makes us sick."

"It made my little sister go to Heaven."

The tears that welled in her teacher's eyes scared Sid. So did the teacher's embrace. Had she made her teacher cry?

For years, germs seemed to live just beyond her reach. They were always there, always on her mind, but she couldn't manage to tame them, or at least tame the thoughts of them. When the announcer on the radio talked about germs in the lake water, and when her uncle told them about germs in the cesspool, she thought about Evelien. She learned that germs caused colds and made her mother's sweet rolls rise. Beer foamed because of germs. Mold that rimmed the cream cheese in the open package at the back of the fridge was germs. But what did the blue-green fuzz on the cheese have to do with Evie's sickness?

The subject of her tenth-grade science-fair project was germs. Her biology teacher brought a stack of agar-filled Petri dishes to class, and Sid planted her palm on one dish and ten of her friends did the same on the other dishes. As her teacher instructed, she stored her Petri dishes in the oven at home, kept its light on for heat. After two days, little dots appeared on the surface of the agar. As the dots grew larger over the next week, she could see that they weren't all alike. There were seven or eight kinds, some gray, some pale yellow, some pure white. Which kind had made Evie sick? On her poster for the science-fair display, she had written that one germ from her palm had reproduced into many, many germs to form one dot on the agar. She described how germs caused bad infections, like pneumonia, impetigo, meningitis, and septicemia. That's what Evie had: septicemia.

"What are you thinking about?" her mother asked. They sat at opposite ends of the sofa, Sid fixing her broken bracelet, her mother crocheting a placemat.

"The day Evie died."

"Oh, God, Sidonie." She lay her crocheting in her lap. "Don't do that to me."

"Don't talk about my little sister? I have so many questions about her that have never been answered."

"We're not going to talk about her."

"Yes, we are. We should. What were you doing when I found her?"

Her mother picked up her crochet hook and began to loop the thread. Her eyes were on her needlework as she spoke. "I was cooking dinner in the kitchen. You were in your bedroom and heard her moans. You yelled to me that she sounded funny."

"Right. When I got to her crib, her face was all twisted like a monster. I think now that she was having a seizure."

Her mother continued to crochet even faster than before.

"You know, Mom, if Evie had lived, you could better understand that it's okay for me to be who I am. Evie would be her own woman, too. Maybe a historian or a pilot or an actress. Who knows, but she'd be different from me, and from you, just as I am different from you."

"Stop it, Sidonie."

"Mom, I want to know about her. All I have are vague childhood memories. I want to hear about the beautiful little girl that she must have been."

Her mother shook her head and muffled deep, gasping sobs with her palms. "I can't."

22

1985 MASSACHUSETTS

Their cab from the airport darted like a nervous moth back and forth across the crowded city streets before jerking to a stop six inches behind a fruit truck. Sid slid forward against her shoulder strap and braced her arms on the back of the seat ahead. An idiot is at the wheel, she thought, and wondered if they'd get to the hotels intact. Dr. Evans, beside her in the back seat, also slammed forward. Eliot, riding shotgun, gripped the dashboard. The taxi driver jolted upright, clenched the steering wheel, cranked down his window, leaned his head out, and yelled to the guy unloading boxes of apples, "Get outta the fuckin' road."

Dr. Evans muttered, "Welcome to Boston." Eliot laughed. Sid winced.

Three blocks later, their taxi pulled to a stop at the Forrester-Handler Suites, and Dr. Evans stepped out. After paying for the ride, he carried his suitcase into the hotel's revolving glass doors. As the president of the society, he had exclusive accommodations.

Four blocks and twenty minutes later, the cab stopped in front of the Ambassador Hotel. Sid and Eliot gathered their bags from the trunk and headed for the door. Eliot said, "You're bunking with Francesca Fungus, right? When's she arriving?"

He was acting like a teenager. Fran Fullini was a graduate student in mycology, studying the cell walls of fungi. "She's not coming because she has to go to her grandmother's funeral in Arizona." At the hotel door, she added, "We had Dr. Evans's new secretary change our reservation from a double room to a single."

The bell captain held open the door and greeted them with a smile. Sid headed to the front desk. "Dr. Sidonie Royal," she said to the clerk. "I have a reservation for three nights." Eliot stood in line behind her.

The clerk tapped on the computer's keyboard and stared at the screen. She tapped again. "Oh, there it is. Dr. Sid Royal?"

"Yes."

"Okay, Dr. Royal." The woman frowned at her and then gazed again at her screen. "I see you're sharing a room with Dr. Eliot Mitchell."

"Oh, heavens no," Sid gasped. "There's been a mistake." She leaned her elbows on the reception desk. "The reservation was originally for me to share a room with Dr. Francesca Fullini, but she had to cancel, so our secretary called to reserve the room for just me."

The clerk looked at her screen again. "Well, it says here the reservation is for one room, two beds, for Dr. Sid Royal and Dr. Eliot Mitchell."

Eliot stepped up to the desk beside her. His jacket sleeve brushed against her coat sleeve. "I'm Dr. Mitchell. Dr. Royal and I are friends, but not the kind that share a hotel room. You'll have to find us separate rooms."

The clerk's fingers fumbled on the keyboard. "I'm sorry, sir. With the big convention this week, we are completely full."

"I need to speak with the manager, then," Sid said.

"Yes, ma'am." The clerk disappeared behind a door.

Eliot drummed his fingertips against the reception desk. "How could they mess it up so badly ..."

"New secretary," Sid said.

Eliot sighed. "Yeah, that's probably it."

Finally, the clerk reappeared, followed by a young man in a stiff, gray suit. His name tag read "David, MANAGER."

"I'm terribly sorry, sir."

The manager spoke directly to Eliot and ignored Sid. She'd let it go, for now. She just wanted to get to her room.

"I'm sure you can understand that Boston is very busy with the convention, and our hotel is completely booked," David the Manager said. "I suspect most of the other hotels are also full."

"I have a confirmed reservation, so you need to find me a room." She pulled a paper from her folder and thrust it toward him.

Eliot passed his reservation confirmation to the manager. The man held them side by side and twisted his mouth. "Okay." He elbowed the clerk aside and began tapping on the keyboard. "I certainly don't understand what happened here." He kept tapping. He scratched his ear and tapped some more. Finally, he looked up from the screen. "I see we have a cancellation for the Diplomatic Suite, and it will be vacant for the next three nights. It has two bedrooms and a living room. Would that work for the two of you? At no extra cost, of course."

"What's the bathroom situation in the Diplomatic Suite?" Sid needed her own.

"Each bedroom has its own lavatory, and there is also one in the entry to the living room."

She turned and looked at Eliot. "What do you think? Sounds like it's either that, or one of us sleeps on the street."

"Fine with me."

"What's fine, on the street or in the suite?" she asked.

"The suite."

"So then it's set?" the manager asked. "You'll both take the suite?"

"Yes." She and Eliot spoke in unison. He smiled at her. She shrugged and smiled back.

It was likely they wouldn't see much of each other—they would spend all day, every day at meeting sessions and dinners with old friends—so the suite would work as long as he didn't pester her about her presentation. If she showed it to him there at the convention, he'd suggest she change at least half the slides.

They rode the elevator to the eleventh floor. Eliot opened the door to their suite and walked in. "Oh, boy," he called. "This is swanky."

She carried her suitcase into the living room. It was indeed elegant. Four overstuffed chairs flanked a huge couch, and a vase of fresh flowers stood on the coffee table. Heavy drapes with sheer curtains covered the windows; wall sconces hung on either side of a large still-life painting of a book, a pen, a bunch of lilies, and an ink pot above a sideboard cabinet; and a sliding glass door opened to a balcony. She had never stayed in so grand a hotel room.

Someone knocked on the door. Eliot opened it. A hotel employee strode into the room carrying a basket of pears, bananas, chocolate bonbons, and grapes. "For your pleasure," he said and set it on the sideboard. He disappeared out the door and reappeared in a moment with a bottle of wine in a silver ice bucket.

Sid pulled a card from the fruit basket. It read, "Please accept our apology for the confusion with your reservations. Ambassador Hotel Management." "David" was scribbled at the bottom in green ink. She handed the card to Eliot. He laughed.

Left or right? She walked into the bedroom to the left. Six throw pillows lay on the bed, and a down quilt was folded on a bench at its foot. "Okay if I take this one?" she called.

"Sure." He headed into the other bedroom.

As promised, her room had its own bathroom as well as a walk-in closet. She opened her suitcase on the luggage rack, hung her clothes on the padded hangers, and stacked her underwear in the top dresser drawer. She glanced at her watch. The opening plenary talk would begin in a half-hour in the convention center, but first she had to get her badge from the meeting registration area. As she wandered through the living room and out the door to the hallway, she heard the toilet flush from Eliot's room. This will be weird, she thought.

The next morning, her alarm rang at six-thirty, and she was dressed and ready to find breakfast at seven o'clock. She opened the door from her bedroom and crossed the living room carpet. Eliot's door was closed, and she thought she heard his shower running. Should she wait for him for breakfast? No, she decided, and headed toward the elevator and into the rest of her day.

That evening, nestled in the club chair in her bedroom, she rested her feet on the hassock and started reading the latest issue of the *Journal of Bacteriology.* She heard the door to the suite open and then a rap on her door. "You home?" Eliot asked.

"Yeah."

The door was slightly ajar, and he pushed it open a bit further. "Want to practice your talk tonight? I'll be happy to listen."

She set the journal on her lap. As far as she was concerned, her talk was complete. She wasn't interested in edits from him. And for sure, he'd want to edit. "I can't change any of the slides now," she said.

"I know. I promise I won't suggest any big changes that would need revised slides. I just thought you might want to practice—you know, pacing, timing, transitions, that kind of stuff. A rehearsal might help with the jitters, too."

She tossed the options back and forth in her mind. True, practice was a good idea; it could smooth the talk and build her confidence. Yet she knew Eliot couldn't restrain himself when it came to making suggestions. Still, a last-minute run-through would be useful. "Okay. If you promise to enjoy it rather than critique it."

"Promise."

She handed him paper copies of the slides, sat on the couch in the living room, and spread her notes on the coffee table.

"Stand up," Eliot said. "Make it as much like the real deal as possible."

She hadn't even started giving the talk, and he already had a suggestion. She didn't acknowledge that standing was a good idea but arranged her notes on the sideboard and stood facing him.

She began with the background information on the BPF project, then described her bacterial killing experiments, how human serum killed the control bacteria but not the BPF strain.

"That was my serum, right?" he said.

"You interrupted."

"Sorry. Continue."

She described the results of the infant rat experiments, how infection with the BFP strain killed most of the rats but the control strain didn't.

"In conclusion," she said, "these results present a possible explanation for the virulence of the BPF bacteria among infected children in Promissão, Brazil. Experiments using additional disease strains will be necessary to confirm our findings."

Eliot applauded. "That was great. You made it sound as if you were telling a story—a logical, well-organized story with a very satisfying ending. This is important stuff, Sidonie. Congratulations, you're all set for a nice presentation."

What had gotten into Eliot? She'd never heard such an effusive compliment from him. He didn't merely say it was good, but he used words like logical. And well-organized. And satisfying ending.

The next day, following the introduction of her presentation by the session leader, Sid climbed the steps to the platform and set her notes on the lectern. She scanned the room. The chairs were all occupied. Eliot leaned against the back wall.

She began by describing, briefly, the outbreak in Promissão. On the background slide, she had included a photo Raven had taken of the clinic. Her hand trembled when she pushed the slide advancer; she hoped her voice sounded steady. She explained her hypothesis that BPF bacteria somehow resisted being killed by blood and, thus, were able to cause serious infections. She showed slides of the methods, detailing the killing assays and the rat experiments, then flicked the advancer to the tables of the results. Now her hand hardly trembled at all. She had practiced the talk so much that it moved along as if blown by a gentle breeze.

After she finished her last slide and thanked the audience, the applause was enthusiastic. The man with the first question complimented her on an excellent presentation and asked a simple question. The second and third questions, too, were easy for her to answer. The fourth question wasn't really a question. Rather, it was a comment on the importance of her work in the world's ongoing quest to understand how bacteria cause disease. She smiled at the audience and glanced toward the back of the room at Eliot. His face was in a shadow, but she thought she saw him smile. This was so different from his no-show in Amsterdam.

She took her seat in the front row and felt a tap on her shoulder. The man behind her leaned forward and whispered, "Very nice presentation." She nodded. It felt as if she were royalty, wrapped in ermine, perched on a throne with a crown on her head, and surrounded by armloads of roses.

Toward the end of the afternoon, the late-breaker abstracts—those submitted after the regular deadline and judged by the organizers to be important enough for special consideration—were about to be presented. She contemplated going back to her hotel room rather than sitting through more talks, but, in the end, she decided to attend the epidemiology late-breaker session.

She took a seat in the auditorium and spotted Eliot across the room. She looked over the program. Her eye caught on the third speaker: Dr. Karla Geiger. The title read, "Outbreak of a Fatal Infection among Children in Serrana, Brazil." She read it again. Her head began to spin. Then, her stomach felt queasy. She heard nothing of the first two late-breaker talks.

Karla Geiger climbed the steps to the podium. In her clipped, German-accented words, she described the outbreak in Serrana. Thirteen children had been infected. Ten of them died. "Blood cultures from all thirteen grew *Haemophilus influenzae,* and unlike other pathogenic *Haemophilus* strains that cause serious infections in children, this virulent strain lacked a polysaccharide capsule."

That was it. The GHA had succeeded. They had identified the cause of the infections. And as expected, the bacteria were unusual. Very unusual. The GHA had thirteen strains; she had one. The next part of Karla's talk was a blur. Something about the biochemical features of the Serrana strains. She showed a photo of the pulsed field gel electrophoresis. All thirteen strains had identical fingerprints. Sid stared at the slide in disbelief. They had won. They found the Holy Grail. She wanted to race from the room but would have had to crawl over five people in her row to reach the aisle. She shut her eyes and bowed her head and took deep breaths.

"In conclusion," Karla said, "We have demonstrated that non-encapsulated *H. influenzae* is the cause of an outbreak of a mysterious, fatal infection among children in Brazil. All thirteen children studied in this outbreak were infected with the identical *H. influenzae* strain, which lacked its major pathogenic factor—a polysaccharide capsule. Studies are underway to understand why this usually non-invasive strain became so virulent."

Karla thanked the audience to a rush of applause. Sid left the auditorium as fast as she could, pushed past the other members of the audience, and walked out the convention center door into the wintery air of the late afternoon.

23

1985 MASSACHUSETTS

It was deep into the night when Sid returned to the hotel. For the past seven hours, she had walked the streets around the convention center. Distracted by her thoughts, she stepped over, and almost into, the open, coin-filled violin case of a street musician. When she stopped for a moment in an art gallery, she found the paintings jarring; the large purple or yellow or red triangles and pentagons were too bright, too angular. She'd wandered past a bagel shop, a shoe repair shop, a bridal shop, and a drugstore. Passing a bicycle shop, she caught a glimpse of herself in the darkened window. The image of a miserable old woman reflected off the glass. Unthinking, she'd ambled through an alley and, upon exiting the other end, realized the possible danger. She didn't care.

Now she wanted to go to bed. Sleep would carry her far away, to a different place, free of Karla and the GHA and BPF and experiments and presentations. If, that is, she could get to sleep. She rode the elevator alone to the eleventh floor and then meandered slowly down the empty hallway. She unlocked the door to the suite and stepped into the entry. The lamps in the living room were turned off, and the door to Eliot's bedroom was closed. She saw no rim of light beneath his door. He must be asleep. Or still out, partying with his buddies.

As she strode toward her bedroom, she saw, from the corner of her eye, something move near the couch. She stopped and stared through the dark.

"Hello, Sidonie." It was Eliot. She blinked to adjust her eyes to the shadows and could now see that he was sitting on the sofa, his feet propped on the coffee table.

"Hello," she said.

"Where have you been? It's late. I was a little worried about you."

Eliot worried? About her? About anything? "Wandering the streets. Trying to forget Karla's presentation."

"Forgetting will be tough to do." .

"I know." She threw her purse on the chair beside her.

"We shouldn't be surprised by it. You knew the GHA was in Serrana, tracking more cases. And collecting strains."

"Yeah, I knew."

"Do you mind if I turn on a light?" he asked. "Are you all right?"

"Go ahead with the light. I'm adjusting to the disappointment."

He stood up and switched on the reading lamp beside one

of the overstuffed chairs. Its dim light was as bright as she could tolerate.

He started to sit down in the chair but stopped. "Say," he said, "did you drink that wine from the management? The bottle the bellman brought when we first arrived?"

"No."

He headed toward the sideboard. "Where'd it go?"

"I put it in the fridge."

He opened the refrigerator door and pulled out the bottle. "We should celebrate your talk. It really was terrific."

She wanted to scream at him, to shriek until her voice gave out. Her excellent talk had no meaning now. Karla's results had completely overpowered the importance of her own work. The GHA had obtained thirteen strains from Serrana, and they didn't share. She would not be able to study a single one of them. But Eliot wasn't to blame for that.

He began twisting the corkscrew into the cork. "Want some?"

She didn't want to eat or drink anything ever again. She shook her head. Then she changed her mind. What the hell. "Sure," she said.

He handed her a glass. "Cheers." He hoisted his goblet into the air.

As she took the first sip, she heard sirens. Screaking and oscillating, the sounds seemed to grow louder, meaning they were getting closer. And closer yet. Then they stopped, and red lights pulsed across the sheers that covered the windows.

Eliot walked to the sliding glass door, pulled aside the curtains, and stared down at the sidewalk. "Someone else is having a bad day," he said.

She didn't care about anyone else's bad day. She took another sip of the wine. It was good, crisp with a hint of fruit. She took another sip.

Eliot's body was silhouetted against the darkened glass. His shirt was untucked, and his sleeves rolled up to his elbows. Beyond him, lights from the surrounding buildings twinkled in the night-time. He took a drink of his wine and continued to stare down at the commotion on the sidewalk. More sirens cut the silence.

She joined him at the window. Firemen were hauling hoses into the building across the street. No smoke. No flames that she could see. Still, something must have been burning. A police car screamed to a stop, and two cops raced away from the cruiser.

Eliot slid open the glass door and stepped out onto the balcony. She leaned on the door frame, felt the cool night breeze against her face.

"Reminds me of the fire at my grandmother's house when I was a boy," he said.

She stepped out onto the balcony, stood beside him at the railing. He told her how sparks from the fireplace had jumped into a pile of kindling. By the time anyone noticed, the living room wall was burning. Neighbors set up a bucket brigade from the kitchen sink to the flames while his grandmother, her hands over her face, rocked back and forth on her feet and cried.

"Sounds scary," she said.

"It was. No one was hurt. We stayed with my cousins until the wall was repaired." He drained his wine glass. "I was most worried about my cat, Henry. When it was all over, we found him quaking among the boots in the back hallway."

Another fire truck arrived. Then an ambulance. "More wine?" he asked.

She nodded. He retrieved the bottle from the sideboard, filled her glass, and set the bottle on the balcony railing.

As she stood beside him in the cool night, the heat of his body stretched to her body, and she smelled the spicy, tangy scent of his hair. It was the same odor she had smelled when they examined lab results together. That was different, though. Very different. Then the air was filled with competing microbiology smells, and the room thumped with the sounds of science. Now, it was quiet except for the sirens, and they were alone.

She began to weep and dabbed her eyes with her sleeve.

For decades into the future, she couldn't explain what happened next. What had come over her? Over him?

His arm slipped around her shoulders. She tightened for a moment—it was merely an instant of hesitation—then relaxed against his chest, against the strength and soul that was Eliot. Would she ever truly understand him? Right then she didn't care. The sanctuary of his warmth and tenderness, of him, were all that mattered. The red lights from the fire trucks throbbed across their faces from the street below. His lips touched her forehead. Her fingertips caressed his cheek, felt the scratch of his whiskers. Together they moved back into the living room to the couch.

They sat side by side, hand in hand, as another emergency vehicle—fire truck? police car? ambulance?—arrived with sirens screaming. The ruckus outside seemed a world away. She couldn't think of anything to say. She wanted to savor the strange but precious moment, to make it last a long time. She took another sip of chardonnay. Finally, he said, "Sid, your talk was really terrific. No matter what Karla presented. I'm very proud of you."

She sighed, wished he hadn't mentioned Karla, then brightened. "Do you realize that you just called me Sid? That's a first."

So was the kiss that followed.

"Sidonie is an interesting name," he said. "You don't hear it every day."

"It was a gift from my Belgian parents. French Belgian."

"Fits you well. Unique, mysterious, feminine, and a bit remote."

"Mysterious? Remote?"

"Yeah. You are indeed mysterious. It's hard to know what propels you. And you keep yourself at a distance. But you're not as remote now as you were a half-hour ago."

She wasn't sure how long they sat there together. The fire trucks eventually rumbled away. The noise from the gawkers on the sidewalk faded. Was it an hour? Three hours?

Finally, he said, "I'm going up to Castine, Maine, tomorrow for a little break before returning to Michigan. Come along."

She leaned away from him and stared into his eyes. Had he said what she thought?

"Please come. I'd like that a lot," he said.

Was he really asking her to join him in Maine? She started to laugh, a gentle rivulet of mirth. She snuggled against his chest. "This is so very strange, Eliot." More than anything else right then, she wanted to go to Maine with him. To another faraway place. A quiet, serene place. "Yes, I'll come."

He pulled her closer. She felt his heartbeat through his shirt, felt his cheek against her forehead. He stroked her arm. She rubbed the back of his neck for what seemed like a long, delicious time.

24

1985 MAINE

Was it mist, or was it rain? The wet, foggy air clung like a velvety film to Sid's cheeks as she and Eliot strolled down the road toward the lighthouse. His hand was warm, its skin softer than she would have expected. She squeezed his fingers slightly, he squeezed hers back. To their left, beyond the grassy field of the old Fort Madison and down the shallow cliff, the waters of Otter Rock shoal slammed against the shore.

"What were you like as a little boy?" she asked. He was the child who took trumpet lessons and whose mother hadn't been around to be bothered by the noise. Where had she gone? What had that done to him?

"I was a pesky kid. One of my first memories is my

grandmother's house in Scotland, the casement windows and stone walls, the candy dish she kept on the table in the living room, the waters of the Firth of Lorn not far away. I hid from Grandma when she announced it was bedtime. Once, I picked almost all her green tomatoes and, shortly after that, I painted her white picket gate with mud. I lived there from the time Mother left until I was five and my father could take me to live with him in South Africa."

His words were gentle, his voice dreamy. This was a side of Eliot she hadn't known.

"Sometimes, I played with matchbox cars under conference room tables while my diplomat dad attended late-night meetings in Pretoria. I remember falling asleep beneath Dad's jacket on banquette benches in smoky restaurants, lulled by the din of mumbly conversation. Then we moved to Washington D.C. Then Amsterdam. Then San Francisco. It felt as if we were chasing something. And we never caught it."

"Where'd she go? Your mom?" She spoke in a whisper, didn't want to disturb the quiet of his story.

He picked up a stone from the middle of the road and sent it skittering into the weeds. He looked at the place it landed and then looked at her. "When I asked my grandmother, she told me not to think about it. My dad was more expansive. He said Mother just disappeared, and they didn't know why or where she landed." In his still voice, she heard the desolate plea of that poor, lonely little boy with no mother.

"What was she like?" She tried to imagine a female Eliot, an older, maternal version of him, and drew a blank.

"I understand she was a poet and a beautiful woman. Dad said she had wild eyes, and her hair was toasty brown, like mine.

Whenever Dad spoke of her, he said she was very unhappy about leaving a great lad like me. Said she loved me very much, but the furies inside her head pulled her away from us."

They walked slowly. The lighthouse was ahead, beyond a clump of trees.

"I often wondered about her furies. I thought they were because of me, that something I had done had wounded her deeply and sent her away. Finally, the weekend after I graduated from high school, I demanded that my father tell me why she left. He told me demons spoke to her, and she couldn't ignore them. He said, 'They told her to go far, far away to places where Druids dance on falling raindrops, where wizards ride on lightning bolts.' Her doctors told Dad she had schizophrenia."

Schizophrenia. She had cared for such patients, those who believed that unreal things were real and were afraid of strange sounds that no one else could hear. She squeezed Eliot's hand again, trying to magically sooth the fallout that his mother's hallucinations, those insistent voices from the other world, must have had on him. She knew it was fairytale thinking on her part, but she wanted to convey a measure of peace to him.

"I didn't remember her face, but when I was little, I could still hear her singing. Sometimes, it sounded like a silver bell. Sometimes like a haunting violin. At least, I thought I heard her singing. Maybe it was just the wind in the bushes."

She nestled against his arm, wanted him to know she, unlike his mother, was there. She remained silent, didn't want to shatter the reverence of the moment.

They continued toward the lighthouse. From a distance, it looked like a white papier-mâché cone with a shining obsidian jewel on top. When they walked the path to the back of the keeper's house, they passed a sign that warned of unstable ground and sat on a bench beside a patch of dried chrysanthemums in the sloping yard.

"How about *your* childhood?" Eliot asked. He slipped his arm around her shoulders. She leaned closer against him.

Where should she start? With her parents moving from Belgium to Oregon before she was born? With her happy memories: playing in the sandbox in the backyard, swinging in the playground, dressing her doll Margeaux in pretty clothes? With the dark, lonely days that overshadowed the pleasant ones? There wasn't an easy place to begin.

She started talking about her father, explained that he was a kind, fun-loving man who took her ice skating in the winter and swimming in the summer. She told him about her little sister's death. And about her melancholy mother who spent days at a time in bed.

She stood up and led Eliot back to the road. She spoke of science club trips when she was in high school, of hearing Dr. Bausch tell of the mysteries of bacteria. She told him about her father's death and kept talking until they reached the city wharf back in Castine.

That night, they lay together in bed under one of the dormers at the Pentagoet Inn. Eliot stroked her hair and asked, "Should we talk about your research project?"

"No." She stared at the ceiling. "Not yet."

Muted words of the song "Twelfth of Never" from the house next door wafted past their window with the breeze. She turned toward him and kissed the warm, tender spot on his neck.

The next noon, they ate lunch at the restaurant on the city dock. The lobster rolls were gooey but good, while the chilly draft off the water nipped at her cheeks and smelled like outdated fish. She tied her scarf tighter under her chin.

Eliot took a swallow of his beer. "While I was in Boston, I met with Jim Henry again."

She remembered. He was the head of microbiology at Minnesota. Eliot's earlier meeting with that man was the reason he had missed her presentation in Amsterdam. Seemed like a long time ago. The thought of it used to make her skin crawl. No longer. Now it was merely a disappointing fact.

"The job is still open there, and he really wants me to come. The offer is terrific. Lots of lab space, a sizable start-up package. What do you think? Should I take it?"

Why was he asking her? Did he need her approval to accept the job at Minnesota? Obviously not. Was he suggesting she might have a part in his future work after he left the Evans lab? That wasn't her plan. She had worked with him long enough to know that continuing would be a bad idea. She tried to read his mind. His face was impassive. "It's your decision, Eliot. You definitely are ready for a faculty position, and the one in Minnesota sounds like a good fit for you."

"I think so, too. I value your opinion about these things. You're a smart and sensible woman."

She took another bite of her lobster roll. Was he saying that he admired her rationality and level-headed judgment? Or that he was fond of her personally and admired her in a caring, kindhearted way? Those were two different things, and she wanted both. She hoped she wasn't a fool for that.

"You asked last night if I was ready to talk about my research.

I'm more ready now." She laid the roll on her plate and took a drink of water. "Obviously, the BPF project—at least my part in it—is over. I simply can't make any meaningful progress without additional strains. And the GHA won't share the ones they've acquired."

He looked down at his plate and then back up at her. "I'm afraid you're right about that. I wish it weren't true, but it is. As I said, you're a sensible woman."

"I can publish the work I ... rather we ... have done, and it will easily fulfill the research requirement for my fellowship. After that ..." She poked her fork into the pile of lobster on her plate. "... I just don't know. By the time I've finalized the experiments and written up the papers and finished the clinical part of the program, my fellowship will be over and I, too, will be looking for a job."

The thought of abandoning the BPF project opened a wide, bottomless chasm beneath her. She couldn't imagine mornings, afternoons, and evenings without BPF as her guide. After all those hours, all the work, all the angst—to just walk away? It was unthinkable. Yet that was what she had to do. The explanation for the deadly nature of the BPF strain was still a terribly compelling question. Maybe someone somewhere would figure it out. She couldn't without more strains. There were other, equally interesting scientific questions out there. She just needed to find them.

"You could continue to pursue your endotoxin idea." Eliot's eyes were intense as they stared into her face. "The GHA won't be smart enough to think of that as a possible virulence factor."

"Maybe. I don't know what I'll do."

"I really hope you continue to do research, Sidonie. You're a natural, with your innate curiosity, your intelligence, your logical approach to problems, your willingness to work hard, your ... ah ... persistence."

"Were you about to say 'stubbornness?'" She chuckled. She knew she was single-minded. She had trouble letting go of important things. Was that bad?

He laughed. "Well, call it what you like, persistence has kept you firmly on track."

The last morning of their visit in Castine, the sun blanketed their breakfast table in shimmering golden beams, and a gull landed on the porch railing outside the window. The bird twisted his head from side to side and then stared at them through the glass. He squawked twice and flew off toward the sea.

The innkeeper refilled their coffee cups and set a ramekin of cheese soufflé in front of each of them. They would have to leave shortly after breakfast to get to the Boston airport in time for their flight back to Michigan. She looked around the room at the soothing colors, at the period furnishings that oozed comfort. Out the window, the ripples on the water glistened in the sun. Before this trip, she had never eaten breakfast while overlooking the ocean. The rhythm of the waves had a calming appeal.

"Eliot," she said, "why did you ask me to join you here?" Hopefully his answer would settle some of her uncertainties about him. Did she want to alter her future plans to fit his? She didn't think so. If that was what he wanted, did it matter to her? She wasn't sure.

He tilted his head at the question and didn't answer right away. "Well, you were so very devastated after that last session at the conference. Karla Geiger's presentation was a terrible kick in the gut. I thought returning immediately to the lab wouldn't be good for you. Are you glad you came?"

"Yes. Very much."

"And," he continued, "I've been to Castine before. It's one of my favorite places to relax, and I wanted company. Your company." He took a bite of his omelet and stared out the window for a moment. "Why did you agree to come?"

She liked the question, had to think about the answer. It was complicated. How much should she share with him? Particularly when she didn't understand it all herself. She folded her napkin into a small square and then unfolded it. "You're right that Karla's talk was devastating. It dashed my research dreams to smithereens in fifteen short minutes." She sipped at her coffee. "In my soul, I knew what the GHA was doing and how it would impact our project. I just didn't want to believe it was true. Now, of course, I *know* it's true. I'll deal with that, but not right now." She sipped at her coffee again. "I guess I was looking for an escape, and fleeing it all with you seemed the right thing to do."

"An escape?"

"Yes, Eliot. Running away with you was absolutely right."

25

1985 MICHIGAN

The lab seemed like a foreign country after Eliot left. For Sid, a giant hole had been blown open in its soul, leaving the place empty, bereft of its lifeblood. The sounds had changed: his commanding, booming voice was replaced by Raven's mutterings, and his clompy footfalls replaced by more gentle steps. Now there were no more opinions from the oracle, no more arguments with him. The sights, too, had changed. No more stealth appearances from Eliot, no sightings of his imposing frame lumbering between the lab benches. Dr. Evans had ordered Eliot's cardboard box bunker dismantled in anticipation of the new postdoc's arrival.

The leaves on the trees outside the lab windows were at their peak fall colors, and the late afternoon sunlight daubed touches of honey on their reds, oranges, and yellows. The phone rang.

"Hey, Sidonie." It was Eliot. "Check out this month's *Preliminary Communications in Bacteriology*. It just arrived in Minnesota today. You'll be very interested in it."

"Don't be coy with me. What's in it?" Same old Eliot.

"The GHA has published the DNA fingerprints of their Serrana strains."

"Really?" She was dumbstruck. They sent out a preliminary communication rather than a final, complete paper? They must feel pressured to publish.

"Yes, really. Dig out that fingerprint analysis you did on the BPF strain and compare the patterns."

At first, she prickled at his suggestion. Once again, he was telling her what to do. But the identical thought had tracked through her mind as he spoke. That was the obvious next step, a grab for the golden ring.

"Absolutely," she said. "I'd bet my car they are alike. So when I prove that endotoxin explains our BPF strain's deadliness, I can assume—or at least make a strong case—that the endotoxin explains the deadliness of all the strains."

"Bingo. One correction ..."

Now what? Eliot always had the last word.

"Please say 'my BPF strain' rather than 'our BPF strain.' It's yours, Sidonie, and you deserve all the credit."

Within an hour, Sid had photocopied the GHA paper from the journal in the library and compared the pictures with those from *her* BPF strain. Their fingerprints, those ladders of DNA fragments that were unique to each strain, were identical. She called Eliot. "That's the missing link I need to proceed. I'm working on experiments to show that the endotoxin from the BPF strain is different from ordinary bacteria related to it. Those fingerprints are exactly what I need to justify a grant application."

"You'll write the grant, get the money, do the research, and be famous," Eliot said.

"I don't know about that. But I'll be happy."

It was midsummer at the height of a hot spell in Michigan when Sid made the announcement. "Good news," she told the lab group. "And we had to wait six long months for it." She watched the anticipation on their faces, and then said, "My NIH grant application to study the BPF endotoxin will be funded." A cheer went up around the room, and, after the meeting, Dr. Evans gave her a hearty pat on the back. The next day, Raven arrived at the lab carrying a bottle of Veuve Clicquot—highly illegal per university policy—and a cherry pie.

"Looks yummy," Sid said. "You are so sweet to bring them."

"It's my mother's recipe."

"You made it?" Sid didn't realize Raven had the skills to bake a pie from scratch.

"Yeah. I hope you like it." She blushed and swept a handful of her charcoal hair away from her eyes. It was a River gesture, and it seemed as if he had remotely joined the party.

Raven unwired the top of the bottle, and, with the final twist, the cork shot to the ceiling, leaving a permanent dent in the textured tile overhead.

"Oops," she said, gazing upward at the divot. "I guess that will forever be the Sidonie Royal Memorial Hole."

Raven poured the Champagne into two 250 ml beakers and passed one to Sid.

"Cheers," Raven said.

While she sipped, Sid sensed something was awry. A glitch in the natural order, an absent element, a staleness in the air. She missed Eliot.

It was Raven who finally said it. "Know what? Eliot should be here. He'd be so happy for your grant."

"And he'd love the champagne," Raven added.

"That, too." Sid took another sip.

And then the flowers arrived. The floral delivery kid had wandered up and down the hallway until he found Sid at her lab bench. "For a Doctor Royal," he said, reading the tag on the package.

"I'll sign," she said.

It was a huge bouquet of roses, lavender lilies, hydrangeas, baby's breath, and shiny dark green leaves, all arranged in a pretty clay vase.

The card read "Congratulations, Sidonie. Well deserved. Eliot." She laid the card in her lap and began to weep. Quietly, softly—the bittersweet beauty and the melancholy of the moment. His kindness. His absence.

"Hey, from a new beau?" Raven asked when she saw the flowers.

"Don't play dumb with me," Sid said. "Must have been you who told Eliot about my grant."

"Well ... yes."

"Thanks for the flowers," she said when she called Eliot. "They're beautiful. That was very thoughtful of you."

"Congratulations, again. Any plans for a big celebration?"

"As a matter of fact, I'm going back to Promissão."

"Really. Cool idea."

"I think so, too. I want to see River and Cibele again. Without their help, none of this would be possible. It'll be a chance to reinvigorate my complicated memories of the place. Promissão is almost holy to me."

"Is Raven going with you?"

"No, she and Doug are going to Santa Rosa to visit her mother."

"Wow. Serious, huh?"

"I guess so."

"Say, Sid." His voice was tentative. "Ah ... would you like company in Brazil? I'd like to see the place. It's pretty memorable, after all."

"You want to go to Promissão?" Her thoughts rocketed all over the room. Where would he stay? What would they do there? His presence would change the character of the trip a lot. Did she want him along? "Interesting idea."

"Think of it this way: I owe you a trip after you went to Maine on the spur of the moment with me."

She shook her head as she weighed his tangled logic. He had invited her to Maine, and now he was inviting himself to Brazil.

Why not, she thought? "Sure. Come along."

"Hi, River. This is Sid." This was not a call she was eager to make. She didn't want to further inconvenience him. "There's been a change in plans for my trip to Promissão."

"Are you cancelling?"

"No, no. I'm still coming. Looking forward to seeing you

and everyone again. But my colleague Eliot Mitchell is coming with me. He's been intimately involved with the experiments on the bacteria from Izabel's blood, and he wants to see where it all began."

"Eliot? He's the gruff one, right?"

"Yes. Sometimes he can be gruff. I'll keep him under control."

"That'll be fine. I look forward to meeting that guy. Do you both want to stay at my place? I can set up the cots in the storage room. Or I could bunk in there, and you two can have my bed."

"No, it's not like that. You stay in your bed, and Eliot and I will take the cots. Thanks a lot. Hopefully this won't be too much trouble for you."

"None at all. It's not like there's a Holiday Inn in Promissão."

26

1 9 8 5   B R A Z I L

Sid led Eliot past the white rocks that littered the boulevard and through the open metal gates of the cemetery. The afternoon breeze was quiet, broken only by the soft rustle of the leaves on the owl trees and an occasional clanky call of a jay. The bright sun that shone overhead belied that place of gloom.

Ahead, a white stucco chapel that stood against the white stucco retaining wall looked old and holy, but newly painted. Sid pointed to the shaggy bird nest nestled in the cross beams of the large wooden cross above the entry.

"What kind of bird?" Eliot asked.

"Don't know."

"Well, here he comes." Eliot ducked as the bird zoomed

over his head and landed in the nest. "Looks like some kind of barn swallow."

The chapel door stood ajar, and Eliot poked his head inside.

"What do you see?" Sid asked. She wasn't sure she wanted to explore the tiny church, the house of the dead, the repository of faith, and of tears, and sorrow. Wandering around the grave-yard was painful enough. In her world, death felt like failure, a breakdown in medicine's mission to keep children alive. She preferred to remain with the living.

Eliot disappeared into the chapel. "Come and see," he called. "It's safe."

The inside, dank and dim, was lit by two small windows high on the side walls. Seven wooden benches stood in rows before the plain wooden altar, which looked like a packing crate. She blinked her eyes until they adjusted to the dark. Two. partially burned candles stood atop the altar, flanking a silver crucifix.

Eliot sat on one of the benches and patted the seat beside him. "This is pretty awesome," he whispered as he gazed around the room. "Reminds me of the chapel in my Scottish grandmother's village. Only hers was made of stone. Same quiet, same damp, same sense of sanctity though. As a boy, I thought it was filled with heavenly beings that, although I couldn't see them, flew around like buzzards. I wanted to catch them and keep them in a cage."

"Kind of reminds me of the mission churches in California," Sid said.

"Yeah, they're both Catholic."

For Sid, the simplicity of the chapel stood in perfect harmony with the rest of Promissão, plain in the sense of staying true to itself. Nothing fancy, but nevertheless it held great worth. The crucifix that hung above the altar, with the figure of Christ woven out of twisted, denuded vines, captured the spirit and serenity of the place better than anything else she could imagine.

"Isn't that wonderful?" She pointed to the vine sculpture. "It's utterly breathless in its austerity and in its depth of meaning and its creativity."

Eliot stared at the vines and nodded.

"Are you a believer?" Sid asked.

"Believer? What do you mean?"

"Well, are you a religious person?"

"Oh, God, no. I'm a scientist. Why on earth do you ask?"

"It was your idea to come to the cemetery, and you seem kind of moved by the chapel. Just wondering."

"I certainly have no use for organized religion. I remember, though, how much my grandmother's faith kept her going from hard day to even harder day. I never understood it and still don't, but I know it was real for her. How about you?"

"I, too, am a scientist and have always viewed religion as mindless hocus pocus. But I've seen the value of their faith in some of the parents of my patients, and that's fine. For them." She straightened her glasses, then continued. "I guess my spirituality resides in my awe of Mother Nature's labors. The vivid colors and delicate intricacies of blooming flowers, the way they gently unfold from their buds as if by magic. The way puppies breathe and cats lick their fur without anyone teaching them how. It's the mystique of DNA. I find it an ingenious system, seemingly serendipitous but designed to favor, generation by generation, the most fit. That's pretty humbling."

"Well said, ma'am." Eliot chuckled. He stood up. "Let's see

if we can find Gilberto."

"Cibele said his grave is near the southwest corner."

Outside the chapel, Eliot shaded his eyes from the sun with his hand. "Let's see," he muttered as he glanced at his watch. "It's three o'clock so …" He turned ninety degrees and pointed straight ahead. "That's south." He turned a bit further. "And this is southwest." He walked ahead a few steps and surveyed the sea of tombstones. "This'll be hard. How on earth will we find his among all the rest of them?"

"We look for the little one," Sid said.

She wandered the narrow grassy paths that separated the stone slabs of the graves while Eliot wandered parallel paths. Moss obliterated the writing from some of the stones, shadows from the owl trees darkened others. She couldn't read the inscriptions written in Portuguese, but she was certain the words declared that the departed had been beloved, had found relief from suffering, now rested in peace. She stopped at two small tombs, but the names and years of death didn't fit. Finally, she found it.

Gilberto Carvalho da Silva

August 3, 1981 to September 20, 1984

A pair of angels—they were actually abstract line-drawings—were carved into the stone beneath the dates. She traced Gilberto's name in the rough granite with her finger. "Eliot," she called. "Here."

Too many lost little children: Evelien, Mariana, Luiza, Gilberto, Izabel, all the rest.

When he reached her side, she said, "I wish you could have

known him. He was a handsome, smart, feisty, lovable little boy." Tears streamed down her cheeks.

On the way out of the cemetery, they again passed the white stucco chapel. A woman in a black dress stepped out the door. An olive-green shawl hung like a shroud over her head and fluttered in the breeze. A tiny baby swaddled in a sky-blue blanket was nestled in her arms. She walked slowly, her eyes focused on the ground. When she looked up and saw Sid, she gasped. "Doctora Royal?" she called.

Sid stared at her. The woman looked familiar. Young, but weary and solemn. Then Sid remembered. It was Dona. And the infant in her arms must be the baby that hadn't yet been born when Sid swabbed the eyes of the neighbor children. Sid introduced Dona to Eliot and explained to him that Dona's daughter, Mariana, was the first child in Promissão to die of the BPF illness. Sid wrapped her arms around Dona and told her, in English, how pleased she was to see her again. She hoped the kindness in her voice, that most universal of languages, would convey the message. Dona lifted the blanket off the baby's face. "Antonio," she said softly.

He was a beautiful baby. Dewy fresh. Healthy. Well cared for in his white, footed onesie and sound asleep in the innocent slumber of children. He was a precious baby, but not a substitute for Mariana, for she would live forever within her mother's being. Nothing could erase her. Dona must have understood Sid's thoughts for she began to weep. Then, with her head bowed, she replaced the blanket over Antonio's face. As she shuffled down a grassy path into the clutter of graves, she motioned for Eliot and Sid to follow.

They stopped at yet another small grave. Several bunches of plastic flowers, some faded, some vibrant, rested in vases surrounding the marker. Dona dropped to her knees and rested her head against its granite face, her cheek pressing on the letters of her daughter's name. Sid sank to her knees beside her and wrapped her arm around the sobbing woman's shoulders. Baby Antonio lay still and silent in Dona's arms.

Eliot stepped up to Sid and laid his hand on her shoulder. His fingers, warm and firm, were the grip of a trusted confidant. She leaned her head against his arm and hoped she could remember that tender moment forever.

"Here you go, Eliot. Something to wet your whistle, Brazil style." River handed Eliot a jelly jar full of hazy liquid and ice cubes.

Eliot took a sip. "Whoa. That packs a wallop." He held the glass up to the light. "What's in it?"

"Sugar muddled with limes and sugarcane firewater. Like it?"

"Yeah.

River handed Sid a glass. "It's watered down a bit, the way you like it."

To Sid, sitting in the same room with River and Eliot seemed like a dream. Never in her wildest fantasies did she expect that to happen. They seemed to enjoy each other, passed easy conversation back and forth. River explained his work with the farmers, and Eliot talked about fly fishing in Montana.

So much remained unsaid. Sid hadn't told Eliot about River's homosexuality, and River himself, as expected, said nothing about it. He talked about fishing in the reservoir with the brothers of the Mosteiro de São Alonzo.

"What do you catch?" Eliot asked.

"A bass-like creature. It's good, right Sid?"

"Sure is."

River hadn't probed about the nature of their relationship beyond the lab either. Sid guessed that he didn't care to know about Sid's sex life, just as she didn't care to know the details of his.

There was a knock on the door. "Must be Cibele," River said. "I knew you'd want to see her again."

Soon, Cibele and Ana, and Ana's husband, Carlos, whose full lips and high forehead and sparkling eyes rendered him an adult version of Gilberto, crowded into River's tiny living room. "When Ana heard you were visiting, she insisted on coming with me. She wants her husband to meet you, and we all want to meet your friend."

The praise for Sid and her work in Promissão was effusive. Ana wept a bit when thanking her, and her husband pumped her hand with a grip of iron. When Eliot got up to get himself another of River's lime drinks, he passed behind Sid's chair and rubbed her shoulders.

They had many questions for Sid: What was Michigan like in the winter? Cold and snowy, Sid answered. Why did the fatal infections happen in the first place? Sid was still trying to figure that out. Why did they go away? She didn't know. Would they come back? She didn't know that, either. And they were fascinated that the BPF strain, the bacteria from Izabel's blood, was still alive, safely stored in Sid's freezer in the laboratory. "It wakes up when we defrost it," Sid explained.

After the company left, Sid and Eliot washed the dishes. "I've learned so much about you on this visit," Eliot said. He held a clean glass up to the light and wiped away a remaining smudge. "I had no idea how important your work was to the people here. It's quite incredible."

"Not really. People appreciate help when they desperately need it. That's particularly true when sick children are involved. You need to trust me more, Eliot."

"Yes ma'am." He swatted her arm with his towel. She grabbed the end of it and tugged it out of his hands.

"Hey, you two," River said as he entered the kitchen. "Take it easy on my towel," he laughed. "And on each other."

Sid was setting River's table for dinner when she heard Eliot yell.

"Damn it." His voice was loud and angry.

She dashed into the kitchen and found a bloody knife beside a carrot on the chopping block. Eliot was wrapping a paper towel around his hand.

"Let me see that," she said.

"It's fine."

"Show me."

"I'm telling you, it's fine."

"Eliot ..." She gave his name a threatening tone.

He peeled the paper towel away; the gaping wound was at the bottom of his thumb. Blood oozed from the slash, and he slapped the towel back over it.

"One more peek," she said. This time she peeled away the paper towel and, pushing against his hand with her thumbs, pulled at the skin flaps beside the gash. Still holding his hand, she walked over to the sink, turned on the cold water, and flushed the cut.

"What in the hell are you doing? That hurts."

"Washing away as many of the germs as possible and cooling

it so it will seal more quickly."

Eliot turned toward River. "Could I borrow a Band-Aid?" He glanced at the wound. "Or maybe three?"

Sid dried his hand and rewrapped it with a clean paper towel. "River, forget the Band-Aids. Would you drive us to the clinic?"

"I'm not going to the damn doctor. It'll be fine."

"Yes, you're going."

"No, I'm not."

Suddenly, in her mind, they were back in the lab. He was refusing to accept her opinion, treating her as if she were an idiot. "Eliot, I'm the medical doctor here. This is a deep wound, and I could see the tendon. It's in a hand, and it needs to be stitched up."

"It'll heal just fine."

"I'm going to pull rank, because I know what I'm talking about, and you don't. This isn't microbial physiology, it's an injured hand. It needs to be stitched."

The clinic was unchanged from her last visit. Same dimly lit hallway with the flickery light bulb, same flimsy wire chairs, same smell of rubbing alcohol. The nurse recognized Sid right away and gave her a tight hug.

As soon as they were seated in the waiting area, Dr. Alancar appeared. "Welcome back. No more cases for a while. None in the past four or five months."

Sid nodded. River had told her whenever a new case appeared. The cases were patchy, sometimes several in a month, sometimes months between one and the next.

"We haven't had the opportunity to use the new antibiotic you brought yet."

That was either good or bad. Good if it was because of

fewer cases. Bad if the children died before they could receive the medicine.

"I'm glad you brought those drugs. So are all the people of Promissão. Sometimes, people here don't trust outsiders, but they found hope in your work here."

She introduced Dr. Alancar to Eliot. "This time, I'm here with my friend, a patient in need of an excellent doctor."

The patient and doctor disappeared into the treatment room, and Sid and River returned to the wire chairs. They hadn't had a chance to be alone since she and Eliot arrived.

"How are you?" She asked. He looked the same: trim body, pale skin, swatch of charcoal hair that fell into his eyes.

He knew exactly what she was really asking. "Healthy." Then he added, "And happy. Work is going well. We're trying out a new variety of corn, and it's working better than we expected, with good germination characteristics and good yields." He smiled at her. "You probably know as much agronomy as I do microbiology."

"Right about that. I'm thrilled all is well."

"As I recall, last time around Eliot was considered an ogre. Things change?" He flashed her a wry smile.

"Eliot and I certainly have had our moments. But we now consider each other good friends."

"How good?" His eyes sparkled with glee.

"Good."

That night, they lay on their cots in River's storeroom. The moon, large as a basketball and bright, shone through the window as it had during their stay together in Maine. She could tell by his choppy breathing that he wasn't asleep.

"Does that hand still throb?" she asked.

"Yes."

"It'll settle down in a day or so." She reached over the gap between the cots to his shoulder and gave it a gentle pat.

"Not soon enough."

Yes, the end of suffering never came soon enough.

27

1987 CALIFORNIA

The waters of Carmel Bay, framed by the gnarly cypress trees that grew between the trail and the sea, stretched before them like a tranquil lake. Eliot led the way, and Sid stumbled behind him over the rocks, roots, and dirt in her new pumps. He had suggested they take a walk at Point Lobos. She hadn't realized the path was not conducive to dressy shoes.

It had been two-and-a-half years since their trip to Maine, and their lives had diverged in more complicated ways than a simple split in the road. She had joined the faculty in Nebraska a year earlier, and he had launched a successful career in Minnesota. They both continued to search for answers to the scientific questions that drove them forward: how bacteria change like chameleons, how they utilize the fairy dust around them to grow, how they make people sick. Now they were in California to speak at the Microbial Pathogens meeting in Carmel-by-the-Sea. He suggested they skip the afternoon sessions. She agreed.

He stopped where a small trail took off through the brush from the larger one and let her catch up with him. They watched the water hurl over the boulders below, sending clouds of sparkling spindrift into the air. "It's so beautiful," she said, wishing she could articulate deeper, more meaningful words to reflect the awe of the sight. The only other way to describe the scenery was "magnificent," but even that didn't fully capture the contrasting colors of the dark green cypress branches and the azure blue bay, the salty smell of the ocean and the piney smell of the trees, the dull roar of the harbor seals in the distance, the energy of the crashing waves, the caress of the sea breeze against her forehead.

"Let's see where this goes." She headed down a narrow trail. He followed. They meandered around moss-covered rocks and clumps of coastal scrub. Tawny rays of the late afternoon sun wove through the tree limbs overhead like streams of butterscotch. Lichen that hung from the dead branches brushed her cheek. She swept it aside.

Near the edge of the water, they stopped at a giant boulder. Weeds grew in its chinks. "Ready for a rest?" she asked.

They sat side by side on a flat spot in the rock. At first, they didn't speak but rather watched the clouds meander to the east. She treasured the grandeur of the place, the pleasure of being alone with him. She broke the silence by asking about his work in Minnesota.

He tilted his head and grinned. "It's going well. That was a good move for me. I just received notice that my newest NIH grant application missed the funding level by a hair. The reviewers' comments were supportive, so I think a revised application has a good chance of making it. That will help a lot. With that money, I can hire at least one more postdoc. Maybe two.

She wasn't surprised at his success in Minnesota. With his determination and laser-like focus, as well as his enviable intellect, he would prosper as an academician anywhere.

"Are they treating you well in Omaha?" he asked.

"Yes, very well. My lab space is generous. And very well equipped. The work on the BPF endotoxin is progressing nicely. We're working on the mechanisms by which it is so deadly. Since my Young Investigator Award will end soon, I'm working on an application for an Independent Investigator Award."

"Good luck with that." He picked up a cedar twig and broke it in half. "Want me to critique it?"

She tightened. It was an old reaction or, rather, an automatic reaction to old fears. About his bossiness. About her not being good enough. In the scientific realm, in her mind, he would always be ahead of her.

Before she could answer, he said, "Here's a thought: I'll critique your application if you'll critique mine. I'd really appreciate your opinion of my revised proposal."

She hesitated a moment and then laughed. "Sounds like a deal."

"Hey, see the otter?" He pointed to a spot in the water. As soon as she saw the animal, it disappeared into a wave. "That guy's full of ambition. He'll reappear soon," he said.

She watched the sea's surface, waiting for the otter to return in the now smooth, empty place where he had been swimming. Ambition. The word had haunted her for a long time. Now it was just a word.

"I assume you received an invitation to Raven and Doug's wedding," she said.

"Yeah. It's in Santa Rosa, right?"

"Correct. I'll be there." She hoped River would make it from Brazil. Last time she'd visited him in Promissão, about four months ago, he told her he wanted more than anything to be there, but he had to be in Hawaii for work at about the same time. His dark eyes had sparkled, and his smile glowed. "I'll figure out a way to get there, even if I have to ride the trade winds across the Pacific."

"Are you going?" she asked Eliot.

"I think so."

"Make it happen, Eliot." She looked forward to a reunion of the BPF three. They had all worked so hard, sometimes together, sometimes against each other, on the mystery of that strain. She wanted to keep that flame alive; after everything they had been through, they couldn't let time pull them apart.

As if he were reading her mind, he stood up, stretched his arms over his head, and asked, "Did you see the article in this month's *Journal of Bacteriology* from the GHA? No surprises there."

"Right. A pile of negative results. They expended a huge effort and spent zillions of dollars only to learn which BPF factors *don't* explain its deadliness." Then she added, "I noticed they didn't find your favorite plasmid in most of the strains." She chuckled and gave him a playful sock on his arm.

"Not every good idea ends up the way one would like." he said, "But your endotoxin idea could be a home run." He smiled at her. It was an endearing smile. He could be charming, beguilingly so.

"The best thing is that the outbreaks seem to have petered out. Cibele—you remember her, she's River's friend whose nephew died while Raven and I were in Brazil—says no more cases have turned up in Promissão in over a year, and Greg says no more in Serrana, either." With no more cases, interest in the cause of the epidemic would also settle down. Even the tenacious GHA would move on to other scientific endeavors.

"Of course, I remember Cibele. She was at the party River threw for us. I can't tell you how much that trip to Promissão meant to me. Every time I think about or read about the BPF strain, I think of the deeper understanding I have of it and of the infections it caused, all because of that visit. There's no substitute for meeting the people affected by it, or for standing in the clinic where it all happened. Merely breathing the air there added layers of context to that microbe."

A young couple rounded the turn in the trail, waved at them, and then sauntered on. Sid wondered what they thought of the two of them, people in their mid-thirties who sat on a rock and ignored the rest of the world, he wearing a sport jacket with a conference name badge dangling from the lapel, and she wearing a pretty business suit and open-toed pumps. The young couple would have recognized them as out of place in their office outfits, there on the Cyprus Grove Trail. They may have thought Sid and Eliot were secret lovers, enjoying each other on a lovely day, in a lovely place. They likely assumed Sid and Eliot were discussing heady things, such as politics or good books. Mostly, considering the aura that stirred the air between Sid and Eliot, the young couple must have recognized their fondness for each other.

Eliot squatted beside the rock and pulled a fist-full of weeds from the chinks. He held them under his nose and took a deep breath. "When are you headed back to Nebraska?" he asked.

"I'm on the red eye that departs about midnight tomorrow." Leaving Carmel would be bittersweet. She had important, interesting work to do at home. Yet being here with him was a hidden, buoyant moment apart from her otherwise ordered life. She would always reserve room in a corner of herself for him. A small wedge was enough; more would be too much. It was a jeweled, treasured wedge.

"Let's have dinner in Carmel tonight," he said. "I'll drop you off at SFO tomorrow night. I'm also on a red eye to Minneapolis then."

They stood and looked again out over the sea. When they turned back toward the trail, she put her arm on his shoulder, leaned toward his face, and kissed him. He wrapped his arms around her. It was a long embrace. Warm. Secure. Easy against the breeze.

Acknowledgements

The making of a finished book is always a team endeavor. I greatly appreciate the thoughtful comments, upon reading repeated versions of Fever, from Danielle Lavaque-Manty, Ann Epstein, Cynthia Jalynski, Marty Calvert, Jane Johnson, and Margaret Nesse. My agent Cynthia Manson has been loyal and diligent to the end, and my editor, Megan Trank, and her associates at Beaufort Books have been incredibly supportive through the publishing phase. Finally, I am forever grateful to scientists worldwide who doggedly, and usually out of the limelight, work to better understand the mysterious ways in which microbes infect people.